Also by Shari Low

The Story of Our Life
A Life Without You
The Other Wives Club
With or Without You
This Is Me

Winter Day Series

One Day in Winter
Another Day in Winter
The Last Day of Winter

Non-Fiction

Because Mummy Said So

THE LAST DAY OF WINTER

Shari Low

First published in the UK in 2019 by Head of Zeus Ltd

A catalogue record for this book is available from
the British Library.

ISBN: 9781788541442

Typeset by Silicon Chips

Printed and bound in Great Britain by
CPI Group (UK) Ltd, Croydon CR0 4YY

Head of Zeus Ltd
First Floor East
5–8 Hardwick Street
London EC1R 4RG

WWW.HEADOFZEUS.COM

To my much loved grandmother, Sarah (Sadie) Hill –
a strong, wise, brilliantly funny force of nature and
a true inspiration to us all.

And to J, C & B… Everything always.

Author's note

The Botanic Gardens in the west end of Glasgow, is one of my favourite places on earth. Inside the lush, glorious, green space sits the Kibble Palace, a stunning glass and iron structure originally built by Victorian entrepreneur John Kibble at his home on the shores of Loch Long. In the 1870s the Palace was moved to the Botanic Gardens and it's been a much loved attraction for Glaswegians and tourists ever since.

When I started writing this book, it was my first and only choice of setting for the day. However, I confess I've taken outrageous artistic licence with the gardens, the buildings and the statues within, tweaking the layout, moving things around, adding a few extras, and turning it into a wedding venue to fit the story.

Please forgive me. And the next time you visit Glasgow, please go there and marvel. I promise you'll love it just as much as Caro, Cammy, Seb and Josie. And me.

Love, Shari x

Who is there…

Caro Anderson – it's the day of her wedding to her love, Cammy Jones.

Cammy Jones – Caro's fiancé, owner of menswear boutique CAMDEN.

Chrissie – bridesmaid number one, lives with her partner, Tom, and their son Ben, 14.

Jen – bridesmaid number two, married to Luke, adopted daughter of Val.

Val – sixty-something treasure, friend and self-appointed surrogate mother to Caro and Cammy and anyone else who needs her.

Josie – in her seventies (she hasn't told anyone her actual age since around 1980), a force of nature, rebel, Val's partner in crime and wedding planning.

Pearl and Bob Smith – Caro's aunt and uncle. Mahogany-tanned Scots, enjoying a very comfortable retirement in Spain.

Yvonne Anderson – Caro's late mum, died two years ago.

Jack Anderson – Caro's cheating, duplicitous father. Married to Louise.

Lila Anderson – Caro's half-sister, daughter of Jack and Louise, former social media darling and selfie addict.

Seb Lloyd – an expat golf pro with a broken heart.

Juliet (Embers) Lloyd – Seb's late wife.

Stacey Summers – Glasgow native living in LA, presenter of *USA Speed Freaks*, secretly in love with Cammy Jones.

Jax Green – Stacey's boyfriend and co-presenter of *USA Speed Freaks*.

Senga Summers – Stacey's mum, Josie's pal, and founding partner in the cleaning company, Manky Scrubbers.

Ida, Ina, Agnes, Jean and Montana – Senga's lifelong friends, self-made family, and co-founders of Manky Scrubbers.

Zac Benson – fashion buyer, Stacey's new-found travel buddy.

Prologue

Website – www.itshouldhavebeenme.com

Members Discussion Forum

Post by member, screen name NotOverYet:

Okay, so the day has come. The love of my life is marrying someone else. Even typing that makes me want to scream. I know this is a forum for mutual support and consolation, but right now I don't want to hear anything that will make me feel better. I'm pissed off and I'm heartbroken. How could he do this? Why isn't he marrying me? Why am I not the one sipping champagne and looking at the white dress hanging on the front of the wardrobe, waiting to say I Do in front of the world? I need to move on, to find someone else, to let him go.

Well, screw that.

I'm not doing it. I want him and if he doesn't want me, then at least I'm going down fighting. I'm going to that wedding today and I'm going to be heard. When you've got nothing left to lose, doing something is better than watching the future you dreamed of slip through your fingers

FRIDAY 20 DECEMBER

8 A.M. – 10 A.M.

One

Caro

Dum dum de dum, dum dum de dum.

The vicar opened his sleek leather Bible as the congregation, the women resplendent in deep jewel tones befitting a winter wedding, turned to watch the bride slowly glide down the aisle. The diamanté edged veil that covered her face scanned from left to right and back again, as if the eyes beneath it were taking in the beaming smiles, the tissues being dabbed under brush-like eyelash extensions, the hats so large they could double as manhole covers and the men who were surreptitiously checking their watches to see if there was any chance of getting out of there and to a TV before the game started on Sky Sports.

The steps of her ivory shoes slowed as she neared the front, where her groom waited. Her soulmate. Her best friend. And all the other clichés that almost every bride spouted about the man she was marrying.

He reached over, lifted her veil and there she was… Caro could hear her own screams now as she took in the scene. It was her father who had lifted the veil, and it was her mother who was standing there at the end of the aisle, dressed in white, her face now revealed, her lips moving... 'Don't do it, Caro,' she was saying. 'Please don't get married.'

There was a fearful gasp as Caro sat bolt upright in bed, her whole body in panicked fight or flight mode. Racing pulse. Shaking hands. Chest tighter than a bride's corset. Every night this week, the same dream – every morning the same reactions. Fear. Dread. Denial. Panic. Realisation. Then a whole lot more fear, dread and panic.

The sound of her rapid breathing was loud enough to stir half of her duo of comatose bridesmaids, the one that was sleeping beside her on the superking bed.

Summoning huge effort, Chrissie managed to open one eye, but it came at the price of a loud groan, followed by a hoarse, 'Are you okay? Holy crap, what did we drink last night?'

Caro paused, the deafening thud of her beating heart drowning out everything else. Until that moment she hadn't realised that it was even possible to hear the functions of her internal organs. 'Tequila,' she murmured, wincing. 'That might be why I can still hear a mariachi band banging in my skull.'

With a low moan of pain, Chrissie pushed herself up until her back rested against the headboard. Her chestnut hair looked like something eagles would nest in. The previous night's make-up gave her a waxy look that wouldn't be out of place in any Netflix series featuring the undead. And her red silk shirt, so sexy the night before, had lost some of its on-point style now that it was on backwards and adorned with a scarlet garland of tinsel procured from an unsuspecting tree in the early hours of the morning.

'You should FaceTime Ben,' Caro muttered, referring to Chrissie's fourteen year old son. 'It would save you the next few years of lecturing him about the evils of alcohol. One sight of us and he'll never touch the stuff.'

'Yeah, but he'd be scarred for life and it would cost me a fortune in therapy.' Chrissie tried to shake her head, but realised the error of her ways when a searing pain shot through her left temple. 'Ouch! I'm going to have to face forwards for the rest of my life.' She continued speaking, using staccato words with absolutely no head movement. 'Anyway, Happy Wedding Day, Mrs Cammy-To-Be. I would have said your new surname, but I think I've got amnesia.'

'Jones,' Caro murmured. How many times had she said that name in her head, yet still it didn't feel real. Caro Jones. Mrs Caro Jones. Wife of Cameron Jones, commonly known as Cammy. Love of her life. Best friend. Easy on the eye.

In just a few hours, that was who she'd be. The thought brought on another lurch of panic and she could feel that familiar sensation of her ribs closing in to squeeze the life out of her.

There was a stirring from the floor at the end of the bed, before a head slowly appeared over the footboard, blinking in the light like someone emerging from underneath an avalanche after at least a fortnight in the snow. 'What did I miss?' Jen croaked.

'It's... it's...' Chrissie struggled to focus on her watch. 'Quarter past eight on Caro's wedding day and we're the worst bridesmaids ever.' Still no head movement, but her eyes flicked to Caro again. 'How could we have let this happen? We were supposed to have you in bed by 9 p.m. so you'd wake up refreshed and glowing like a goddess for your big day. I remember a…' she squeezed her eyes closed as her memory disc kicked into action, 'Christmas party at the next table. And then dancing. And singing. And climbing on a chair and telling the whole restaurant that you were getting married today. And then… drinks. Vodka.'

'Tequila,' Caro corrected her.

'Yes! Tequila. And a…' Another squint. 'Was there a mariachi band playing Christmas songs or have I completely lost it?'

'There was,' Caro reassured her.

'Oh, thank God. I keep hearing myself sing Santa La Bamba in my head. I'm sorry, Caro, we should have done a much better job than this. I'll understand if you sack us.'

'I really should,' Caro told her, feigning gravity. The truth was, sacking her bridesmaids would be a mere drop in the swirl of emotions that were currently sucking her down a dark well.

Her wedding day. Taking place, for extra cute points, on the last Friday before Christmas, exactly two years after she and Cammy first met. In fact, it was also two years since she'd stepped foot in Glasgow for the first time, after travelling there from her home in Aberdeen, in search of the father who'd deserted her and her mum. To her devastation, she'd found him – and a whole load of secrets and lies that she could never have anticipated. But it wasn't all bad news. Thanks to that trip, she'd also found a new home, an incredible group of friends, a city she loved and a fiancé she adored.

Yet, right now, head thumping and stomach churning, it didn't feel like she was in a fluffy haze of counting her blessings.

Breathe. Just breathe. It'll pass. It has to.

Still dangling over the footboard at the end the bed, her eyes bloodshot, her mascara verging on panda, Jen squinted at her watch. 'Oh Jesus, Val and Josie will be here soon. I haven't had a bollocking from Val since I was fifteen and she found out I'd been smoking at the school disco. Somebody save me.' Val had been Jen's surrogate mum since she was a young teenager, when Val and her husband Don had swooped in to take care of a girl whose mother had died and whose father preferred a drink to raising his daughter. Val, and her best friend Josie, were the matriarchs in that incredible group of friends that Caro had found here. Some related, some not, they were a big, happy, mutually supportive, caring group of strong women and decent men, most of whom worked in the same row of shops in Glasgow's Merchant City, a stylish area of the city centre packed with high-end boutiques, trendy bars and great restaurants. Back in Aberdeen, Caro had been a primary school teacher, but she was taking a sabbatical and enjoying working with Cammy in CAMDEN, his upmarket menswear boutique, while Jen and Chrissie were partners in Sun, Sea, Ski, the one-stop holiday shop next door.

Thankfully, extra staff had been brought in to run both shops that day, to let the bosses enjoy all things marital.

If they ever got there.

Despite the throbbing hangover, a mental image of Val chiding thirty-two year old Jen made Caro grin. Perhaps it was more of a grimace. 'Nope, you're on your own. But if you need coffee, I can just about cover that.'

Reacting to Jen's strained nod, she tentatively placed her feet on the floor and pushed, managing to stabilise herself in a standing position, despite a sudden wave of nausea and another searing temple pain. Her legs hurt. Her body hurt. Hell, even her eyelashes hurt.

Wobbling with every step, she made it through to the kitchen. Morning coffee was normally Cammy's domain, but he'd gone off to stay in a hotel last night, the first one they'd spent apart since becoming a couple.

After downing a large glass of water in one go, it took a few welcome moments of solitude to make three coffees and then load a plate with croissants and the butter dish. When all else fails, turn to carbs, Caro decided, popping a chunk of pastry in her mouth. It didn't help, but it took her mind off her woes for a split second, before another wave of fear kicked in. She couldn't. She just couldn't.

She pressed her shaking hands together, attempting to stop the sheen of sweat that was forming on each palm.

The doorbell cut through her thoughts, as did an audible, 'Fuck, I bet that's Val. I'm a dead woman. Don't answer it,' coming from Jen in the bedroom.

Caro shuffled down the hall. 'Ignoring it isn't an option. She'd only call emergency services and demand they break the door down.'

No arguments came from the other room – mainly because they all knew it was true.

'Jesus!' Val exclaimed by way of greeting, shock at Caro's dishevelled appearance turning her religious, her eyes so wide her blue eyeshadow almost disappeared.

'Shhhhh,' Caro chided her, as she stepped back to allow the new arrival to enter, standing flat against the wall to give enough space for Val's blonde bob, a structure of unfathomable height and width and sprayed to the consistency of steel, to pass.

Caro paused, confused, as she waited for another arrival to materialise behind Val. It didn't come.

'Where's Josie?' she asked. Josie. The other half of the dynamic duo – a woman with a birth certificate that stated she was in her seventies, a face and body that suggested she was in her fifties, and a brain that remained a bitchy, rebellious, outrageous twenty-something. She was also chief wedding planner, having stepped in to organise every single aspect of the day with her trademark bolshy brilliance. Right from the moment they set the date, Josie had it all covered.

'She texted to say she'd been held up and she'd meet us here. No doubt she'll wander in any minute.'

There was a bang and a howl from the bedroom.

'What's that?' Val asked, her instincts immediately going to deeply suspicious. This was a woman who had the interrogation skills of a trained intelligence agent, so Caro knew lying would be futile.

'Jen and Chrissie are in there with hangovers from hell and a look of the walking dead about them.'

Despite the automatic purse of Val's lips, Caro could see the amusement in her eyes.

'I'll let you go and shout at them in a minute, but can you help me with the coffees first?'

Val obliged, following Caro into the kitchen.

'Jesus,' she repeated. 'Has this place been ransacked while you were sleeping?'

Caro sighed as she surveyed the scene through Val's shocked gaze. More than a few empty wine bottles, some of them on their sides. Several lipstick rimmed glasses. An overturned bowl of popcorn. Plates containing what was left of... Eeew, were those kebabs?

'We may have slightly overdone things last night.'

Val automatically lifted the marigolds from the sink, pulled them on and got to work as she talked, her superpower being the ability to do absolutely any domestic task to perfection while concentrating on a dozen other things. 'You do know you're getting married today?'

Caro felt a violent surge of panic.

Oblivious, Val chirped on, 'I was expecting glowing cheeks and flawless hair and a bit of giddy excitement.'

Racing heart now. Chest tight again. Can't breathe.

'Or, you know, at least for you to have had a shower.'

'Understandable, but...' The words stuck in Caro's throat.

It took Val a couple of rounds of the sink with a scourer before she realised Caro had choked up. Glancing over, she saw two tears streaming down Caro's cheeks.

'What? Oh God, love, what's wrong? Is it nerves? I was bricking it when I was marrying my Don.'

There were a few pained, excruciating moments, before Caro could get the words out. 'I don't want to go through with it, Val. I don't want to marry Cammy.'

Val's jaw dropped and her marigolds froze, mid scour, while Caro gasped oxygen into her lungs, her cardiovascular system kicking in due to the sheer relief of admitting that out loud.

Today was the day that Caro Anderson wanted to call off her wedding.

Two

Seb

'Can I take that from you sir?' The flight attendant was smiling and, to her credit, giving no indication that she'd probably done this trip a thousand times and just wanted to get home, put her feet up and watch a bit of Netflix, Seb decided.

'That'll be great, thank you,' he replied, handing over an empty coffee cup and a KitKat wrapper. Chocolate. And there had been two sachets of sugar slipped into the cappuccino. His body could go into shock from the unfamiliar sugar overload at any moment, but he found himself not caring. Nothing about this week so far had been normal or familiar or in character, so he wasn't going to give a second thought to this momentary lapse in discipline. Not that he was fanatical about his diet, but – vino aside – he generally stuck to a healthy lifestyle. At fifty-five, living in the south of Spain and working as a golf pro at the kind of place he would have called 'swanky' in his younger years, it was an easy choice. Although, the truth was that since Juliet had been gone, he had little interest in slap-up meals anyway.

His eyes automatically drifted to the leather bag between his feet and he had to make a conscious effort to block the place his mind was going to. Instead, he distracted himself with playing over the events of the last week for the millionth time.

On the previous Saturday night, he'd been at his usual night-time spot – the bar at the golf club. Yep, he knew there were gossipy whispers. He could imagine the kind of things they must be saying.

'Pathetic,' they'd mutter. 'He's not been himself since... well, you know.'

'I don't know how he can live with himself after what he did. Drowning his sorrows won't change that.'

'Juliet was such a wonderful woman. No wonder he's in the state he's in.'

And of course, there undoubtedly be would be the others, the ones who felt that the injustice should be righted.

'Can't believe he's still here. He should be in jail, if you ask me. Poor Juliet.'

He didn't disagree with any of their thoughts. Was he there too much? Absolutely. It beat going home to an empty house. Was it easier to eat there rather than sit at home and stare at an empty chair across the table? Yes, it definitely was. Was he drinking too much? Yep, he couldn't argue with that either. He wasn't putting vodka on his morning cornflakes, but a few glasses of wine at night seemed to seal the void of Juliet's absence, allowing him to find a way around the guilt and the emptiness for just a few hours, until he woke up the next morning, felt the empty space beside him and was consumed by that black hole all over again. And did he deserve to be in jail? Yes, he absolutely did. At least then, he'd feel that in some way he was paying for what he did.

Right now, though, he was thirty-five thousand feet in the air, more than a thousand miles away from those whispers, heading to Glasgow. It had all started with that chance meeting in the bar just six nights ago.

'Seb? Seb Lloyd?' A woman's voice. Scottish. He'd placed the accent as being from Aberdeen, but softened, perhaps through time spent away from the city. When he'd first left Glasgow in his early twenties, he'd spent a couple of years in the Granite City coaching wealthy oil executives, his first stop on a career that had taken him all over the world. But that was more than thirty years and a heartbreak ago.

He'd turned to see an attractive woman, perhaps also in her fifties, dark hair, wearing the standard expat uniform of floaty top, linen trousers and gold sandals. Beside her, a tanned bloke in a polo shirt and chinos was sporting a bemused expression.

His wine glass had clinked as he laid it on the marble bar top. He'd thought about lying for a moment but had decided it wasn't worth the effort. 'Yes.'

'Wow, it's a small world.'

'Is it?' he'd replied, his tone undoubtedly conveying the conviction that he had absolutely no idea who this lady was.

'I've been sitting over there all night…' she'd gestured to the restaurant tables to the side of the bar, 'staring at you, trying to place the face. And it just came to me, didn't it, Bob?' she'd gushed to her nodding companion. Enthusiasm and incredulity were oozing from every pore of her skin now. Seb had decided he really needed another drink.

'Aberdeen Golf Club! 1985!'

The wine had dulled his arithmetic skills, so it took him a moment. 'Yes, I worked there then.'

'I knew it!' the stranger had beamed. 'I'm Pearl Smith! Well, Pearl McCann, I was back then. I worked behind the bar.'

Nope, he still had nothing. He was saved from admitting that when she went on…

'You would always chat to me and my sister, Yvonne.'

A synapse in his brain had flashed, made a connection. Yvonne McCann. She'd worked behind the bar too. Long, dark blonde waves. Gorgeous smile. Great fun. They'd been best friends, but for him it was so much more. For a moment in time, he'd thought she felt the same. Thankfully his tan concealed the slight flush of his face as a memory surfaced. One cold evening, Yvonne, him – it was Pearl's night off so he was helping her clear up the empty bar in the early hours of the morning. Madonna was singing 'Crazy For You' – Yvonne's favourite song – over the speakers, Yvonne was singing along, smiling for the first time since her boyfriend had ditched her and gone off on holiday with his mates. The guy was a fool, Seb had told her a dozen times over the previous few days, meaning every word. He'd been quietly falling in love with her since the moment they'd met about six months before, but now wasn't the time to make a move. She was hurt, confused and… Her arms were around his neck and she was kissing him, her hips still moving in time to the music.

That night they slept together in his room at the club, and they'd spent the next glorious week sneaking off to be together whenever they could. It was bliss, the first time he'd thought that a fling could be so much more… right up until the moment her ex had sauntered back into the bar and it had been obvious to them all that the person she was crazy for was the one with the newly acquired suntan. There had been an embarrassed apology and a few awkward weeks of watching them fawn over each other, before he'd packed up his bruised heart and dented ego and moved on to a new role down south.

'Well, isn't it a small world, right enough?' he'd said, the sheer unexpectedness of the encounter giving him a genuine cheer that he hadn't felt in a while. 'Would you like to join me?' He hadn't had to ask twice, before the adjacent bar stools were pulled out and the couple climbed on board.

The barman, Miguel, had served up two glasses and another bottle of Rioja, and they'd passed the first hour in easy chat, discussing what had brought them to the same place at the same time. Pearl and Bob had taken early retirement, having made enough in the Aberdeen boom years to enable them to live a comfortable – if not extravagant – life in the sun. They'd come to this golf club, about twenty miles away from their home, because friends had raved about the food here.

Second bottle opened, they'd moved to the more comfortable armchairs on the terrace, the air thick with the intoxicating scent of bougainvillea, to continue the conversation. Chatting to people had always come easy to him. Skill on the green aside, it's what made him so good at his job, that ability to make people feel at ease and relax, whether he was talking to a complete beginner or a professional fighting for his career at a top level tournament.

'How is Yvonne?' he'd asked, as they sat in the luxuriously upholstered rattan seats.

Pearl's face had fallen, Bob stared at his moccasins, and the sudden chill wasn't down to a drop in the evening temperature.

Pearl's voice went from cheery to choked in an instant. 'Och, she passed away a couple of years ago now. Early onset dementia. It was a heartbreak.' She wiped away a solitary tear. 'For goodness sake, what am I like. All this time has passed and I still fill up when I'm telling anyone for the first time.'

Seb knew that feeling all too well. He still struggled for words when anyone asked him anything about Juliet. How could he explain? What could he say? He took the coward's way out every time, fudged over the truth, omitted the details, changed the subject.

'I'm so sorry to hear that,' he'd sympathised truthfully. She'd been great, Yvonne. A little unsure of herself sometimes, but so full of life, and always quick to giggle.

'And what about you, then? Married? Kids?' Pearl had asked, out of both curiosity and a desire to change the subject.

'No children. Married,' Seb had answered automatically, before correcting himself. '*Was* married.'

Pearl had nodded knowingly. 'Nothing wrong with that. I'm a big believer that life's too short and if you're not happy, you should move on, find happiness elsewhere.'

Shit. Seb could feel this conversation going down a rabbit hole of misunderstanding, and while he couldn't think of anything worse than correcting her, he realised he didn't have any choice. If they became regulars here, they'd no doubt hear about it from the gossips anyway.

'No, we didn't divorce. We... She... died. Six months ago.' He'd stopped, feeling the familiar blockage in his throat, praying that a couple of extra blinks would stem the excess moisture behind his eyes. Every bloody time. Why was saying it still so bloody difficult? Because he missed her, because he loved her – and because he knew that it was his fault that she was no longer here. He'd done this.

Pearl's jaw had frozen, her mouth forming into a circle, before her shocked expression crumbled into a head tilt that Seb had become way too familiar with since the moment the paramedic, bent over his wife's body, had raised his head, then slowly moved it from side to side. Nothing. No hope. She was gone. And as the police pulled him away, all he could do was howl with pain.

'Oh God, I'm so sorry,' Pearl had whispered, her shock undeniable.

'Christ, that's awful,' Bob had added, with genuine feeling.

Seb could see that these two were just ordinary, decent people. It was the only thing that was stopping him from getting up, going to the bar and ordering a dose of anaesthetic in the form of a large brandy. At least in jail, he wouldn't be getting this kind of sympathy. 'I did it,' he'd wanted to roar. 'Don't feel sorry for me. Hate me. Tell me how despicable I am.' He should tell them, right then, what happened. Watch their faces curl into disgust, see them back away, change their opinions of him.

'What was her name?' Pearl had asked gently.

'Juliet.'

'Juliet,' Pearl had said softly. 'Well, I'm very sorry we never got to meet her.'

It was such a tender, lovely thing to say that Seb had almost lost it. Almost. He'd almost said how the pain of missing her was like a knife that was twisting in his gut, every second of every day. He'd almost said that he deserved every bit of this agony he was feeling and more, and that he would regret what he did to his dying day. He'd almost said that his utter devastation was stopping him from fulfilling a promise they'd made to each other the day they married.

Instead, in a well-practised act of subject changing diversion, he'd cleared his throat, forced a smile, and said, 'I am too. Anyway, let's not dwell on the sad stuff. Do you get home to Scotland much?'

Pearl had hesitated, and Seb could see she was briefly deliberating whether to offer more sympathy and consolation or to go along with his charade of resolve. He prayed she'd choose the latter. It was the kindness that killed him every time. He could be stoic and composed, and yet the minute he heard genuine words of compassion, or felt a warm hug of empathy, the threads of his strength would begin to unravel.

His shoulder muscles had dropped with relief when Pearl decided to go with his diversion and shifted the conversation back to cheery banalities. 'We're actually heading to Glasgow on Wednesday,' she'd announced, with an unmistakable glimmer of excitement. 'Our Caro, that's Yvonne's girl, is getting married on Friday. Our son Todd and his partner Jared are meeting us there, so the whole family will be together and...' She'd paused, and Seb had seen a flash of embarrassment as she had a realisation. 'Oh, listen to me rambling on about happy families and you suffering such a loss...'

Seb had immediately jumped in. 'Please, don't worry. I'm interested and, trust me, hearing about happy families is good for me right now. Reminds me of the stuff that life is worth living for. Where's the wedding going to be held?'

Pearl had beamed, like someone given carte blanche to talk about their very favourite subject. 'In the Kibble Palace at the Botanic Gardens. Have you been there?'

Another twist of the knife in his gut. Seb had instinctively glanced downwards, so they wouldn't see the flinch of pain cross his face. He knew the place so well. Juliet had taken him there on one of their first dates, and many times since then on their visits home to Glasgow. It was one of her favourite places, a stunning Victorian glass and iron structure, home to a magnificent collection of statues and plants from around the world, and situated in the glorious green surroundings of the Botanic Gardens.

He'd promised Juliet they would return there next summer, yet another vow he was destined to break, just like one of the many things that he'd been tortured by for the last six months.

Seb had realised an unanswered question was hanging in the air. 'Many times,' he'd answered. 'It's beautiful.'

'It is! It might have taken our Caro a while to get there, but she's doing it in style.'

Determined to ensure the focus didn't return to himself and his loss, Seb had grasped for a question that would keep the conversation going until he could recover his balance. 'A while to get there?' he'd asked.

'Well, I mean, not nowadays, I suppose. But she's such a lovely lass and I was beginning to get worried that she'd never find the right person. Soon as she met Cammy though, that was it. And I said to her, "Caro, love, you're only thirty-four – still plenty of time if you want to start a family, but best get those eggs frozen just in case."'

At the time, Seb had given it no further thought, just grateful that they'd steered the conversation back on to ground that didn't make him feel like his pain receptors were on the outside of his skin. It was later though, when he lay in bed, unable to sleep, that the words came back to him, the calculations threw up questions, and he wondered if the coincidence that had brought Pearl and Bob into his life that night was more like a twist of fate, a sign sent by the woman he loved and whose life he had ended. Perhaps she forgave him and this was her way of showing him that? Or maybe she didn't, and this was a way to make him hurt, make him pay for what he did. Perhaps his punishment was going to be raised hopes and searing disappointment, the reaffirmation that he had nothing left to live for.

Now, as the 'fasten seatbelts' sign pinged on above him, and the cabin crew prepared to land in Glasgow, he knew he had to find out.

Either way, no matter what the answer was, he would take it, because after six months of avoiding the subject, that chance meeting had compelled him into action. Live or die, happiness or devastation, he had one thing he had to do first.

Staring at the bag between his feet, the one containing the ashes of his love, the guilt ebbed for just long enough to feel an incredible sense of relief that he was close to fulfilling the promise that they'd made to each other on their wedding day. If either of them were to die, the other would scatter their ashes in the city that they loved.

Today was the day that he was finally going to keep that promise.

And then he was going to do everything he could to find out if a bride who was getting married today could possibly be his daughter.

Three

Josie

'Message received on Thursday 19th December at 5.05 p.m.'

Another voice took over.

'This is Margaret Rosemund, secretary to Dr Ormond at Glasgow Central Hospital, with a message for Mrs Josephine Cairney. Dr Ormond has the results of your recent scan and requests that you make an appointment to discuss them. Please call me back as soon as possible to arrange a convenient time.'

Josie pressed the red button to end the playback. She'd listened to that message at least twenty times during a sleepless night, trying desperately to glean any kind of hint of her fate from the intonation in the caller's voice. Nothing. She was none the wiser. She'd called back yesterday evening, five minutes after receiving the call, but the secretary was already gone for the day. Who made a call like that and then darted out of the office? Josie had been left with no choice but to wait until this morning to call back.

So far, it had been the longest fifteen hours and forty minutes of her life. Now, at 8.45 a.m., standing in the open doorway, looking over her back garden, she took a long, intoxicating drag on the cigarette that dangled between her fingers. There was a bloody irony right there, she decided. These were the fecking things that had got her into this mess in the first place. A rasping cough interrupted her thoughts and as soon as it subsided, she pulled her dressing gown tighter around her, then lifted her mug of tea to her lips.

She was going to catch her death standing there, but this had been part of her morning routine for so long that – rain, hail, sunshine or snow – it just wouldn't feel the same to start her day any other way. Up, dressing gown on, downstairs, make a cuppa, open the back door, have her first cigarette while casting her eyes over her the daily changes in her garden.

A robin watched her from the ancient oak birdhouse that she kept fully stocked in winter, its red breast puffed out, eyes beady. The sight would normally have made her smile. Not today.

She stubbed out the cigarette in the ashtray that sat on the worktop just inside the door and took a deep breath, setting off another coughing fit.

'Bloody hell, you sound like you're on yer last legs there,' Val had said to her a few months ago after a similar episode. 'You need to get that checked and then get some big handsome bloke to rub that Vicks menthol stuff on yer chest.' The two of them had creased into cackles, then continued wandering around Topshop. It was one of Josie's favourite pastimes, watching the shocked looks on the young ones' faces when she trotted into the dressing room, all seventy-ish years old (she refused to calculate the exact number and threatened to staple shut the mouths of anyone else who even thought about blurting it out), and came out looking deadly in a pair of black skinny jeans and a slinky top. Other than the obvious landslide situations caused by age and gravity, her figure had barely changed a jot since she was a teenager, nor had her fashion taste. Still a size 8–10, still wore black, still channelled a cross between Emma Peel from the Avengers and – with her white spiky hair – Billy Idol. Add a bright red lip, an attitude of defiant indestructibility and an over-fondness for profanity, and that formed the armour that had kept her enjoying every moment of her life for seven decades.

The cold morning air was making her shiver now, so she closed the back door and retreated to the kitchen table with her steaming mug. How many people had sat around this table and bared their souls over the years? Her daughter Avril used to call it Drama Central, because the moment anyone within a five mile radius had a disaster, trauma or problem, they'd show up here and out would come the biscuit tin, the teabags and the kitchen roll for mopping up tears. Josie would listen, console them and offer sweary wisdom until the poor soul felt better. Now the kitchen roll was on her side of the table.

She'd been looking forward to today for months and she should be long gone by now, on her way to pick up Val, before heading over to Caro's flat to spend the morning on the Buck's Fizz, bossing everyone around while delighting in every second of the anticipation and revelry before tonight's ceremony.

Yesterday's phone call had changed everything.

The old wooden wall clock ticked relentlessly, but to her relief the sound was drowned out by the sudden ringing of her mobile phone. She snatched up the handset and checked the screen. Not the doctor's office again. The word 'Cammy' flashed at her. Summoning every ounce of strength she possessed, she pressed the green button and launched into one of her usual barbed but affectionate greetings. 'What is it? I'm a busy woman and my time is expensive.'

'You know if I was thirty years older I'd be marrying you today,' Cammy's smooth, amused voice promised her.

'You couldn't keep up with me,' she shot back with a wry chuckle, trying desperately to sound as normal as possible. Cammy. Her friend for well over ten years, since they worked together in a 'his and hers' lingerie boutique, a riotous time of her life that she'd absolutely adored. The laughs they'd had, forging a friendship that had been instant and full of mischief. Outsiders may have judged them an unlikely pairing, but Josie didn't give a hoot what anyone else thought. Many of her circle of friends were in their thirties, forties, fifties... Age had no relevance for her, given that she refused to pay any attention to her own. Besides, she thought of Cammy as family, joining Michael and Avril, her adult children, at the top of the Christmas card list. Not that she actually sent cards – not with the price of bloody stamps these days.

'Sad but true,' Cammy agreed, feigning sadness. 'Anyway, I'm just phoning to check on you. Are you on your way to pick up Val?'

'No, there's been a slight... erm... change of plan.'

'Oh God, what's happened?' he groaned. 'You've been arrested. You've fallen down a pothole. You've—'

Josie decided to set him straight. 'I spent all night shagging George Clooney and Amal just turned up at the door demanding I give him back. Stroppy cow, that one. So now I just need to get shot of her, freshen up my lady bits, go pick up my wedding togs and then I'm meeting Val there.' Josie sent up a silent prayer to the gods of maledom that the mention of lady bits would throw Cammy and he'd skip over the change of plan and decide there was nothing to worry about. She didn't give him a chance to counter. 'Anyway, how are you feeling this morning? Ready to marry a woman who is far too good for you?' she teased. It was the least he would expect.

'Absolutely. Not quite sure how I got this lucky,' he added, with a tone that hinted at both honesty and uncharacteristic seriousness, before switching back to more familiar humour. 'I just hope she doesn't see sense and ditch me at the altar.'

'If she does, I'll step in and marry you. I'm thirty years too old for you, but it'll make the papers and we'll score a fortune from the scandal. They'll have us on *Good Morning Britain* by the end of the week.'

Cammy's laughter was low and infectious. 'Done. Anyway, I'd better go and drag my best men out of whatever gutter they landed in last night. Josie, thanks again for everything you've done to help us today. You know we love you.'

Josie felt her throat constrict, and this time it wasn't because of those damned cigarettes. 'See if you're still saying the same when you get my bill,' she joked, before hanging up.

Her head immediately went into her hands, pained by the effort of the cheery façade. Fuck. Keeping this up all day was going to be a nightmare. Of course, she might not have to. Maybe it would all go swimmingly. Maybe she was reading too much into yesterday's call. Perhaps she only had good news ahead.

The clock chimed 9 a.m. and her finger hit the number she'd programmed in earlier.

'Dr Ormond's office, Margaret Rosemund speaking, can I help you?'

'Yes. This is Josephine Cairney. You left a message on my answering machine yesterday about scan results.' It was a wonder the woman on the other end of the phone could hear her over the sound of the fireworks that were going off in her head.

'Let me just check...' A pause. 'Ah, yes, Miss Cairney. Dr Ormond would like to discuss your results. The first appointment I have is Friday, January the third, at 3 p.m.'

'No,' Josie said simply.

The woman on the other end of the phone sounded puzzled. 'No?'

'I'm sorry, but that's unacceptable. I am in my advancing years and I don't suppose I have many Christmases left in me. I'm not going to spend this one in a state of panic because I don't know if I'm about to be dealt some bad news from Dr Grim Reaper. So I need to see him today.'

'I'm sorry, but that's not possible. He's fully booked and—'

Josie creased as another coughing fit hijacked her body, forcing a pause before she could answer. 'Margaret, I'm sure you're a lovely lady and I know you're doing your best. But the reason my son added me to his extortionate private insurance policy was because I'm closer to the exit than the entrance. The stress of worrying about what the good doctor has to tell me will kill me before Christmas Eve. So here's the thing – I'm going to head on down to his office right now. I know he starts at ten o'clock, so I'll be there at 9.45. He can choose to either put this old dear out of her misery and tell me the verdict, or he can have me ejected. I hope he'll do the festive thing and go for the first option. See you then.' With that, she hung up, leaving a dumbstruck Margaret stuttering out an objection to an audience of no one.

Josie Cairney hadn't got this far in life by playing to other people's rules and limitations and she wasn't going to start now. This was too important. All she wanted to do was go and see two people she loved get married and start a glorious existence together.

But first, today was the day that she was going to find out if this Christmas would be her last.

Four

Stacey

The guy in the seat next to Stacey had been casting sly glances at her since the seatbelt sign had gone off five minutes after leaving Dublin. Out of the corner of her eye, she could see he was wearing an expression she was all too familiar with – curiosity as to whether she really was who he thought she was, coupled with an internal dialogue of indecision as to whether or not he should ask her. She really hoped he wouldn't. It felt like the last twenty-four hours had lasted a week and she just wasn't up to idle, awkward chit-chat.

She'd done everything she could to avoid this kind of encounter – she'd pulled her hair back into a ponytail, wasn't wearing a scrap of make-up and – the ultimate disguise – had thrown on a baggy sweatshirt that drowned her figure. It had worked on the first leg of the journey from LA to Dublin – to Stacey's relief, the woman sitting next to her on that flight hadn't a clue that she was chatting to a TV celebrity whose face had made it on to billboards. Instead of fending off the usual questions, Stacey had spent all of the eleven hours listening to the stranger, who'd introduced herself as

Coleen before she'd even got her bag in the overhead locker, sharing every detail of her Christmas plans, including the intricacies of every dynamic in her extended family. By the time they'd crossed the Atlantic and Coleen had hugged her goodbye and headed off to baggage reclaim, Stacey knew that Coleen's niece, Orla, and her feckless husband, Seamus, were heading for post-Christmas splitsville, her grandson, Kayden, could do with a severe dose of discipline, her sister, Linda, had scandalised the town by flirting with the priest, and her late husband, God rest his soul, had been a saint who had adored her to his last breath, even if he did like a drink. Stacey had managed to squeeze in her first name, and the fact that she was heading back to Glasgow for a friend's wedding. It was only a partial truth, but the other woman hadn't stopped for breath long enough for Stacey to elaborate even if she'd wanted to. Which she most definitely didn't. The last thing Stacey Summers wanted to talk about was herself, her life in LA, her star status, or the real reason for her trip back to her homeland this weekend.

Unfortunately, the man who was now sitting next to her hadn't received that memo and decided to go for it. 'Excuse me, I guess you must get this all the time, but are you...'

The accent was American, he was in his late thirties, maybe well maintained early forties, and the biggest demographic for the show, so Stacey knew he was probably going to get this right. Her fame hadn't quite reached the British side of the Atlantic, but in the USA, she had gathered quite a following, not all of it welcome. Still, this guy looked fairly respectable, with no obvious signs of pervdom, so she wasn't going to be rude.

'Stacey from *USA Speed Freaks*?'

'Would you believe me if I said no?' she asked, not unkindly. She could see now that he was actually quite good-looking – smart suit, maybe Boss or Tom Ford, Movado watch, good haircut, a bit of stubble that was to be expected if he'd also travelled from the USA with a Dublin stopover. It was the route that Stacey always preferred to take when she was coming home, mainly because on the way back to LA, a special agreement between the American and Irish governments meant that she cleared US immigration at Dublin airport. No three hour wait trying to get through the arrivals queues at LAX, just off the plane and out of the door.

Perfect teeth flashed at her. 'Not now that I've heard your accent.'

USA Speed Freaks was one of the most popular shows on the car channel, featuring a weekly competition between rival garages tasked with renovating similar sports cars. Stacey's role as co-presenter had been – let's be honest – fairly decorative at first, thanks to a uniform of tiny vests and miniscule Daisy Dukes, but over the last five years she'd won over even the most critical of viewers with her quick wit and sassy put-downs, all delivered in a Scottish accent that was still as strong as the day she'd left Glasgow twelve years ago. Now, at thirty-five, she was practically prehistoric in Hollywood years, but thanks to a long overdue wave of resistance against sexist ageism, the unparalleled knowledge she'd built up about cars, and a workout schedule that left her with a body that had barely changed in fifteen years, she was still a firm favourite with the show's viewers.

Getting the role had been the biggest thrill of her life. After working as a dancer for years (yes, there were poles involved) and doing the odd bit of modelling, she'd gone to

America after landing a part in a condom advert, which led to a relatively well paid campaign for a Scottish brand of bras that had been gaining increasing popularity overseas. At first, living there and trying to break into the entertainment industry in a land of unfeasibly beautiful people had been daunting, but when her mate, Cammy, had joined her, the life of a struggling actor/presenter/model suddenly became a lot more fun. Cammy had picked up enough retail and modelling work to stay afloat for nearly a decade, until he'd left, almost three years ago. A shudder reminded her that was a goodbye she didn't want to think about.

She fast forwarded her mind to the present. Now, both professionally and personally, she'd had more success than she could ever have hoped for. Her role on *USA Speed Freaks* had gained her a huge following, she'd moved into a gorgeous apartment in West Hollywood, and she was in a relationship with Jax Green, her co-presenter for the last three years. Brought in to replace her original co-star, Taylor Lawrie, after he was involved in a drug fuelled pile up that wrecked his Lamborghini and his career, Jax was an immediate hit with the male viewers for his car knowledge and straight talking cheek. But he also gained an adoring female fanbase thanks to the fact that he was charming, drop-dead gorgeous, with a ripped and toned body that was close to perfection and the kind of tattoos that screamed 'edgy' without tipping over into trashy. Their relationship had been swift and the cherry on top of what seemed like a gilded existence. Yep, on the outside, it all looked perfect, but on the inside...

'I love that show,' the guy was saying now. 'I'm Zac.'

'Stacey,' she replied, stating the obvious, making an effort to be pleasant but not over friendly. She didn't want another new-found travelling companion. She was fairly sure Coleen had given her tinnitus.

It seemed he wasn't great with subliminal messages. 'That makeover you guys did with the '54 Mustangs was awesome.'

Engage. Don't engage. Engage. Don't engage. Stacey checked her watch. Half an hour left until landing. May as well make polite conversation, so he didn't think she was arrogant. The last thing she needed was some random guy tweeting that she'd been rude, and then she'd land to a hundred bitchy barbs from trolls. Ah, the joys of the social media age. Her decision to engage was delayed by the flight attendant placing a tray with a ham and cheese roll and a plastic cup of orange juice on the tray in front of her.

'Yep, they looked great. I actually bought the white one after the show,' she eventually replied. It had been one of the highlights of her life – buying the kind of car she'd only ever seen in movies when she was growing up. It sure beat the rust-ridden, MOT-failing, ancient Micra that had been her family car until she started work and helped her mum buy a new one.

His eyes widened with interest. 'Seriously? Man, that's cool. That was a beauty.'

'It still is,' Stacey said. 'I love it.'

Maybe that would be it. Small talk over. Time to return to a comfortable silence.

Or not.

'Are you going home to visit family for the holidays?' he asked, then grinned again, this time with sexy self-deprecation. 'Sorry. It's four days before Christmas. I guess that's a pretty dumb question.'

Putting him at ease was instinctive. 'I am. But I'm also going home for a wedding tonight. A... friend's wedding.'

There was a narrowing of his brow. 'And yet, you don't look too happy about that. An ex?'

Both his perception and his frankness surprised her. It was one of the things that she usually loved about the people she encountered in LA – they had no filter and no concept of privacy. It reminded her of home. In the area of Glasgow she grew up in, you couldn't wait for a bus without getting the complete life story of the person standing next to you.

'Kind of. Not really. No.' It was difficult to explain, especially because she couldn't really make sense of it all herself. Cammy had come over to LA a few months after her and for years they'd shared a flat, partied their asses off, built up a great gang of mates, supported each other through relationship make-ups and break-ups, and been like the brother and sister neither of them had ever had. Cammy eventually found his own place, but that changed nothing.

For every moment of their time in Tinsel Town, she'd loved him. The problem was, she hadn't realised that 'loving him as a best friend' had turned into 'being hopelessly in love with him' until it was too late. She'd met Jax, he'd moved in with her, and they were a few months into a turbulent on-off relationship when Cammy had decided to return to Scotland.

The memory of his last night in LA came flooding back, as vivid as the inflight movie she'd been watching until her seat buddy had struck up a conversation.

Her relationship with Jax had always been rocky, with enough drama to keep the tabloids busy. They'd been on one of their many splits, when Cammy came to stay with her the night before his flight, because he'd already given up the lease on his place.

They were up on the roof terrace of her apartment – a space that was small but glorious. Stacey had put a gorgeous rattan daybed up there, big enough for two, with side tables for drinks and sun cream. Or, in this case, bottles of beer and tacos from her favourite Mexican restaurant. She was in jeans and a vest top, her feet bare, and lying next to her, Cammy had on just a pair of shorts, the rest of his stuff packed away for the flight the next day. He'd picked up enough modelling and bar work to fund his time in LA and she could see why. His six-pack was cut to perfection. His shoulders wide. His grin infectious.

'Will you miss it?' she'd asked him.

'What, LA?'

'Yeah. The life here. Me,' she'd added, laughing.

'You, more than life itself,' he'd teased. 'The rest of it? Yeah, no doubt I'll miss some things,' he'd admitted, running his fingers through his hair. He always did that when he was perturbed or had something on his mind, so Stacey's curiosity was piqued.

'So why leave then? Stay and keep me company until they decide I'm an old hag and toss me out of the city. I've heard that happens the minute you turn forty.'

He took a sip of his beer. 'That answers the question. I'm already hitting forty. Time to go home, be a grown-up. Do something with my life.'

'And what about that stuff you'll miss?' It was a glib comment until the last word was said, and his gaze fixed on hers, his face so close she could feel the exhalation of his breath.

Something changed. She'd never know what. Maybe he just finally had a now or never burst of courage. But when they came, his words were no longer flippant and joking. They were soft, loaded with a depth of emotion that didn't usually factor in their relationship.

'Maybe one day she'll realise we should be more than friends and she'll come home too.'

Sledgehammer to the solar plexus, arrow right through the heart, as she realised what he was saying.

She was never sure if he kissed her first, or the other way around, but suddenly they were naked, they were making love and it was the most incredible, mind blowing sex she'd ever experienced.

They'd found their way to bed, made love again. 'Have I mentioned that your timing sucks?' she'd asked. 'Why now? If you felt this way, why not mention the not so insignificant fact that you wanted to remove my underwear before now?'

He'd kissed her collarbone, her neck, her fingers. 'Too much to lose. I couldn't risk freaking you out and losing you.'

'And now?'

'Now you know. And now it's up to you.'

'Smashing. Great. No, really. Superb.'

His smile did things to her insides. In the name of all things platonic, what was happening here? It was like slipping into some kind of alternate universe, one where she found her best friend irresistibly sexy and could come up with absolutely no explanation as to why this had never happened before. Even his voice was turning her on now.

'Look, Stacey, you have a great life here and I could never ask you to give that up. It's time for me to go home and I know that, but I'm not sweeping in here and begging you to come with me. You've been my best friend for ten years and I love you. If you think we can make it work, you know where I'll be. Either way, I'll always love you. Christ, I came over all Dolly Parton there.'

Her laughter had been stopped by kisses, then hands, then tangled limbs, and they'd made love until the sun came up. He hadn't asked her again, she hadn't offered. This had to be thought through. She had a job, a life, a boyfriend here.

When she'd woken up the next morning, he was gone. Jax had appeared at the door an hour later, flush with apologies and promises of redemption. Unable to face another drama when she was already in the middle of an emotional shitstorm, she'd let him in, but held him at arms length, saying she needed time to think.

Cammy had called her when he landed.

'How long?' she'd blurted, as soon as she heard his voice.

He didn't have to ask what she meant. 'Years. Two or three.'

'For God's sake, Cammy – has anyone told you your communication skills need work?'

'You. Many times.'

He had her there. She'd been telling him forever that he was way too laid back when it came to expressing his feelings. He blamed it on his Scottish genes. 'It's a part of the DNA,' he'd tell her. 'Like the ability to go out in sub zero temperatures wearing just a T-shirt, or track down a kebab shop at the end of a night out. It's in the blood.' And then he'd grin, and so would she because he was completely unfazed by his character flaw.

'Jax came back,' she'd admitted.

'He'd have been a fool not to.'

'Cammy, I don't know what to do.' How could she give up the life she'd worked so hard for here? But yet, how could she not explore this new landscape with Cammy?

'Then do nothing,' he'd told her softly. 'I love you, Stace. You know where I am. If it's meant to be, it'll be.'

'You're doing Doris Day now.'

'I'm going to go before Celine Dion kicks in. Listen, I don't want this to change things between us, so I'm not going to mention it again. Let's just say it didn't happen, unless you change your mind. I'll be waiting. I love you.'

And then he was gone again.

She'd almost come back. Almost. But the following morning an offer had come in to do a six page photospread in Hawaii for the biggest selling car magazine, Jax had done the whole 'post-split making an effort' thing, the show's shooting schedule had been crazy and...

So many excuses. All of them valid, all of them – as she looked back on it now – completely irrelevant. The truth was she'd been confused and pissed off with Cammy for blindsiding her. By the time she'd caught up, realised he was right, life had moved on. Since he'd left, they'd spoken once a month or so on the phone, just friendly chat, like two great old friends. True to his word, it was like that night had never happened and neither of them ever mentioned how they parted. However, every call cemented what she knew – she was in love with him, and by the time she was ready to tell him, he'd met Caro.

This was her last chance. She just had to steel up the courage to take it. Thinking about how she'd messed the whole thing up made her stomach tingle and her hands shake as she pushed the in-flight snack away.

She realised she'd left her answer hanging in the air, and her travel companion was politely waiting for something more. 'An ex-roommate. And friend. I'm just not big on weddings,' she added, not quite truthfully, but realising that didn't quite cover her obvious reticence. A change of subject was required. 'What about you? Why are you going to Glasgow?'

'Two days of meetings there. I work for a menswear brand in LA and our next collection uses Scottish tweed. I'm going to meet with our supplier tomorrow to nail down some details.'

A menswear brand. That explained the snappy suit. Stacey was surprised at the timing though. 'On a Saturday?'

He nodded, flashing that self-deprecating grin again. 'It's amazing how accommodating people can be when there's a generous budget. And I need to get in and out in two days. Don't want to risk not making it back for Christmas.'

A vision of this man, next to a picture-perfect wife, with two sweet little kids that looked just like mommy and daddy came to life in her head. Of course he needed to get back for Christmas. He was a normal guy with a normal life, not someone whose whole shiny existence was based on a lie because inside she was aching for the one missing piece.

The flight attendant came by to clear their trays, giving Stacey momentary relief from having to make conversation. Moments later, the seatbelt sign came on, just as the pilot announced that there were ten minutes to landing.

'Listen, I don't know if it's possible, and I swear I don't ever do this, but would you have time to catch drinks or maybe dinner with me before I fly back on Monday?'

It was all Stacey could do not to roll her eyes. As if her life wasn't complicated enough. 'I'm sorry, but I have a boyfriend in LA. I don't think he'd be too happy about that.'

Yep, the boyfriend. Sometimes she wondered if she'd ever really given her relationship with Jax a chance. Her feelings for Cammy had always held her back, yet the guilt of that had, in some ways, kept them together. It was the perfect 'showmance', great in the press, and sure they had a lot of fun together. Their sex life was sensational and underneath all his cocky arrogance – and if you overlooked his fairly typical LA self-obsession – he was a good guy. She couldn't have stayed with him this long if he wasn't. But soulmate? Forever love? He just didn't make her feel that way. Unlike Cammy. Damn it.

The wave of nausea she was currently experiencing had nothing to do with the fact that the plane dipped suddenly as they came in to land in stormy weather. She'd walked out. Left Jax a note with just the briefest explanation. 'Decided to go home to the wedding after all. Be back for Christmas,' she'd written yesterday, before flying out of the door to make it to LAX for the booking she'd made only ten minutes before.

It had been a spur of the moment thing. A decision that was probably up there with Pretty Woman's big mistake. Huge.

Jax had been filming down in Palm Springs, but Stacey reckoned he'd be getting home around now. It was too late to worry about how he'd react, but hopefully he'd be fine with it. She was pretty sure he had no idea how she felt about Cammy. Her acting skills had never threatened the future bank balance of Meryl Streep, but she'd always tried to pull off 'casual and nonchalant' when she'd spoken of him.

Not that it mattered.

Right now, the only thing that she cared about, that made her heart beat faster, was telling Cammy how she felt. The urgency had crept up on her, shifting her attitude from bitter regret to grasping at one last chance. When she'd woken up yesterday, she'd realised that she would never forgive herself if she didn't at least let Cammy see the full picture. That's why she was here this morning.

As the wheels of the plane touched down on a wet Glasgow runway, she took a deep breath and strengthened her resolve. She had to do it. There was no choice.

Today was the day that Stacey was going to tell Cammy Jones that she was in love with him.

Five

Website – www.itshouldhavebeenme.com

Members Discussion Forum

Post by member, screen name NotOverYet:

Okay, so the day has come. The love of my life is marrying someone else. Even typing that makes me want to scream. I know this is a forum for mutual support and consolation, but right now I don't want to hear anything that will make me feel better. I'm pissed off and I'm heartbroken. Why isn't it me? Why am I not the one sipping champagne and looking at the white dress hanging on the front of the wardrobe, waiting to say I Do in front of the world? I need to move on, to find someone else, to let him go.

Well, fuck that.

I'm not doing it. I want him and if he doesn't want me, then at least I'm going down fighting. I'm going to that wedding today and I'm going to be heard. When you've got nothing left to lose, doing something is better than watching the future you dreamed of slip through your fingers.

Comments:

CarolSaidGoodbye: Hey NotOverYet, I get how you're feeling. Been there, done that, messed it up and watched him be with someone else. I didn't fight for him. I wish I had. You go, girl!

NancyBirmingham: No! Don't do it. Only two possible outcomes. 1. His bride will mess you up. 2. You'll look like a tit.

10 A.M. – NOON

Six

Caro

Val's jaw had dropped so low it took her a moment to get it back up to a position that facilitated speech.

'Caro, love, are you trying to give me a stroke? What do you mean, you don't want to get married? Of course you do. Oh, dear God, I've seen this on the news. Roofies. Someone slipped something in your drink last night and you've lost your mind. We need to get to the hospital and get your stomach pumped and… I'll bloody kill our Jen and Chrissie. How the bugger did they let this happen?' Val turned her head to the side and ramped up her volume, voice now steeped in menace, so she could be heard by the hung-over matron of honour in the next room. "Jen, you'd better start running, love, because I am NOT BLOODY HAPPY.'

Caro sighed, leaning against the kitchen worktop for support. 'Val, no one spiked my drink. And it's nothing to do with Jen.'

'What's nothing to do with me?' Jen asked, appearing in the doorway.

If Caro didn't feel like her heart was being ripped out of her chest without an anaesthetic, she'd have found the sight amusing. Last night's shirt on backwards. Make-up smears on her face. Stray pieces of tinsel matted in her hair and snowman earrings, one of which had suddenly begun flashing, probably out of sheer terror at Val's furious glare.

'What the hell did you do to this poor lassie last night?' Val demanded, her platinum bob trembling with outrage.

'Got her pissed, made her lead a conga, forced her to sing with a mariachi band and fed her a kebab.' Jen then shrugged apologetically at Caro, only a twinkle in her eye giving a hint that she had no idea of the gravity of this situation. 'Sorry, Caro, she's always been able to crack me. My spine removes itself the minute she gives me the glare.'

In any other circumstances, Caro would have found this hilarious. Not this morning.

Val's hands went to her hips. 'She's saying she doesn't want to get married.'

Jen chortled. 'Of course she does! She's winding you u—' she broke off when she saw the absolute agony that was written all over Caro's face. 'Oh bollocks. I need caffeine and a seat for this. So do you, Val. Your varicose veins will be fit to burst. Chrissie, get in here and help.' While Caro stared at the floor, Jen took charge, clearing the shiny white gloss table, putting the three cups of coffee and a newly added cup of tea for Val in front of the four seats that surrounded it.

Chrissie wandered in just as the other three were sitting down and, drawn in by the coffee aroma, joined them at the table. 'What did I miss?' she asked glibly.

'I don't want to go though with the wedding,' Caro said, more definite this time than when she'd just plucked up the courage to tell Val. 'I can't. I just can't do it.'

Like Jen, Chrissie giggled at the sheer ridiculousness of the statement. 'Yeah, right. And I'm Vera Wang...' The last word trailed off as she caught the other women's wide-eyed horror and, like Jen a few minutes ago, realised that this wasn't a joke. 'Shit, you're serious. Is this some kind of alcohol poisoning psychosis?'

Val stepped in, making a real effort to regain some of her trademark composure. Freaking out, shouting at people and generally steamrollering her way through life was Josie's job. Val had always tried to maintain a more warm, accepting, understanding attitude to her loved ones. 'Okay, love, start from the beginning. What's happened to change your mind?'

There was a pause as Caro struggled to find the words. Eventually, she settled on, 'I don't think I've really changed my mind, so much as gone along with something I was never sure I wanted to do. When Cammy proposed, I said yes because I love him and would never want to hurt him. I still do. It seemed like the natural way of things and I didn't give it too much thought. But then when we set the date, the anxiety started. Not about Cammy, but about the wedding. I feel sick every time I picture myself walking up the aisle, or when I think about saying vows and hearing him say them to me. Everything about it makes me want to run away and forget about the whole thing. I thought I could handle it, but I can't.'

'So it's not that you've changed your mind about Cammy, it's the wedding bit that you don't want to go through with?'

Jen asked, hangover now forgotten while her foggy brain attempted to make sense of a senseless situation.

Caro nodded. 'I just don't want to do it.'

Chrissie was a bit more forthright. 'I hate to ask the obvious question, but why didn't you say anything before now? Talk to Cammy? Or to us? You know you can tell us anything.'

'I think I was hoping that something inside me would change and that it was just stage fright. Cold feet. I should have told him and I tried so many times, but as soon I brought up the subject of the wedding, he'd immediately go on about how much he couldn't wait and how excited he was and then… I'm such a coward. I just couldn't tell him. What was I going to say? "Sorry, darling, you're wonderful, but you can forget that wedding lark because I've changed my mind?" So I just pushed my feelings back down and I prayed I'd get over it, but it just gets worse every single day and now I'm here and I know I can't do it. I hate myself for it, but I just can't.'

The three other women shot each other helpless glances before Val took charge, putting her hands over Caro's shaking fingers on the table. The others weren't sure whether it was an act of consolation or a move to stop Caro from fleeing.

'Look, love, nobody is going to make you get married if you don't want to. And, God knows, that man of yours is so in love with you he'd forgive you anything. But let's not be too hasty and rush into anything. Tell me exactly what you feel when you think about the wedding. What is it that's scaring you?'

Caro took a sip of coffee, misery seeping from every pore as she thought about her answer. She didn't have a logical explanation, just a vague explosion of thoughts that seemed to crash around in her mind, battering her 'until death do us part' gene into submission.

'I've had the same dream every night for the last week. A wedding. My wedding. Only it's not me. The bride gets to the end of the aisle and the groom is my dad, and he lifts her veil, and it's my mum and she's crying and begging me not to do it.'

'Oh love…' Val murmured, sympathy and compassion in every crease of her pained expression.

'And I know why she's saying it. Look at them. Married for thirty years and the whole time it was a sham. What's the point? Did it make my dad stay faithful? Did it make my mum happy? Was there a single thing about their marriage that I'd want for myself? Nothing. All it brought was misery. My mum died alone and only the fact that her mind was long gone saved her the agony of finding out that my dad had been cheating on her for thirty years and walked out when she needed him most. That's what marriage is to me. A sham. A complete farce, but worse than that, it was the thing that wasted my mum's life. From the moment she married my dad, she lived for him, and she ended up dying alone while that bastard lived it up with someone else. I know this won't make sense to you, but marriage destroyed my mum's life. And now…' she was forcing herself to speak through her sobs, 'I feel my mum is telling me not to do it. I know that sounds completely messed up because I don't even believe in that kind of stuff, but this isn't making me happy, Val. It's making me miserable, and anxious and so, so scared. This isn't how anyone should feel on their wedding day.'

An air of shock now mingled with the fetid aroma of last night's revelry.

Chrissie reached over and pushed Caro's messy hair back from her face. They all knew the shocking story of Caro's discovery when she first came to Glasgow and found out that her father had been living a double life. Two families in different cities. 'But, Caro, your parents are not you and Cammy. You two are so different.'

'I know that. And I love him and I am absolutely sure he loves me and we're meant to be together. I just can't marry him. And I'm pretty sure if I tell him that now I'll break his heart. I don't know that he'd ever forgive me.'

'Of course he would,' Val argued, hoping she was right. He was a good man, Cammy. She couldn't imagine any circumstances under which he'd walk away from Caro. But then… if there was one thing that life had taught her it was that you never really know the people you love as well as you think you do.

Caro didn't even register Val's uncertainty, too lost in the hopelessness of her situation. How had she let it come to this? She was a good person. How could she even consider hurting the man she loved? Yet, the very thought of pulling on a white dress and making those vows turned her stomach.

The ring of the doorbell interrupted her thoughts.

'That'll be Josie,' Val said, with definite relief, as she got up to go answer the door.

Caro, meanwhile, slumped down further in her chair, consumed with dread and regret. Josie had done so much for them, planned and sourced everything that they would need to make the day perfect. She'd even bought a clipboard on eBay and had taken to making lists and ticking things off. She'd wholeheartedly embraced the project and now it was all for nothing.

Val's footsteps retreated down the hallway. They'd faded out of earshot by the time Caro made a snap decision and jumped up from her chair.

'I have to go,' she blurted to Jen and Chrissie. 'I can't just sit here and do nothing about this.'

'Caro, wait, we'll sort it all out and...' Jen ended up speaking to an empty space as Caro grabbed her bright red duffle coat from the back of the kitchen door, thrust her feet into a pair of boots, picked up her bag and bolted.

Out in the hall, she was greeted by a huge white cloud coming towards her. Not Josie. Claire, her wedding dress designer, complete with a four-month pregnancy bump, was negotiating her way past Val while holding aloft a huge white garment bag containing the bride's dress for the big day.

Caro wanted to throw up. Instead, she kissed Claire on the cheek, took the garment bag off her, hung it on the back of the living room door and then shimmied past her. 'I'm sorry, Claire. So sorry.'

'For what?' her friend asked, confused.

'The wedding is off.'

'What... what... what...?' Claire couldn't process the information.

Val took over. 'Where are you going then? Caro, love, stay here, we'll help you. You don't even have a hat and gloves – you'll catch your death of cold out there today.'

'Then it'll save me cancelling everything,' Caro murmured. 'I'm sorry, Val, I really am. I just can't stay here and face this.'

'Let me come with you then,' Val offered, as Caro whizzed past her.

'No. I appreciate it, I really do, but this is something I need to do on my own. I need to sort this out myself.'

Leaving two stunned friends, two hung-over bridesmaids, a house that looked like it had been ransacked and a pristine wedding dress, the bride-to-be walked out and closed the door behind her.

Seven

Seb

The terminal building was heaving with people as Seb made his way through arrivals, smiling when he spotted a large group of women with Santa hats, party blowers, and a 'Welcome Home Stacey!' banner. Whoever Stacey was, she was lucky to have a welcome like that waiting for her. A bolt of reality struck him. He had no family, and he'd led such a nomadic life, he had no large groups of friends anywhere either. There was nowhere in the world that he could go and be greeted by a crowd of eager faces waiting for him.

In the corner of the terminal, Christmas music was coming from speakers near a huge white Christmas tree. It must be eight metres high, yet it wasn't having any effect on his lack of festive spirit. This had been Juliet's favourite time of the year. They'd always spend the afternoon together, just the two of them, and they'd have a huge party at night, with everyone invited. There was a big expat community in Estepona, so many people that were far from their loved ones and Juliet was wonderful at making them forget that, just for one night.

Seb stopped at the car hire desk to collect the vehicle he'd booked online when he'd decided to come here a couple of days ago. The choices were slim, with this being the busiest weekend of the year, and he'd ended up with a...

'Here's the key to your Mercedes, Mr Lloyd. Enjoy your stay in Glasgow,' the rental clerk told him with a cheery smile as she handed over his paperwork and key.

A white E-class Mercedes. It had cost more for the car than it had for the west end hotel that he'd reserved at the last minute too. That's what happened when you had no family left in your home city.

Glasgow held such bittersweet memories for him. The happiest times and the saddest of times too. He'd grown up here, he'd discovered his love of golf on the courses here, he'd married in the city, and he'd said goodbye to people he loved too.

He'd been an only child, and both his parents had passed away in the last five years. His last few trips home had been to visit them when they were sick, and then to watch as they were placed in the ground. He'd thought that was the extent of the heartbreak he'd have to endure for a long time. How wrong he'd been.

Juliet had no family left here either. Her parents had split twenty years ago when she was at university in Glasgow, and now her father lived with his second family on the south coast of England, while her mother lived with her third husband in a very lovely retirement village on Majorca. That lack of family was one of the things that had bonded them so tightly. Both of them grew up without siblings, and neither of them had ever had children. Just two souls, who knew from the first moment they met that they were destined to be together.

He found his car in the bay that was noted on the top of his paperwork and put his bags in the boot, with the exception of the brown leather satchel containing a sealed urn. He wouldn't let that one out of his sight and was just grateful that it hadn't raised any flags when he'd gone through security. That was one item of hand luggage that he didn't want to have to explain.

The clock on the dashboard said 10.15. Too early to check into his hotel. Ironic. He'd had days to think about this trip and yet now that he was here, he wasn't sure whether or not he was crazy to carry out the things he'd planned to do. At the end of the day, he knew he had to let Juliet go, to fulfil his promise and scatter her ashes somewhere that had meaning to her. He still wasn't sure exactly where. That's why he planned to step back in time, to visit all their special places, to remember, to feel the pain of what he'd lost and to seek some kind of atonement for what he'd done. He told himself that he'd know when it was the right time and place to say their final goodbye. Although, he wasn't entirely sure he'd have the courage to do it when the time came.

He joined the motorway slip road, heading west, away from the direction of the city centre. Thirty-five minutes later, he pulled into the car park at the Lomond Lodge Hotel, situated next to one of the most prestigious courses in the country. He saw his hands were shaking as he switched off the engine. The car park was busy, as he'd known it would be. He'd been the golf pro here when they'd first met, fifteen years ago, and while the course would have no business in this weather, the grand stately home beside it was a favourite with families who had money to spend on the festivities. He took a moment to steady himself, until he felt his legs had the strength to climb out of the car and walk inside.

The lobby was a riot of tasteful colour and decorations, all traditional golds and reds, a grand tree soaring into the vaulted ceiling above. An orchestra played over the speakers. He recognised Handel's Messiah – one of Juliet's favourites at this time of year.

He made his way through to the lounge bar, a stately, wood-panelled room with one wall of floor-to-ceiling windows overlooking the loch. Every table was occupied, except... He watched as a couple got up from the table he and Juliet had always considered theirs, placed some cash in the leather wallet containing their bill and then walked off arm in arm.

Seb smiled at them as they passed him, then raised his eyes heavenwards. If ever he needed a sign that Juliet was there with him, this was it. He made his way over, sat in the familiar seat and looked out over the view that took his breath away, even now, when sheets of rain were battering against the window.

This was where they'd met. Seb had been sitting at this table, updating his schedule in his Filofax – he hadn't yet embraced the digital era back then – when he'd heard the sound of a throat clearing.

Turning his head to the window so no one could see his face, he closed his eyes, desperate to be back there, to experience that moment all over again. He blocked out the present, and felt every nerve in his body surge with happiness as he returned to the past.

'Excuse me, is anyone sitting there?' the voice said, with a hint of an apology.

Seb glanced up from his notes to see the most endearing smile, the kind that immediately warms you to a stranger. The woman's eyebrows were raised in question, and only then did he realise that he hadn't answered her. 'No. I mean yes. I'm... sorry, what was the question?' Crap. What had just happened? Some kind of mind fart had robbed him of all powers of articulation. She must think he was a complete idiot.

'Is anyone sitting here?' she repeated, her hand resting on the back of the velvet armchair positioned opposite him. Thankfully, he could see that she seemed to be finding his ineptitude amusing.

'No,' he said, very definitely. 'No-one is sitting there. And yes, you're very welcome to take the seat. And no, I won't talk nonsense to you any further. Actually, I can't promise that.'

'I'll take my chances,' she replied, her low throaty chuckle attracting the attention of some of the people sitting nearby, who automatically smiled.

She was infectious, he realised. And beautiful. Her long chestnut hair fell in waves past her shoulders, creating a curtain for green eyes that had an intoxicating feline slant. But more than that, from the easy way she moved and held herself, he could see that she had absolutely no idea just how stunning she was.

Seb had always mocked the concept of love at first sight. Over the years, he'd had a stream of relationships with beautiful, interesting women. The golf world was an extremely sociable environment, especially for a good-looking, successful pro with an easy-going manner and a genuine interest in the people he met. He'd come close to a more long-term commitment a few times, only for life to get in the way. A career move. An offer from another country. The chance to join a professional player on a tour. His professional aspirations and enjoyment had always been his priority. Some people might call him a loner, and they were probably right, but he preferred to look at it as making the most of a fantastic lifestyle. Good friends, great parties, an exciting job, and a transient existence – but one that allowed him to fully enjoy the experience.

Right there, in that instant, he changed his mind.

'I'm Seb,' he said warmly. 'I'm the golf pro here at the course. And I won't say any more if you just want to read or relax and ignore me. I can take rejection.'

'Juliet,' she replied. 'I'm here for a teaching conference that I'm supposed to be embracing, but it's far too beautiful a day to be stuck in a windowless room with two hundred strangers, so I'm skiving for an hour. Playing hookie. And I don't care if I get caught because this view is worth it.'

'Yes, it definitely is,' he agreed. 'There are few that can match it.'

He was looking straight at her when he said that. And he meant every word.

'Sir, can I get you anything?' The waitress's voice snapped him back to the present, to a rainy December morning so different from that first meeting.

'A coffee, please,' he answered, trying not to show his desolation at the spell being broken. He tried to step back in time again, but it wouldn't come. Instead, he stuck to his memories.

Juliet's one hour break had lasted for twelve. They'd walked along the loch, come into the hotel for dinner, then gone back outside and sat under the moonlight with brandies, Juliet wrapped in a blanket to keep out the summer evening chill. They'd swapped stories, they'd laughed and they'd fallen in love as the stars shone and the water glistened.

Later, there had been no questions, no words, no doubts, when they'd gone back to his suite in the golf club wing of the hotel and made love until dawn. That was it for them. A done deal. Juliet had left her school a few weeks later at the end of the term, and they'd moved to Portugal together, where Seb had been offered a lucrative post on a stunning new course. It had been the start of a nomadic life, a couple of years in each place – Portugal, Spain, a stint in the USA, then latterly back to Spain again, with several short trips back to Glasgow to see his parents, and to revisit old memories and make new ones. The thought that he'd only ever come on his own now made his chest tighten.

The waitress placed down his coffee, in a china cup with a square of Scottish tablet on the side, and retreated with a smile. She would be far too young to remember him, and he doubted that any of the old staff still worked here, yet the feeling of familiarity was undeniable. He and Juliet should have come back to this hotel more often. They'd only managed it a couple of times, on their fifth anniversary and then again on the tenth. It had always seemed like they had plenty of time. Now he knew different.

A commotion over by the entranceway attracted his attention. A bride and groom passing by to cheers from the crowd of family and friends that surrounded them. This was a popular wedding spot, with sometimes two or three on the same day in different function suites. He'd even attended a wedding on the eighteenth hole for one of his most regular golfers, a woman who'd persuaded her fiancé that there was nowhere else she'd rather say I do.

Seb and Juliet had thought about marrying here, but somewhere else seemed even more perfect. He'd get there today too. But first, he watched as the bride turned around and threw her bouquet over her head to squeals of delight from the bridesmaids waiting to catch it. For a second he wondered if that could be... No, he immediately dismissed the thought. Pearl had told him that her niece was getting married in the Kibble Palace in Glasgow at 7 p.m. tonight, so, of course, this couldn't be her.

However, the thought of 'what if' was harder to dismiss when it came to Pearl's niece. He and Yvonne had spent the week together, around – from what he could gather – the same time as her daughter had been conceived. It was all pretty vague, though. The dates matched up – he remembered exactly when it was because only a few weeks later he'd left Aberdeen – but that was only one half of the equation. He had no idea if Yvonne had carried the baby for nine months or whether she was premature or overdue. She had been with her boyfriend in the week before their brief affair, and gone back to him the day it ended. The chances of the child sharing his DNA were so slim. Yet... just for today, he was going to let himself believe that there was the slightest possibility it could be true. Right from the beginning of their relationship, he and Juliet had accepted that they wouldn't have children. They'd both been forty when they met and it just hadn't happened. Perhaps if they'd got together in their twenties or thirties, there would have been a hole there that they'd have felt a longing to fill, but that had never been the case – they'd been so blissfully happy with each other, so grateful for what they'd found together, that it had been enough.

However, that was when he had his love by his side and no idea that having a child was even a possibility for him. Now, the thought consumed him and he had to know. But not yet.

He finished his coffee and tucked a five pound note under the side of the saucer. Time to go. This was the last day he would spend with Juliet and he still had places to go and more memories to share.

Eight

Josie

The secretary – Margaret, Josie presumed – glanced up with barely disguised resentment when Josie entered the office suite.

'Josephine Cairney for Dr Ormond. And if you're going to call security, could you give me warning because I'll never be able to outrun them in these boots.'

Margaret Rosemund's eyes instinctively moved downward, to check out the black leather, pointy-toed stilettos, complete with silver studs around the ankle. Despite herself, she found the edges of her mouth turning up in amusement. This woman was outrageous, stroppy and demanding, but she couldn't half rock a pair of killer heels. Not the usual attire for a lady of her vintage.

Despite the antagonistic phone call, Margaret felt herself defrosting. The patient was stressed and upset – a bit of high-maintenance, demanding behaviour was totally understandable. 'I told Dr Ormond that you were coming in and he's happy to see you.'

'Thank you,' Josie replied with complete decorum, as if she hadn't threatened to storm the building if the good doctor refused to see her.

She plonked herself down on the chair nearest Dr Ormond's door. She was a woman who never got nervous, who rarely felt fear, yet – for the first time in her life – she was utterly consumed by panic. She also felt sick, exhausted and weary, but she'd hidden all those things under such a heavy blanket of denial that she found it difficult to admit the truth even to herself.

A sudden bout of coughing sprang from nowhere, making her bend forward at the waist as she gasped for some relief. The cough had been around for the best part of a year now and, yes, it was ridiculous that she'd waited this long to get it checked out, but she was a busy lady. She had a life to live, friends to enjoy, family to shock with her behaviour – there was no time to be sick. Besides, what was the point in wasting someone's time with something as minor as a common cough?

The bark had barely subsided when the door next to her opened and Dr Ormond proffered his hand. 'Miss Cairney, come on through.'

Josie wondered, not for the first time, if he was the kind of man who kept his socks on during sex. His voice was clipped and on the far end of the posh scale, and he had an introspective manner that suggested he'd always been more studious than sexy. However, right now, she didn't care if he wore his wife's slipper on his willy in bed, just as long as he delivered good news.

'Please take a seat.'

Josie did as she was told, biting her tongue to stop herself breaking the tension by saying something rude or crude. Old habits die hard.

'Thank you for seeing me at such short notice. I couldn't have waited until after Christmas. I hope you understand.'

'Of course, yes. Although, normally we do ask that you bring a family member or friend with you as it can be useful to have someone else taking everything in too.'

An icy cold grip of fear started at Josie's toes and began to work its way through her veins. What was there to take in? She was hoping for a packet of pills, an instruction to take two tablets twice a day and to be sent on her way. Instead, the man with the answers was pulling out a large manila file and removing a sheaf of documents.

This wasn't good. She could feel it in the bones that were being consumed by that cold terror.

'As you know, Miss Cairney, we carried out extensive tests, including blood analysis, chest X-rays and a CT scan of the lungs. Unfortunately, those tests identified abnormal cells in both lungs. I'm going to be direct with you, Miss Cairney – I'm terribly sorry to tell you that you have what we call small cell lung cancer.'

Josie's first thought was, *Jesus, he could have sugar coated that.* Her second thought, she vocalised. 'I. Have. Lung. Cancer?'

'I'm afraid so.'

'How bad is it?' The words were made terse by cold, blind fury. Fucking lung cancer. She couldn't have that. Absolutely not. She wouldn't allow it.

He sighed, and once again, Josie knew that whatever he was about to say wasn't going to be good. 'Miss Cairney, we need to do more tests and scans to see the extent of the spread of the disease into other organs. We can already see signs that it's in—'

Josie put her hand up. 'Spare me the details. I don't want the doom and gloom. I just want you to tell me what you can do about it.'

That threw him, but he remained impeccably calm and professional as he changed direction. 'Well, what I can tell you, is that in the lungs, we can see that it is in a late stage of progression, and we are therefore extremely limited in our options. It's actually quite remarkable that you are maintaining your current quality of life, given the extent of your illness. For this type of cancer, surgery is not an option. I would recommend an intensive course of chemotherapy, possibly combined with radiotherapy, with the hope that an aggressive course of treatment will slow further spread.'

'You mean you can't cure it?' she asked, hearing her voice but strangely detached from what it was saying. She was still stuck on his assertion that she had cancer. That couldn't be right. It was simply unacceptable.

'I'm sorry, Miss Cairney—'

'In the name of God, call me Josie. It's the least you can do when you're telling me my lungs are up shit creek.'

He nodded, and she could see the sympathy all over his face. For some reason that made her even angrier. *Do not pity me*, she wanted to scream. *Do not feel sorry for me.*

'Josie,' he said kindly. 'There's no easy way to say this. Your cancer is terminal. Chemotherapy and radiotherapy will prolong your life, but there's no way to reverse or cure this.'

There was a minute of silence as they both allowed time for Josie to digest this.

'How long do I have?' Her words were slow and deliberate, waging a desperate fight against the rapid beats of her heart.

'We don't give specifics, Miss... Josie.'

'Doctor, I really don't care about protocols and what you do or do not do.' Her statement was harsh, but it was out of desperation and he seemed to understand that because he nodded thoughtfully. 'If you're going to be my own personal Grim Reaper, at least fill me in on the details.'

'In my experience—'

'That'll do,' Josie assured him.

'With no treatment, three to four months. With treatment, perhaps six months to a year.'

She leaned forward, only stopping herself from sliding to the floor by grasping the desk until her knuckles were white.

'I've checked our schedules and we can begin treatment on the twenty-eighth of December. I've made an appointment for you at 10 a.m. with our head of oncology. Again, I'd advise you to bring a family member or friend along with you. I'm so sorry to be giving you this news, Miss... Josie. But I promise you we'll do everything that we can to support you over the coming months. Do you have any further questions for me?'

She had many and none. What was the point? What would they change? She was dying. Three months, ten months, what did it matter? A death sentence was a death sentence and there was nothing that could make that go away.

In a semi-trance, she rose from the chair, leaned over and shook his hand. 'No questions. Thank you, Dr Ormond.'

Turning on her steel stiletto heels, she walked out, passing the secretary, who gave her a weak smile. She knew. Josie could tell.

'Goodbye, Margaret. Have a lovely Christmas,' she said, for some reason feeling the need to redeem herself after giving the woman such a hard time on the phone. Karma. That's what this was. She always thought that on the grand scale of karma, the fact she adored her family and friends, and would do anything to help anyone, made up for the fact that she could be a bolshy cow. Now she was fairly sure that wasn't the case.

Outside, the bitter cold hit her face and the rain seeped into her hair, but she barely noticed. She walked along the road with absolutely no idea where she was going. Walking. Just walking. Mind racing. Thoughts ricocheting through her brain. She should call her son, Michael, in Italy. Or her daughter, Avril, in London. She should tell Val.

Oh God, Val. They'd been friends for so long and they did everything together. Hadn't Val had enough heartache? It was only a few years since she lost her daughter Dee after a hit-and-run caused by a drugged-up driver. The thought of bringing her more pain was unbearable.

Walking. Still walking. She was almost past the café when the aroma of fresh coffee made her glance in the window. Without a conscious decision, she stepped back and made her way inside. She wasn't hungry but she just needed somewhere quiet, somewhere alone to think.

Her back ached as she slid into a seat beside a white painted table. The owners had made a real effort to decorate it for Christmas with gold and green sprayed pine cone arrangements in the middle of every table and tinsel draped around the top of every wall. In one corner, a miniature silver tree, already twinkling with white lights. Band Aid played in the background and she remembered the first time she heard that song, back in the eighties. She'd joined in, belting out the chorus as she watched the Live Aid concert on a big screen at a huge bar in the city centre. She'd outlasted a few of the folks who had been on the stage that day – Bowie, Freddie Mercury, George Michael, all of them bloody marvellous – and she'd thought she was so indestructible that she'd outlive them all. Not now.

She ordered a coffee, then nodded gratefully at the young woman who brought it to her table. Usually, Josie would be the first to strike up conversation, but today she had nothing to say. Instead, she just smiled in thanks, then tried to gather her thoughts and calm the swirls of emotion that were carrying her off in wave after wave of despair.

Dying. Well, fuck it, it came to everyone, she told herself. The bugger of it was that it was coming to her now. She still had so much to look forward to. Watching Michael's children grow up and being the most outrageous granny she could be for them. Seeing Avril, a make-up artist on movie sets, achieving brilliant new highs in her career. Even just the everyday stuff, with the people she spent her time with – she loved it all and didn't want it to end. However, she honestly believed that she'd had a great life, made the most of it. If she had to go back and do it all over again, she wouldn't change a single thing. That had to be a reflection of a life well lived, didn't it?

What mattered now wasn't the past but how she handled what little time she had left. That's what would break her heart – not that she was going, but that she was about to cause pain to the people she loved. Her job in life had been to make theirs better, to help when they needed it and to support them in tough times. Now she was about to be the reason for sorrow and heartache and she couldn't bear it.

A single tear dropped from her right eye and she brushed it away. She wasn't a crier. That was Val's department. She was a fixer, a solver, the one who stayed strong when the rest of the world was going tits up. And that, she instinctively knew, was what she was going to do now.

There would be no treatment. She wasn't going to prolong the agony of this for the people who loved her, not when it would only buy her a few weeks or a couple of months more. Nor was she going to put herself through that. She'd held the hands of friends who'd succumbed to cancer and she'd willed them to fight, demanded that they do everything they could to live.

Right now, she was choosing otherwise.

No debilitating chemo, no time spent hanging around hospitals waiting for radiotherapy, no rake of doctors probing and prodding her, delivering more bad news as they reached the end. For however long she had left, she wanted to spend every moment with friends, doing the things that they loved – drinks, songs, sarcasm and laughter just about summed it up.

That was how she was going to go.

She'd tell them all at some point, but not now, not today.

Today she had a job to do. She was Cammy and Caro's wedding planner, and they were relying on her to pull this off. If ever there was a day that would take her mind off her future – or the future that she no longer had – then this was it.

Another coughing fit sealed the deal, giving her a kick of a reminder that she had to get off her arse and get things done.

Cammy and Caro needed her and she had to be strong for herself and for everyone else, so it was time to get up, get to work and pretend that this morning never happened.

Tomorrow was for thinking about dying – but today, she was choosing life.

Nine

Stacey

'Stacey! Stacey! Stacey!'

Oh. Dear. God. Every single person in this airport that didn't know her name definitely did now.

'Friends of yours?' her new-found companion, Zac, asked. 'Because right now I'm jealous that there's no welcoming party like that for me.'

Stacey had surprised herself with how much she'd enjoyed his company. They'd continued chatting while they'd waited at the baggage reclaim. 'Look, I know this is weird, but can I have your number?' he'd asked. 'In case I maybe get lost or something? I've never been to Scotland before, so it could happen.'

'You know we have fantastic technical advances like satnavs and maps here? We try not to lose too many visitors to our country. It hurts tourism,' she'd joked, trying to deflect the question. He was cute. No, more than that. He was seriously good-looking. He was also articulate, sexy, and smart. Yep, it would be a terrible idea to give him her number. Awful. Her life was complicated enough. 'It's sweet of you to ask, but I'm in a relationship, and my life's... complicated.'

'I like complications,' he'd bantered back. In another life, in another time, she'd be seriously attracted to his confidence and charm.

'Trust me, I'm one that you don't need,' Stacey had answered, with just a little regret.

He'd accepted the finality of the answer, but still they'd walked together down the endless hallways of Glasgow Airport, up to the point where the huge glass doors slid open to reveal the people waiting for their loved ones.

The chorus had been both instant and hilarious – her mum, Senga, with five of her pals, Ida, Ina, Agnes, Jean and Montana – all wearing Santa hats and somehow managing to dance while holding up a 'Welcome Home Stacey' banner. Some of them were shouting her name, others were blowing on party hooters and then cheering, causing much hilarity to everyone that passed.

'Aw crap. Some people are actually filming this. Look!' she nodded to a handful of travellers who had their mobile phones out, documenting the spectacle. 'This will be bloody viral by lunchtime. I'm mortified.'

Despite her words, she couldn't help but giggle, as a wave of sheer bliss consumed her. Regardless of all her worries and woes, and the stress that had her wound tight as a drum since the wedding invitation had arrived, it felt like a suffocating weight was being lifted from her chest. It was so good to be home. It was even better to see her mum and 'aunties' there. None of the aunts were related by blood, but these women had been a gang all her life, supporting each other like sisters. Stacey loved every single one of them. Which was just as well, because they were now charging towards her, almost taking her down as they surrounded her and enveloped her in a hug.

'Ma!' Stacey exclaimed to her mother, Senga, the first one to reach her, who now had her in something between a headlock and a full body, unbearably tight, embrace. 'You'll burst my boobs!' Stacey squealed, still laughing.

'Freeze!' Senga bellowed, and it took Stacey a second to realise she was shouting in the direction of a departing Zac, who stopped and turned around. 'Who are you?' she asked tartly. 'And what's your relationship to my daughter? Ida, get the thumbscrews – he'll be easy to crack.'

Stacey beamed with embarrassment. Her mother had been doing stuff like this to her all her life. Senga and her chums thought it was hilarious, but Stacey threw up her newly released arms in despair. 'Ma! He's just someone I met on the plane. Leave the poor guy alone.' She turned to Zac. 'Sorry. She does this. She should have been a spy in a past life. Or maybe in jail.'

Thankfully his (admittedly ovary-twanging) grin suggested he was finding this whole scene entirely entertaining. 'Good to meet you, Stacey. If I get lost, I'll send up a flare.'

'Take me ten minutes to track him down on a dark night,' she heard Montana whisper behind her.

He gave a parting wave. 'Enjoy your wedding.'

'Enjoy your… buying,' Stacey replied weakly, then watched as he sauntered off. Poor guy. He'd probably avoid all trips to Scotland in the future in case he got accosted by wacky Senga and her chums.

'How come I never get someone like that sitting next to me on a plane? I always get the one with bad breath that snores like a moose,' Senga said.

'Don't talk about me like that! I brushed my teeth twice before we flew to Benidorm,' her pal, Jean, said archly, making the rest of them hoot with laughter.

Stacey couldn't resist joining in. Oh, how she loved this lot, she thought again, as Senga linked her arm through hers. Anyone would be able to spot that they were mother and daughter. They both had the same sapphire eyes and the kind of high, perfect cheekbones people now got surgery to achieve. Over the years, Senga had sported every hair colour from purple to red to blonde, but now she was back to her natural ebony black, which she still wore long and flowing, defying all those bloody *Daily Mail* articles that hinted women should cut their hair short and cover their cleavage the minute they turned fifty.

Senga clearly paid no attention to that either. Her décolletage was barely concealed under a low-cut red furry jumper that sported a snowman on each breast. Which wasn't as bad, Stacey thought briefly, as the time this lot had turned up at her school nativity play dressed in flowing robes, announcing that they'd rewritten history to make it more realistic, and they were therefore here to represent the forgotten heroes of the nativity, the 'Six Wise Women'. Stacey's primary school teacher had turned a shade of puce that matched Rudolph's nasal cavities.

The seven of them, all arms linked now, like a chorus of the Moulin Rouge, walked in a line to the exit. They crossed the road outside the terminal, breaking into a jog to minimise the damage from the torrents of rain that were pelting from the skies. As soon as they reached the ground floor of the multi-storey car park and saw the line of waiting cars, Stacey knew immediately which one belonged to them. Three back in the row of vehicles parked in the pick-up bay was the bright pink minivan, with borders of flashing lights around the windows, and a sign along the side in silver glitter, announcing that it was the 'GoGo Party Bus'. Over the years, she'd visited Vegas, land of ostentatious tackiness, many times, but never had she seen something so gloriously crass.

'Hurry up,' Senga said conspiratorially. 'Ida needs to get this back to The GoGo Club before they realise it's missing.'

'Auntie Ida! You stole it?' Stacey gasped.

Ida immediately flipped to outrage. 'Absolutely not! I erm... borrowed it. And if the buggers would pay a decent rate for their cleaners then I wouldn't have had to!' she finished with a defiant wink. 'We only keep them on because they've been clients for so long.'

Many years ago, the women had realised there was strength in numbers, and they'd formed their own cleaning company, Manky Scrubbers. All equal partners, they'd built up a wide base of new customers but still retained most of their existing clients. One of them was The GoGo Club. Formerly Sparkles. Before that, ten other names. It was just one of many places that Stacey had spent her childhood, going there after school, while the club was closed, to do her homework on freshly wiped tables as her mum or one of these women cleaned around her. While today's climate of political correctness and nanny states might find that idea abhorrent, Stacey could honestly say that she'd had a brilliant life growing up. They'd never had money, but she'd known nothing other than overwhelming love, great laughs and strong women who never let her feel alone or unsupported for a single second. They'd all been there for every event she'd ever had – her first school play, her first gymnastics win, the first time she donned a sequined thong bikini and danced on a pole (in Sparkles, and yes, their cheers almost drowned out the music). As a thank you for everything they'd done for her, Stacey had flown them all to LA for the first screening of *USA Speed Freaks*. They'd cried with pride, then headed to a karaoke club, the first stop in a party that had lasted for two days. Stacey wasn't sure that Hollywood had recovered.

Now, they piled on to the pink vehicle, where two bottles of Prosecco were chilling in the large ice bucket next to the back seat. Before they'd even shook the rain from their shoulders, Senga had distributed the glasses. 'Stacey, love, I can't tell you how happy we are that you're home. It's the best Christmas present I could have hoped for,' Senga declared, and to her shock, Stacey could see that her mum was blinking back tears.

Her heart strings tightened. Her poor mum. She'd lost her husband, Edwin, to a sudden heart attack just before Christmas last year, so this month and the festivities were always going to be tough for her. Stacey had been so happy for her mother when she and Edwin had got together twelve years ago, around the same time as Stacey moved to the USA, and they'd had a truly happy marriage. It had broken Senga's heart when he'd passed away and only the support of her friends and Stacey had kept her going. It still swamped her in guilt that she hadn't made it back to Glasgow for Edwin's funeral, but shooting commitments had made it impossible to get there on time. Instead, Stacey had flown Senga out to

LA the day afterwards and they'd spent a month together, her mum hanging out on set every day and sharing a double bed at night. Jax wasn't thrilled about it, but it didn't matter because Senga said the change of environment was the best thing that could have happened for her. By the time she left to return to Scotland, Stacey could see a glimmer of her mother's joy in life returning, and knew she'd be ok. Since then, they'd spoken on Facetime every day at least once, but nothing beat the feeling of being right next to her now and watching her face crease into the widest grin.

The others all raised a toast and then they laughed, chatted and caught up with the gossip all the way back to Senga's home. When the bus stopped at the end of the gravel path to her semi-detached home in Paisley, a town about fifteen minutes from the airport and twenty-five minutes from Glasgow's city centre, they all hugged and made plans to meet up before the wedding ceremony. Stacey and her chums had known Cammy since he and Josie – another of Senga's closest friends – worked in an underwear boutique in the city centre a million years ago and he employed them again now to keep his current shop spotless. To Ida's delight, he was very happy to pay their standard rate, although they'd offered him a loyalty discount. He'd refused, saying they were worth every penny, and they'd all fallen in love with him just a little bit more. They had no idea that Stacey knew that feeling all too well.

Pulling her large gold suitcase behind her, Stacey followed Senga through the door, dropping her bag and coat as soon as she stepped into the hall and throwing her arms around her mum again. 'I'm so glad I came home,' she told her, emotion distorting her words.

'I'm thrilled you're here, ma love. I've missed you so much. Come on, I need a cuppa.'

In the kitchen, Stacey chatted away while Senga made two cups of tea. The room they were in now was a far cry from the one they'd had in the tiny council flat they'd shared until Senga and Edwin got married. After the wedding, Senga had moved in to Edwin's home and they'd decorated it together. Now the kitchen was a large square, with white Shaker units and yellow walls, cream worktops and a long pine table – with, of course, enough seats for six – in the middle. Even though Stacey had never actually lived here, it was so 'Senga' that it felt like home.

The teas were finally brought to the table, along with a biscuit tin, a pot of jam, and a plate piled high with warm buttered toast, bringing on another swell of happiness and nostalgia.

'There you go, pet,' Senga said, as she slipped in to the chair across from her daughter. She picked up her own tea and watched with undisguised love as Stacey lifted a slice of toast and smeared it with strawberry jam. 'Thirty-seven and it still warms ma heart to watch you.'

Stacey's toast stopped in mid-air. 'Ma, I'm thirty-five.'

'Really?' Senga asked with an air of mock innocence, making Stacey giggle as she realised she was being played. She rolled her eyes. 'Can't believe I fell for that.'

'Aye, you've been in Hollywood too long. Now eat your toast. Although, that body has been deprived of carbs for so long there's every change it'll kill you. Death by pan loaf.'

Stacey's jaws were beginning to ache from laughter. She needed this. Needed to be here. Needed to get her head together. Needed to tell her mum what had brought her here, but she suddenly realised that she didn't know where to start.

Senga put her mug down. 'So come on, then. Tell me what's going on.'

Damn, it was like she could read her mind.

Her courage failed her and she decided to wait. She should speak to Cammy first. What was the point of upsetting Senga, of causing a drama, when there was no need for it? No, she should just plead innocence, talk to Cammy, and then, when he rejected her – which she was fairly sure he would – she could skulk back to LA knowing that the damage had been contained and her humiliation was strictly between her and the man she was in love with.

'Tell you what? I just decided to come home to spend Christmas with you.' Stacey was fairly sure she'd nailed the innocent act, until her mum's eyebrows rose in the same way that they would when Stacey was a teenager and she would tell Senga she was going out with her pals, when really she was meeting some boy from school and planning to snog him outside the youth club. She got caught every time.

'And you just happened to come home on the day of Cammy's wedding?'

'Yes, well, I thought I'd go. He sent me an invitation ages ago, but I didn't know whether I'd be filming this week, so I couldn't commit to coming.'

Senga absorbed her explanation for a few moments, finally going quiet.

Stacey chomped on her toast, her insides relaxing with relief. Yes! Her mum was buying it. She'd always kept her feelings for Cammy to herself and she was positive that

Senga had no clue how she felt. Success! Victory! The teenage Stacey would be so proud.

'Ah, that's great then,' her mum said, with calm insouciance. 'I'm glad it's got nothing to with the fact that you've had a thing for that man for years and you've not come here with some daft notion to tell him.'

Stacey's inner teenager put her toast down. Caught, cornered, and left with no option but to make a full confession.

'Sorry. Bugger. Sorry,' she spluttered. Yet she still didn't make a move to get out of the cab. She couldn't do this. She should just give him her own address and go back home. Or go to the hotel and speak to Cammy and tell him she couldn't marry him. Rip that plaster right off. 'Sorry, I've changed my mind. Could you take me to...' her request tailed off, cut short by a visceral reaction to what she'd just seen. The house. The window. Someone standing there. Their reaction suggested that they'd seen her too. They'd put their hands on their hips, staring at her, as if throwing out a subliminal challenge. *Come ahead*, they said.

Run. Stay. Run. Stay.

'Look, I can see that you're having a day of it,' the driver went on, spotting her renewed hesitation, 'but I need to keep the meter ticking here. My missus will kick my arse if I don't come home minted tonight.'

'I'm so sorry,' Caro said, meaning it. She hated to put people out.

Snap decision. She pulled twenty quid from her pocket and thrust it towards him, more than covering the fifteen pounds showing on the meter.

'Merry Christmas,' he said, as she clambered out of the cab.

'You too,' she replied, with a forced cheeriness she definitely wasn't feeling.

The taxi accelerated off, leaving her standing there, a lone figure in a very conspicuous scarlet duffle coat, just staring at the stationary silhouette in the window.

She could still run and...

No. Decision made.

It was time.

She'd been avoiding this family for two years now. How could she move on, build a new life, when she hadn't settled her old one? Today had already gone from what should have been the happiest of her life to potentially one of the worst, so she may as well pile on the misery.

As she stepped forward, she lifted her head and jutted her chin. Even if she didn't feel confident, she could at least act like it.

At the door, the huge brass knocker reverberated as she lifted it, then let it fall against the wood.

Five seconds. Maybe ten. No one was going to answer. Spineless bastards.

She reached up to knock again and...

The door opened. Caro stared at the woman in front of her, suddenly struck silent. Lila. The half-sister she'd only found out about two years ago. They shared a father – the one who had been cheating on her mother for almost the entire duration of their marriage. The one and only time she'd seen Lila, on the night she'd confronted her father, she'd been a vibrant, blonde, Marilyn Monroe-esque beauty, flawlessly groomed and spectacularly turned out. Back then, Lila posted every detail of her life on social media and was rewarded with hundreds – sometimes thousands – of 'likes' and fawning comments. Caro remembered the figure she'd seen when she last checked Lila's Instagram profile – 246,000 followers. Yep, 246,000 people cared what Lila thought, what she wore, what she said. That blew Caro's mind.

The woman standing here now was the same person but in a different shell. There was no make-up. Her hair was scraped into a ponytail. Her cheeks were sunken, the circles under her eyes a dark contrast to the red of the spots that had broken out on her chin.

'Lila?' Caro said, tentatively. The woman nodded, saying nothing, leaving it to Caro to proceed. 'I'm—'

'My sister,' Lila said bluntly. 'I know who you are. My dad told me all about you.'

Caro hid her surprise. She'd no idea her father had revealed the truth to his other daughter. They'd all been in the same room only once, but the two women hadn't actually come face to face and Lila wasn't even aware that Caro was there. They were in a restaurant where Lila was having dinner with her mother, their father, and...

Cammy. Yep, Lila had been dating the man Caro was supposed to marry today, but she'd ceremoniously dumped him the same night Caro met him. After Lila had ditched him, Caro had got talking to Cammy outside and he'd offered to drive Caro home to Aberdeen. How crazy was that? Caro had come looking for a father and had ended up with the love of her life. Her half-sister's cast-offs. Probably the only gift her sibling would ever give her.

'I was hoping to speak to my... our... Is Jack in?' Caro stuttered over the words. Calling him 'dad' seemed so wrong, given that he'd never been a father to her. Not really. He'd come home a week or so out of every month, allegedly back from his travels with his big-shot job in the oil industry, but now she knew it was actually a week away from his other family. How convenient for him that his job was based in both Aberdeen and Glasgow, so it fitted his duplicitous life. When he was around, he'd pretty much co-existed in the house with her. Her mother had worshipped the ground he walked on, but Jack had never taken an interest in his daughter's life, never shown any fatherly affection. Caro hadn't realised dads could be any other way until she was a teenager and met some of her friends' fathers.

It seemed though, that he'd been a very different father to Lila. Her social media posts were packed with pictures of the two of them together on special occasions, and gushy declarations about how great he was and how much she loved him.

Now, though, even the most observant person would be hard pushed to recognise this woman in those pictures.

'He's out, but he'll be back soon,' Lila said, her voice completely flat.

'Okay,' Caro sighed and realised that her overwhelming emotion was relief. This was confirmation that confronting him today was a mistake. She shouldn't have come and she wasn't even sure why she was here. Was she looking for understanding? For explanations? For some shred of reason that would restore her faith in marriage and everything it stood for? Or was she looking for revenge, to let go of her hatred by taking on a battle her mother hadn't even known she had to fight?

What was the point? What could she possibly gain?

She managed a half smile at Lila. 'Thanks anyway,' she said, as she turned to walk back down the path. Time to go.

'Do you want to come in and wait?' Lila blurted. 'He won't be long.'

There was something in her tone, an edge of anxiety maybe? Caro wasn't sure, but it was enough to make her hesitate.

'I don't think…' she began.

Lila rolled her eyes. 'Seriously? You've, like, come all the way over here to speak to him and you're just going to leave? That's, like, so lame.'

Caro immediately felt her hackles rise. Lame? That should definitely be a cue to get out of there. Yet, something in Lila's challenge, combined with curiosity, an emotional whirlpool and a dose of pride, made her hesitate. This was her half-sister, but she didn't know her at all. It suddenly seemed important to her not to let Lila think she was some cowardly 'lame' individual.

The words were out of Caro's mouth before she could change her mind. 'Okay, I'll wait then.'

Lila opened the door wider to let her in, then led the way down the hallway. Scanning from left to right, Caro could feel her teeth begin to clench. Dotted the whole way along the walls on either side of her were large black and white photos, on white mounting boards surrounded by black frames, depicting a lifetime of happiness for the occupants of the house. Lila and their father holding hands as they walked on the beach. Jack Anderson and his other wife, Louise, throwing their heads back as they laughed on a windy day. Their wedding, the bride and groom standing in front of an altar. That one almost made her flee. From the picture, Caro could see that Jack would have been about thirty – when he was already very definitely married to her own mother. The lying, cheating, duplicitous bastard. For over thirty years he'd lived a double life and got away with it: two wives, two families, two homes, two cities. It was the kind of thing you read about and questioned... how did no one find out? Caro discovered later that his second wife knew about their existence and chose to ignore it, but her mother had never so much as suspected her husband of infidelity. She'd absolutely believed that he was working away to support them and she'd adored him unconditionally, spending her whole life waiting for him to walk in the door, ecstatic when he was there, almost shutting down when he wasn't. Her marriage claimed her whole life and it was all a sham.

Caro steadied herself, took a deep breath and kept walking, with a new resolve to face him down, to get answers, to say what she had to say.

The kitchen took her by surprise. Her dad had always been notoriously tight with money, and he'd shown absolutely no desire to splash cash on the house she'd grown up in. It had been a perfectly nice home, but it had the same kitchen all her life, and nothing else much had changed either. This space, on the other hand, was gorgeous – black gloss units, with top-of-the-range appliances and an island in the middle, crowned by a stunning chandelier. No wonder he'd been so disinterested in their Aberdeen home, when he had this house waiting for him in Glasgow.

Caro could see that there was a half-full glass of wine already sitting on the centre island next to an open copy of… She strained to see the words at the top of the page. *Vogue*.

Lila slid onto the cream leather bar stool that was already pulled out beside it and motioned to Caro to sit on one of the others. The noise of the metal base of the stool moving across the marble tiled floor jarred as Caro pulled it out and climbed on, while trying to make her pulse slow down to something approaching normal.

Okay. Maybe this wasn't going to be so bad after all. Lila had invited her in, so she was clearly making an effort. Perhaps this was a good thing, a chance to build even a small foundation for a relationship with a woman who was, after all, her half-sister. *Be positive. Be open. Give her a chance.* It would be okay. Perhaps she was actually a lovely person. Perhaps she'd been wronged by their father too. Maybe they could chat. Share experiences. Build a bond.

In a split second, all heart-warming thoughts were immediately wiped out by the narrowing of Lila's eyes as she spat out her opening line.

'Surprised to see you here today. Isn't this the day you're meant to be marrying my ex-boyfriend?'

Eleven

Seb

The drive to Glasgow gave Seb a chance to settle his mind. He'd been right to come back here. Even if Pearl's niece was absolutely nothing to do with him – and let's face it, that was a very strong probability – the potential consequences of that chance meeting had forced him to come back to Scotland, to finally fulfil the promise he and Juliet had made to each other. He hoped that somewhere, wherever she was, Juliet could see that. It was the least he could do, although when the time came, he still had no idea if he'd be able to let her go. The very thought of that made his mouth go dry and his stomach heave. The same words played over and over in his mind. *I'm sorry, Juliet. So sorry. I hope you know that.*

It was a strange thing. He'd never believed in the afterlife, or spirits, or loved ones sticking around to watch over you. How that had changed. Perhaps it was desperation. Maybe a coping mechanism. But at some point since Juliet died, he'd convinced himself that she was still with him, that he could feel her, sense her, that she was seeing everything that he did, that she knew how tortured he was over what he'd done. For the last few months he'd been drowning in a quagmire of grief and guilt. He regretted every single second of the day that she was killed and it felt like part of him had died with her. The good part. Nothing else left but sorrow and self-loathing and a void that not even the bottom of a bottle could fill. He realised this was the first day since Juliet died that he hadn't thought about opening a bottle of wine at lunchtime and downing a couple of glasses to take the edge off. Maybe later.

Traffic got busier as he left the motorway, going through the Clyde tunnel and then on to the expressway in the west of the city, cutting off at the Partick junction. Despite the rain, the streets here were busy, the mass of young people sporting backpacks a testimony to the fact that this was the university area and heavily populated with students. There were all age groups though: elderly people carrying umbrellas and plastic bags of shopping, mums juggling kids as they darted in and out of shops, flash cars going by, representing the other prominent demographic in this part of the city: wealthy professionals and members of the arts community. This was the side of town that Juliet hailed from, growing up in the garden-flat conversion of the ground floor of the stunning curved Victorian terrace that Seb had just turned in to.

He drove slowly, watching the building come towards him, imagining his love in the rooms of the home in front of him. She'd brought him here shortly after they'd met, pointed out her old bedroom window, regaled him with stories of her childhood, playing in the communal garden outside their front door, a green haven for the residents of the street.

With a sad smile, he drove on, navigating the damp West End roads, lined with shop windows decorated for Christmas. A few miles further on, he reached his destination. The car park was quiet when he drove in, understandable when most people were busy preparing for Christmas instead of spending a leisurely day in the grand halls of this building.

Kelvingrove Museum and Art Gallery had special meaning to them both. They'd come here for the first time in 2006, when it had just reopened after a three-year refurbishment. After that, on every one of their many visits home to Glasgow, they would return to wander the halls. Art had never been his thing, but Juliet's enthusiasm had been contagious and he'd found himself enjoying the trips every bit as much as she did. That was Juliet's gift – the ability to make people see things through her eyes, to get them excited and enthusiastic. It was what had made her a great teacher and partner. Seb suddenly realised that, in that thought, he'd used the past tense. Maybe a lunchtime wine wasn't such a bad idea.

Before he could act on that, he chided himself. *Stop being such a fucking coward and face this. Face the past. Face what you did. Face the pain.*

He inhaled. Exhaled. Reset. Time to go.

He lifted the brown leather bag, unable to let it out of his sight, and sprinted to the entrance to minimise the soaking from the pounding Glasgow rain. At the door, the security guard gave him a nod and a smile, which he reciprocated. It still astounded him that entry to this incredible building was free. No wonder the twenty-two galleries within its grand walls were a magnet to locals and tourists alike.

Inside, he was, as always, immediately struck by the sheer scale of the main hall and the magnificent curved ceiling, exquisite chandeliers dropping down past stunning arched windows. Above him, grand balconies ran around all four walls of the building, and in front of him, soaring up the far wall, was an awe inspiring organ encased in deep, rich walnut. It was spectacular.

Seb climbed the stairs to the second floor, then walked along to the middle arch in the upper balcony. If he looked down to his left, he could see where he'd been standing just a moment before. To his right, the brass pipes of the organ. This was it. The very spot he'd proposed. And even now, almost fifteen years later, he could remember every detail.

'Why are you looking at me like that?' she'd asked playfully, her wide smile making her cheeks dimple. Her long chestnut hair was loosely pulled back into a plait that fell over one shoulder, escaping tendrils framing her face. It was June and she looked tanned and healthy in her white cropped jeans and pale blue T-shirt, white trainers for comfort because they planned to wander around the city all day. They'd been together for a year, living over in Portugal thanks to a two year contract with a new course on the Algarve, and had flown back for a friend's fortieth.

'I was just thinking I got lucky,' he'd said, tugging her towards him, and laughing as her arms went around his neck and they kissed.

'Eeeeeew, that's gross,' came a voice from a few metres away.

They'd turned to see a whole class of children, obviously on a school trip, all staring at them, disgust on their faces, their spokesperson a little guy, around eight years old, with wide, horrified eyes, freckles and a mop of curly brown hair.

'Sorry,' their teacher had winced. 'We haven't covered tact and diplomacy yet,' she'd joked, as she herded them away. That had made them laugh even more.

As soon as they were alone, Seb knew it was the right moment. It wasn't where or when he'd planned it. It was supposed to be later that evening, over a candlelit dinner in a beautiful restaurant. But he'd had the ring in his camera bag all day, too scared to leave it in the hotel room.

He'd lifted the top flap of the black bag that dangled over his shoulder, removed the little navy velvet box, and opened it. He didn't go down on one knee – Juliet had mentioned once that she found that too cringe-inducing. She always laughed, covered her face with a cushion and made 'Eeeeew' noises when they got to that bit in a romcom. Instead, he'd reached over, gently cupped her chin, drawing her astonished pale green eyes back from the ring box in his other hand. Nothing in his life, right up to that point, had ever felt so right.

'Juliet Embers, I have loved you from the moment I met you. You are everything I could ever want and I know that I will adore you until the day I die.' He had to clear his throat, given that his tough, West of Scotland male façade seemed to be temporarily choked. 'Will you please marry me?'

Her eyes were still locked on his and there was a slight pause before the most beautiful, intoxicating burst of laughter escaped her. 'Yes!' she'd cried, and he'd scooped her up, swung her round, both of them lost in the absolute joy of the moment.

'I love you,' he'd murmured into her hair.

'I love you right back.' Every word oozed happiness.

'Eh, mister, I think you dropped this,' came the same kid's voice from earlier, and that's when they'd realised that the entire class had returned and were standing by the entrance to the balcony, except the wee romantic who'd offered his disdainful opinion during their last encounter. He was right next to them, holding up the tiny velvet box that Seb had managed to drop in the excitement.

Seb retook custody. 'Thank you."

'No problem, mister. Still think all that kissing is pure yuck though. My mammy says it can give you cold sores.'

The mortified teacher had swooped in and shooed him off, with a quick 'Congratulations' and a thumbs up.

'Cold sores?' Seb had asked his fiancée, grinning.

'I'll take my chances,' Juliet replied, kissing him again, a long, slow touch of her lips. No one else existed. Not the tourists, the schoolkids or anyone else in the outside world. It was just the two of them.

Engaged. He was forty-one years old and he'd finally found the person that he wanted to share his life with. Even better, by some miracle, she felt the same. That night, they'd gone to dinner at the West End Grand Hotel just a couple of miles away, and they'd drank champagne, eaten delicious food and then made love until sunrise. The next day, they'd crossed the road to the Botanic Gardens and wandered in the sunshine, making plans for their wedding, their future life together. 'I can't wait to grow old with you,' she'd whispered.

Hearing those words in his head now made him buckle at the waist, as if he'd been sucker-punched in the stomach. She never got to grow old. Her life had ended far too soon, before she'd fulfilled all her dreams, ticked everything off her bucket list, enjoyed her sixties, her seventies, her eighties.

Sometimes he wondered... if, by some cosmic power, Juliet could decide whether to go back and make the same choices, would she do it?

Would he?

Standing here now, looking down as a group of kids just like the ones who'd been there that day made their way through the hall, squealing their 'wow's of amazement, he knew the answer to that.

The last fifteen years had brought him the kind of happiness that he hadn't even known existed, an exquisite love that he could never replace. They'd travelled the world, they'd had incredible experiences, they'd truly loved each other, and while no marriage was ever perfect, they'd come pretty damn close. Their time together had given them a lifetime of highs.

But it had also brought him the very worst of lows.

Would he do it again? No, he wouldn't. Because if he hadn't proposed to Juliet that day, if she hadn't married him, if they hadn't spent the last fifteen years together, then that day, six months ago, wouldn't have happened.

He'd killed Juliet. And if he could go back, he'd undo their lives together, because then, somewhere out there, the love of his life would still be alive. And he wouldn't be back in their home city under a cloud of bitter guilt, trying desperately to find the courage to say a final goodbye.

Twelve

Josie

'Where the hell have you been?' Val screeched, as she swung the door open at Caro and Cammy's flat. 'I've been texting you for the last two hours!'

The outburst startled Josie for a split second. Shit. She'd had her phone on silent since she went into the doctor's office and hadn't thought to check it. And the look on Val's panic-stricken face… Crap, she knew. How could that have happened? How could she have found out already? Oh, bugger. Damage limitation.

'Look, Val, it's not the end of the world…'

'You knew?' Val screeched back. 'You knew she was going to do this?'

Hang on. Who was going to do what? Josie immediately grasped that they were on different pages and thought on her feet. 'Knew what? I don't know anything, but whatever it is, it's not the end of the world. Now let me in because if I don't get a cup of tea and a caramel wafer in the next five minutes, there's every chance I'll start a riot.'

Val stepped to the side to let her pass and she spent the time it took to get into the kitchen recalibrating her demeanour. Chrissie and Jen, Caro's bridesmaids, were already sitting at the kitchen table, looking like someone had stolen their tiaras. Okay, whatever was going on here clearly wasn't good. Had Caro changed her mind about the dress? Or the flowers? Or the bridesmaids?

'What have I missed?' she asked suspiciously, flicking the kettle on and taking a mug from the draining board. They all spent so much time in each other's houses that there was no standing on formality and waiting to be served. Besides, neither of the owners of this abode appeared to be present at the moment. She knew Cammy was staying at a hotel, but… 'And where's Caro? In the shower?'

'We don't know,' Jen admitted woefully.

Josie froze. Turned. 'You've lost the bride?' She sounded like Liam Neeson in every *Taken* movie, when he realises that there's a serious problem and his voice goes low and deadly.

'Not lost her, exactly,' Chrissie jumped in.

Josie took in the pale complexions and bloodshot eyes on both of them. She'd been to Hangover Central enough times to know what it looked like. Her first thought was how stupid they had been to have a wild night out the day before the wedding. The second thought was outrage that she hadn't been invited. She'd never turned down a party in her life.

Val came barrelling in behind her, her blonde bob trembling with panic. 'Caro says she's changed her mind and she doesn't want to get married today.'

Fuck. Shit. Bugger. Well, this day wasn't panning out the way Josie had expected. Somebody in the Gods was clearly having a laugh at her expense.

Josie placed her mug back down on the worktop. Now she knew why Liam Neeson never had time for a cuppa in *Taken* either. 'What?'

'Says she's not doing it,' Val went on. 'She woke up this morning and decided she can't go through with it. It's not that she doesn't love Cammy, it's just... you know, all that business with her parents. She feels like marriage ruined her mum's life and it's all just too much for her and she's having some kind of meltdown.'

'Dear God, I take my eye off the ball for five minutes and this is what happens... Could she not just have done the sensible thing and took a hit out on that bastard father of hers?' Josie murmured, dolloping an extra sugar in her tea. She was going to need all the strength she could get. Right, focus. What was important here? Track down Caro. 'So did she say where she's gone?'

Val shrugged her shoulders. 'No. She just said she was going to sort it out, and she bolted out the door.'

Josie was incredulous. 'And you didn't rugby tackle her to the ground? I expect more from you, Val Brennan.'

'The shock threw me off,' Val retorted archly. 'And anyway, where have you been? If the wedding planner had been here then maybe there would still be a flipping wedding to plan.'

'Last minute details,' Josie shot back, unwilling to elaborate. 'Right, we need a plan. Chrissie, love, throw me a caramel wafer,' she said, gesturing to the biscuit barrel that was sitting in the middle of the table. She caught it, unwrapped it and took a bite in one fluid motion.

The few seconds it took gave her space to think.

'Right, where would Caro go?' she asked, after she swallowed her first bite.

Jen came up with the first suggestion. 'Her Auntie Pearl, Uncle Bob, and Todd and Jared are all staying over at the West End Grand at the top of Byres Road. Maybe she's gone to see them? Or maybe she's gone to see Cammy. He's staying there too.'

Josie nodded. 'Yep, I booked them all in. They're having lunch together at two o'clock, with the other out-of-towners that are staying there.'

The hotel had been the obvious choice as it was directly across the road from the Botanic Gardens, home to the glorious Kibble Palace where the wedding ceremony and reception would be taking place. Josie had booked rooms for the whole bridal party to stay there tonight too. At the time, she'd thought it was a great idea, because they could continue the celebrations long into the night. Now, she wasn't even sure there was going to be anything to celebrate.

'Maybe we should just wait and see if she comes back,' Val offered. 'We don't want to go tearing over there and make everyone panic.'

Josie couldn't conceal her exasperation. 'Val, I have spent the last two months planning every last bit of this wedding. I've got a celebrant, I've got dinners, flowers, cars, hotel rooms, guests, frocks, suits and speeches organised down to the smallest bloody detail – all of which is completely irrelevant if I don't have a fecking bride. I think if there was ever a time to panic, this is it.'

'Fair point,' Val agreed. 'Panic away.'

Her quip made Josie smile. God, she loved that woman. For a moment, she wanted to grab her and share her news, cry on her shoulder and seek some comfort, some moral support, but now wasn't the time. *Let's get past the wedding crisis before moving on to the next one.*

A catch of emotion in her throat set off another coughing fit, this one so severe that she had to clutch on to the worktop to steady herself.

'In the name of God, Josie, when are you going to get that seen to?' Val demanded. 'How many times have I nagged you to get to the doctor's? Sounds like you're coughing up bloody Brillo pads there. If I see you so much as lighting up a cig, there'll be hell to pay.'

Josie waited until she thought she could get a sentence out without choking before she retorted, 'Val, I love you, but I haven't listened to you for the last ten years, so the chances of me starting now are about as slim as my bony arse.'

She ignored Val's pursed lips and eye roll of disapproval and snapped into action. There was no way she was letting this day fail, not while she had a breath left in her fecked lungs.

'Okay, you three stay here and if she comes back, call me immediately.'

'Where are you going?' Jen asked, her voice still hoarse from all the singing the night before.

'If Caro says she's gone to sort it out, that can only mean she's gone to see Cammy. So I'll head over there and suss it out. I need to pop in to the venue anyway and check that everything is going to plan. Try not to lose anything else, like a bridesmaid, while I'm away,' she added, with a droll wink to Val.

'I'll come with you,' Val offered.

Josie immediately declined. Normally, she'd want Val right by her side for a situation like this, but today she didn't trust herself not to blurt out the truth about her health, so she came up with an argument on the spot. 'No, Val. If she comes back she'll need you here to talk to, because these two don't look like they're up to the job.' She cast a disapproving glance at Jen and Chrissie, who didn't have the energy to argue.

Val reluctantly agreed. 'Okay. We'll get everything back on track at this end, so that if you come back with Caro, we'll still be on schedule. And I'll call you if she appears.'

'Good plan. See you later,' she said, giving Val a kiss on the cheek as she passed. 'And look on the bright side...'

Val's bewilderment was obvious. 'What's that?'

'If they don't get hitched, you and I can go on the honeymoon. Two weeks in the Maldives coming right up.'

Despite herself, Val giggled. These two had used humour to get them through some of the very worst things in life, and dealing with situations this way was second nature to them.

Besides, this wasn't a disaster yet. It could still be saved if she could just find Caro and get to the bottom of what was going on.

Downstairs, she whistled to a passing taxi, and watched with satisfaction as it pulled into the kerb in front of her. It had been a conscious decision not to bring the car today, as she knew that at some point she'd probably succumb to a vino or six. She'd assumed they would be in celebration. Now she knew differently.

Again, she pulled her mind back into focus. Concentrate on the problem in front of her, worry about the other stuff later. Today, the wedding. Tomorrow, her health. Until then it could stay in a box, firmly held shut with nails and a large roll of gaffer tape.

The wet streets sped by as they travelled from the Merchant City in the centre of Glasgow, out to the more picturesque grandeur of the West End.

As they drove, Josie prepared herself and thought through the problem. Caro and Cammy loved each other, that much she was sure of. But there was no denying that Caro had been through a rough time over the last couple of years, what with her mum dying and finding out that her father had been lying to her since she was a child. That had to be hard to take, and yet Caro had held it all together, taken everything in her stride and seemed to have coped with it all without any long-term damage. At least, they all thought she had coped. Who really knew what was going on under the surface though? Her whole life had changed in such a short time – her mum dying, meeting Cammy, moving to Glasgow, changing her job, her friends, her world... No wonder it had bubbled up and become so overwhelming now. Josie's heart went out to her, but at the same time, she didn't want Cammy getting hurt. That boy was like a son to her, and she loved him as much as she loved her own brood, Michael and Avril.

Twenty minutes later, she gave the driver ten quid and jumped out at the entrance to the hotel. It was one of her favourite buildings, a Venetian-style terrace built in the mid1800s. She'd had too many lunches and lovely dinners in here to count, often followed or preceded by a wander round the Botanic Gardens across the road.

There would be no one wandering around there today in this rain – except, hopefully, the caterers who would be setting up for tonight's ceremony in the Kibble Palace, a stunning glass structure in the gardens. She considered nipping over there to check on the preparations first, then changed her mind. Let's see if she could get the wedding back on track before worrying about the bloody salmon vol-au-vents.

It was almost two o'clock. She had five hours to turn this around. She just prayed that Caro was here and that she could sort it.

She skipped up the steps, and into the lobby, immediately warmed by the stunning decorations and the sound of an orchestra playing 'Silent Night' oozing from the some hidden speakers. This was Christmas card perfect. If the Christmas card in question featured a fleeing bride, a clueless groom and a whole heap of wedding guests who'd showed up for a union that might not happen. Where were the three wise men when you needed them?

She marched over to the one free receptionist. 'Could you call one of your guests for me please? Cameron Jones.'

'Certainly. Who shall I say is looking for him?'

It was out of Josie's mouth before she could help herself. 'His escort service. He'll be thrilled that I've got here so quickly, what with the hassle of parking my mobility scooter.'

The receptionist stifled a laugh as she picked up the phone, behaving as if this was a completely normal interaction.

After about thirty seconds with the phone to her ear, she shook her head. 'I'm sorry, but there's no answer in his room.'

'Damn,' Josie sighed, before a thought came to her. Everyone who was staying here was due to meet for lunch at two o'clock. Surely Caro wasn't in there right now, breaking it to them all at the same time? Bugger. 'Thanks anyway,' she said, smiling graciously, before taking off in the direction of the restaurant. She pushed the brass handles on the heavy wooden door and burst inside, scanning the room.

To her right, she saw the long table and... yes! There was Cammy. And Pearl and Bob. Todd. Jared. Some of Cammy's family, who'd travelled down from Perth. Definitely no Caro. But... Fuck.

It took her a moment to make sure she was seeing correctly. Cammy had his arm around a woman and was in deep conversation with her. Josie could only see her from the back, but she knew immediately that it was one of the two people she just could not handle seeing today. Her eyes went to the left, and there, bloody hell, was the second face she didn't want to see.

No. Absolutely not. Those Gods were messing with her again. She couldn't do this. Just couldn't.

Cammy suddenly caught her eye. 'Noooooo,' he yelled, his words alerting the woman in front of him and the man to his right. 'It was supposed to be a surprise!'

His two companions turned to see her, laughing as they threw their arms up in exasperation.

'She's like a bloody ninja. I told you some freaky superpower shit would alert her to the fact we were here,' the woman said, laughing. They all were. They all looked so happy, and it was all Josie could do not to run, to flee the scene. The interlopers both came towards her, arms outstretched.

'Admit it, Mother – you put tracking chips into us years ago,' the guy said, as they descended and enveloped her in a hug.

Michael. Avril. On any other day, they would be the best thing she could possibly see, but not right now, because by God, it was hard enough to hold it together today and these two had just made it impossible.

Thirteen

Stacey

Stacey's phone buzzed, saving her from Senga's inquisitive stare. She picked it up and checked the screen. Jax. A text.

WTF is going on? Where are you?

Her heart sank. It had been a shit move, running out on him like that. They'd been planning to spend Christmas up at Mammoth Mountain, a ski resort about five hours north of LA, and she'd just ditched him. Not only had she ditched him, but she was in love with someone else and had decided to fly halfway around the world to do something about it. And the Oscar for rubbish girlfriend in a leading role goes to Stacey Summers.

Sorry Jax. Had to come home. Last minute decision. Hope you understand. Xx

No reply. That's when she noticed that his original text had been sent hours ago. It must have just come through now because her phone had connected to her mum's Wi-Fi. She did a calculation – it was now just after 4 a.m. in LA. He'd probably be in bed or in a club – either way, she didn't expect him to answer her text. And she very much doubted that he understood anyway.

That was a problem for another day. Right now, her biggest issue was staring her in the face, in the form of a decidedly unamused mother, who was giving her the evil eye over the rim of a mug that said, *I lost my heart (and my knickers) in Benidorm*. She really hoped that wasn't true.

'I should have seen this coming,' Senga said, with a sigh. 'Jean bet me a tenner years ago that you and Cammy would get together, but I didn't believe it. You were such good mates and I didn't think you'd risk your friendship. I don't know if I hate it more that you're hurting, or that Jean was right.'

Stacey smiled, grateful that at least her mother wasn't flying off the handle.

'When did you realise how you felt about him?'

Stacey's shoulders slumped. 'Years ago. The night before he left LA to come back here. We had a wild night of passion—'

'Given that I'm your mother and don't want to hear these things, I'm taking that as being a wild night of playing Jenga,' Senga interjected.

Stacey couldn't resist the bait. 'Yep, wild, brilliant, madly passionate Jenga. And afterwards, he told me that he was in love with me. I'd had no idea.'

'That bloody Jean is psychic. So what did you say?'

'Nothing. I just... fumbled it all. Then he left and told me I knew where to find him if I felt the same...'

'And it's taken you the best part of three years to realise it? Why didn't you tell him back then and we'd never have got to where we are today? Hells bells, Stacey, didn't I always teach you to say what was on your mind and be honest about how you feel? What happened to you?'

'You've no idea how many times I've asked myself that too. I should have said something. It was...' she paused. 'Complicated. He'd already decided to leave and I wasn't ready to give up my life there. By the time I realised that I wanted him, he'd met Caro, and I thought it was too late...'

Senga's sigh interrupted her. 'It is too late, love.'

'Is it though?'

'Yes! Why now? Why didn't you come back six months ago or a year ago or last bloody week? Why the weekend of his wedding? Come on, Stace, love, you've got to see that's crazy.'

'I know! But I thought he and Caro would burn out and I was waiting until that happened. My life is in LA now and I was sure he'd miss me, miss his life there and come back. When the invitation to the wedding arrived, I was stunned. What happened to long engagements and plenty of warning? It's all I've been able to think about for weeks and then a couple of days ago, I realised that if there's a choice between living in LA without Cammy, or living here with him, I'm ready to come back.'

'You don't mean that.'

'I do. I love my life there, Mum, but I honestly think I'd give it up for him now. I'm thirty-five. How much longer have I got in hot pants? I want to get married, to have kids, to have a normal life and I want to do that with Cammy.'

As she was saying it, Stacey could hear how it sounded – like someone who was nervous about her future and looking for a safety blanket. Maybe that was partly true, but that wasn't the crux of it. She blurted out the next argument before Senga could nail her on the last point.

'The thing is, Mum, what if he's only marrying Caro because I rejected him? What if I'm the love of his life and the one he's meant to be with? We were best friends, inseparable for over ten years. That's tough to beat.'

'And yet it didn't turn into anything more in all that time.'

'Because we were stupid! He was too scared of damaging our friendship and I was too blind to see how he felt. But what if we were meant to be together? What if he's settling for second best because his first choice didn't work out?'

'Or what if his feelings have changed since he met Caro?'

Stacey swallowed the last bite of her toast. 'But what if they haven't?'

Senga thought about that for a moment. 'I want it noted that I'm doing my best to be calm and non-judgemental...'

'Thanks, Mum.'

'So I won't say you're a daft boot and you should have done something about this long before now.'

'I appreciate that you're not pointing that out,' Stacey added with a wry roll of the eyes.

Senga took another sip of her tea. 'And I won't say that I think you're wrong, but I do. Caro is something special, love. I've never seen Cammy so happy. They're right together. Are you absolutely sure you want to do this and risk looking like a complete tit?'

'Pathetically positive.'

Senga continued to punctuate every line with a sigh. 'S'pose at least it means you're done with Jinx?'

'Jax.'

'I know, but Jinx sounds better. Easy on the eye – Ida said he made her insides flip for the first time since the eighties – but you two have been on and off more often than my bloody boiler.'

Stacey didn't rise to it. The last thing she wanted was an invasive dissection of her relationship with Jax. She didn't need her mother to tell her that it wasn't right. One way or another she would sort out things with him when she got back to LA.

'Okay. So tell me the plan,' Senga went on.

Stacey lifted her mug, mostly as a diversion because she could feel Senga's disapproval wafting towards her. 'What plan?'

'The plan that you've hatched in your head as to when and where you're going to speak to Cammy,' Senga retorted. 'Because if I'm to be pure mortified by my daughter's behaviour, then I want to at least be wearing fresh lippy and have something to hide behind.'

'I don't... I don't have a plan.'

She wasn't lying. Get back to Glasgow, go see him, get him alone and blurt out her feelings. That was as far as she'd got. And even then, she wasn't sure she'd be able to say it.

Looking from the outside, she could see that it was crazy. Insane. Who did this? Who actually set out to tell someone that they loved them on their wedding day to someone else? She'd obviously spent too much time in LA, and begun to believe that life turned out just like a romcom, with a big dramatic twist and then the right girl getting the guy. She'd lost it. Her mother clearly thought the same.

'Are you on drugs?' Senga asked, with the same tone she'd used to check if Stacey was smoking after the youth club when she was twelve. Back then, she'd been guilty. Not now.

'Of course not!'

'Right,' Senga answered, satisfied. 'Just had to ask. Ina has been on the cannabis oil for her arthritis and she's come out with a few wild ideas in the last wee while. She decided she was madly in love with some bloke that works in Morrisons and propositioned him in the frozen food aisle. They're going out for a curry next Friday night.'

'Ma, I'm not on drugs. I just... love him. And I can't stand the thought that I haven't told him. I know my timing is terrible and this makes me look like a really shit person, and I know that he's going to marry someone else and I don't stand a chance anyway, but I need to say it. I need to know for sure, because then I'll stop torturing myself about whether I've let the best thing in my life pass me by.' She was furiously blinking back the tears now. 'Look, if you tell me not to do it, I won't.'

'Stacey Summers, you haven't taken my advice since you were ten years old and I think it's highly unlikely that you'll start now.'

'I will,' Stacey argued.

'Okay, don't do it. It's crazy. Cammy is marrying Caro. She's a lovely girl and they're blissfully happy together. I'm sorry, love, but you're right – you don't stand a chance. And if you try to get in the way of the biggest day of their life, you're only going to fall flat on your face and lose his friendship. If you want to change your life, then do it. Find a good guy, settle down, have kids. But that guy isn't Cammy. So there's my opinion. Don't do it.'

Stacey stared at the table. Her mum was right. Of course she was. How bloody stupid had she been, charging all the way over here, on some kind of crazy mission to land the guy she was in love with?

She wouldn't do it. She would stay here, change in to her comfies and spend the afternoon on the sofa, cuddled up with her mum, watching some of their favourite movies... except *My Best Friend's Wedding*. Probably a good idea to give that one a miss. And then she'd go to Cammy's wedding, and sit there with her mouth welded shut while he promised his life to the woman that he was actually in love with. Afterwards, she'd go back to the USA, face Jax and build a new life plan. Yes, that was what she'd do. Definitely. Absolutely.

Nodding slowly, she gave her mum a weak smile. 'You're right. I know you are.'

The relief in Senga's voice was palpable. 'So you won't go charging over there?'

'Nope, I'll stay here with you. Sorry, Mum, I know I'm acting deranged, but I just... Ah, bugger, I don't know what I was thinking. I love him. But that's my problem and I need to get over it.'

Senga reached over and put her hand over her daughter's hundred dollar Beverly Hills manicure. 'You're right. And I'm proud of you for coming to your senses, love. No good would have come from it and you'd only have hurt yourself. Now, bung the kettle back on and I'll go and run you a bath and then we can have a lazy afternoon before we get ready for the ceremony. And at the "does anyone object to this couple marrying" bit, me and Ida will sit on yer hands so you don't make a show of yourself.'

The mental picture of that made Stacey giggle, and all at once the tension she'd been feeling since the moment the invitation had dropped into her mailbox lifted. She wasn't going to do anything. Yes, it would hurt to see the man she loved with someone else, but she'd get over it. Other people did. This wasn't the end of the world. She'd just focus on all the other good things in her life and wait for the pain to subside, then she'd move on, find her happy ever after somewhere else. Maybe this would even clear her mind enough to give her relationship with Jax a fair chance. Maybe this temporary aberration would turn out to be the best thing that ever happened to her.

Senga was halfway out of her seat when Stacey's phone buzzed. That would be Jax, Stacey thought as she picked it up and checked the screen.

Nope, not Jax.

Senga caught the change in expression on her daughter's face. 'Here we go,' she muttered. 'Cammy?'

Stacey nodded, to a knowing eye roll from Senga.

Her heart, which had reverted to a normal rhythm for a whole two minutes, began to thud again as she opened the text.

Silence.

'Oh, for feck's sake, what's he saying?' Senga blurted, her buttocks now firmly back down on her seat.

'He saw the footage Ida tweeted of my arrival at the airport. He's invited me over to his hotel for lunch at 2 p.m.'

Senga gave her the one raised eyebrow of warning, a facial gesture that had once been enough to strike terror into her heart. 'But you're not going to go, are you? Because we've just discussed this and you know that upsetting the biggest day of his life will only lead to heartache, most of it yours.'

Stacey nodded, saying nothing, mind racing. A few seconds ago, she'd been so sure of what she should do. Hadn't she conceded that her mum was right and going near him would be incredibly stupid? This didn't change a thing. She'd just text him back, refuse his invitation, wish him well and turn up like all his other friends and family to watch him getting married.

That was what she'd do.

Unless... what if this was a sign? Did she really want to give up this easily? Isn't that what she'd done last time? She should have been bold, brave, should have told him exactly how she felt.

Now she had a second chance.

'Stacey Margaret Rosina Summers, are you listening to me?'

Crap. Her mother only used her full name when she was seriously pissed off with her.

'I'm listening, Ma.'

Senga sighed. 'And you're going to ignore me and go charging on over there, aren't you?'

Stacey put her mug down, closed the biscuit tin and made her decision.

She wasn't that girl in the romcoms. Rushing over there wouldn't be cute, or romantic, or lead to a happy ending.

But she was going to do it anyway.

Fourteen

Website – www.itshouldhavebeenme.com

Members Discussion Forum

Responses to post by member, screen name NotOverYet:

Comments:

CarolSaidGoodbye: Hey NotOverYet, I get how you're feeling. Been there, done that, messed it up and watched him be with someone else. I didn't fight for him. I wish I had. You go, girl!

NancyBirmingham: No! Don't do it. Only two possible outcomes. 1. His bride will mess you up. 2. You'll look like a tit.

JessieInAJam: Two words – restraining order.

NotOverYet: I can't believe I'm getting negativity on here. I'm just doing what every single one of you wishes you'd done. Couldn't care less about the haters tbh.

BethanySunshine: You're right and I so admire your courage. I should have done this ten years ago when my Rodger left me and married my best friend. Wasn't brave enough. Still haven't found anyone #SineadO'Connorunderstood #nothingcomparestoyou

RealityCheck: Remember to pack a bag and put in something warm. Police cells get cold at this time of year.

2 P.M. – 4 P.M.

Fifteen

Caro

Shock robbed Caro of her words for a few seconds, as Lila's challenge echoed in her head: *Isn't this the day you're meant to be marrying my ex-boyfriend?*

And given the tone of her half-sister's voice, it wasn't a friendly opening to a casual conversation. Caro, always a people pleaser who avoided confrontation, found the strength to fight fire with fire. She wasn't going to let her sister bully or dominate her. Not here, not now.

'Yes,' she replied, deadpan. 'How is the man you ran off with on the same night that you dumped Cammy?'

As far as Caro knew, Lila had last been seen heading off into the sunset with a French footballer she'd picked up the night their worlds collided. Caro had instigated the showdown with her father five minutes after Lila had ended her relationship with Cammy and stormed out of the building. At the time it looked like Caro and Cammy were the losers – both rejected by people they'd loved, but that had turned around when they'd got talking and it had led to so much more.

As for Lila, hooking up with the footie star had been a social media sensation. Caro didn't have so much as a Facebook page, so she hadn't kept track of what had happened to Lila after that. She'd had no interest whatsoever in the new-found side of the family.

However, she was interested enough to notice that Lila squirmed before spitting out. 'It didn't work out. Not my type.'

Caro highly doubted that was true. The guy had money, celebrity and over half a million followers on Instagram. From what she knew of Lila, that was exactly her type.

It still baffled her that Cammy and Lila had been a couple. Cammy struggled to explain it too, his only reasoning being that Lila had come along at a time in his life when he'd just moved back from LA and was finding it tough to transition to being back in Scotland. Caro hadn't delved any deeper into it. It was the past. All she'd cared about since the moment she met Cammy was the future. The one she was about to blow away by pulling out of their wedding.

Not that she was going to reveal that information to her sister. 'But yes, I am getting married to Cammy today. How did you know?'

Lila looked at her like she was stupid. 'Because he put it on his Facebook page. A whole load of soppy crap about marrying the love of his life. Urgh,' she groaned, 'That's, like, so basic.'

Caro had absolutely no idea what that meant, but she was guessing it was in the same category as the 'lame' from earlier.

A maelstrom of irritation settled down as sheer loathing for her sister. How dare she mock Cammy? And how dare she speak about their marriage with such contempt? What. A. Bitch. A wave of guilt came swooping right over that feeling – in a bitch competition, Caro's actions today beat any petty barbs that Lila could come out with. Maybe they had more in common than she wanted to admit. Despite this, she fought fire with fire.

'So, you look… different from last time I saw you.'

Lila's eyes flared. 'I'm taking some time out while I decide what I'm going to do with my life.'

Caro didn't respond, feeling bad that she'd lashed out. That wasn't her. She didn't resort to this kind of stuff. She was someone who lifted other people up, who ignored negativity and whose first instinct was always to help anyone. Her self-reproach compelled her to speak, but before she could get the words out, Lila got in there.

'Or is that not what you want to hear? Do you want to hear that I lost my job, my new boyfriend publicly humiliated me by shagging someone else and then dumping me, my followers on social media all disappeared as soon as my life crashed, and I'm back here, living with my parents because I have absolutely nowhere to go, and I feel like my life is over?'

Caro's jaw dropped as Lila's voice cracked on the word 'over'. This was definitely a very different soul from the one Caro had seen across a restaurant two years ago, and she could sense now that underneath the bravado she was… broken. That was the only word to describe it. Caro felt a pang of pity.

'Look, I'm so sorry. I didn't realise all that happened to you.'

Lila shrugged. 'I think now that I probably deserved it. I was a selfish cow. But you don't see that at the time, do you?'

Another pang of sympathy. Caro immediately felt regret that she hadn't reached out to Lila before now, but it had just been too complicated, too sore, too damaging.

'Maybe we could...' Caro began, planning to take the first step in establishing some kind of relationship, but then stopping, interrupted by the banging of the front door.

She froze as she listened to the steps coming down the hallway, then watched as her father's frame filled the doorway. An immediate clutch of disgust twisted her stomach, but she forced herself not to react to his evident surprise. Or maybe shock was a better way to describe it. Either way, he didn't throw his arms open to welcome her.

'Caro,' he nodded, as if it was completely insignificant that she was there. Another thing to add to the list of reasons why she hated him. Apparently she wasn't even worthy of some kind of hurried apology or hug or a gasp of relief that the daughter he hadn't clapped eyes on for two years was standing in his kitchen.

Also on the list? He looked exactly the same as he had the day he walked out on them for the last time. His hair had greyed over the years, but he was one of those blokes who looked better as they aged. Blue eyes. Golf course tan. Still in great shape, thanks to a health and fitness schedule that he maintained religiously.

Suddenly, Caro realised that she couldn't make small talk, couldn't stand on ceremony. She wasn't here to play happy families. She wanted to understand, to find a way to untangle her feelings about her parents, so that perhaps, just perhaps, she could gain enough insight to explain to Cammy why she couldn't marry him today.

The words of castigation poured out in one long rant. 'I need to know why. Why did you marry Mum, why did you stay with her when you had someone else, why did you lie to us for all those years? Did your marriage mean nothing to you?'

He tossed his keys and a newspaper down on to the kitchen island and pulled out a chair. Caro could see that Lila was as interested in the answer as she was.

'Caro, what do you want me to say?' he asked, with almost disdainful disinterest. Bastard. 'It's all in the past. There's no point in dredging it all up now.'

A torrent of uncharacteristic rage began to build inside her and she fought to control it.

'Answer the questions,' she said, through gritted teeth.

She could see that he realised he wasn't going to be able to palm her off.

After a pause, he spoke. 'I married her because I loved her.'

The rage in Caro built again. She didn't believe that for a second.

'But then I met Louise and fell in love with her too. Your mum wanted to stay in Aberdeen because her family was there and you were settled there, but my work was in Glasgow. When Louise fell pregnant, it just made sense to go between the two. I suppose I didn't want to hurt anyone.'

'Bollocks,' Caro spat. 'You didn't think you were hurting Mum by only giving her half your life? She shut down completely when you weren't there, spent her whole existence waiting for you to walk back in the door. Meanwhile, you were off fucking around and living it up down here.'

'I can't change any of that now,' he snapped back.

'Why didn't you do the decent thing and leave her when she was still young enough to start a new life? Instead, you waited until she was sick, until she had no chance of real happiness, and you walked out the door for good. Is that what marriage meant to you?'

He snorted. 'Marriage is just a piece of paper.'

Caro reeled like she'd been slapped. There it was. The whole crux of her issues today. Marriage was just a piece of paper.

'Not to Mum. She stayed faithful and loving to you until the day she died. Your marriage made her life a lie. I think you were hedging your bets. I think you didn't leave Mum because she adored you, and you loved the fact that you were the centre of her world. I think you knew she was sitting in an expensive house that could give you both a very luxurious retirement if she'd lived longer. And I think you couldn't make up your mind what wife...' her eyes flicked to Lila, 'or what family you wanted to live with. So you tried to have both. And then when Mum got sick, that made your decision for you and off you fucking trotted.'

He barely flinched at the onslaught.

Caro remembered reading somewhere that the opposite of love wasn't hate but indifference. This man, who shared her DNA, who was responsible for her life, could not be more indifferent to her right now. None of this was even permeating his shell of nonchalance and that was driving her crazy.

'Like I said, nothing I can do to change that now. You're entitled to your opinion and I can see I won't change that. We all just need to move on.'

Two years ago, when she'd first discovered his treachery, she'd kicked his chair, the only time in her life that she'd ever lashed out in anger. Right now, she wanted to do that again. But what would she gain from that? Not a thing. He truly wasn't worth it. She wasn't sure what she'd come here for, but she should have known he'd give her nothing. Story of their lives.

For a moment, Caro thought Lila was going to speak, but she said nothing. Two peas in a pod, like father like daughter, Caro decided.

But she couldn't be like him. She just couldn't. She didn't want to have anything in common with this lying, cheating, vile excuse for a human being.

She loved Cammy. But for her, marriage would always be tainted by her parents. She had to see him, had to explain it, had to make him understand why she wasn't going to be at the altar tonight. And she had to hope that he would accept that, because if he couldn't then there was no hope for them. She couldn't live on someone else's terms. Her mum had done that her whole life, and it had only brought her loneliness and betrayal.

She picked her bag up off the kitchen island and slipped it over her shoulder. 'You know, you really are a soulless prick. I sometimes wondered if there was any hope for us to forge some kind of redefined relationship. Now I know that there isn't. But I hope that one day you find out that karma comes back and bites your arse and I hope you suffer. You deserve to. Good luck, Lila. You're going to need it if you stick around here.'

With that, she turned and walked quickly down the hall, knowing that he wouldn't follow her. She jerked open the Yale lock on the front door.

'Caro!' Not her dad's voice. Lila's.

Caro paused, her gaze meeting her half-sister's face. All the defiance and anger that had been in Lila's posture when she'd arrived earlier was now gone. Caro waited, unsure of why Lila had stopped her at the door.

'I just wanted to say… that erm…' This clearly wasn't a woman who was good with emotions or expressing regret. 'I just wanted to say…' she repeated. 'I'm happy for you. Good luck with your wedding tonight.'

Caro couldn't believe what she was hearing, but there was something there, a genuine undertone that convinced her that Lila really did want to reach out to her and this wasn't some twisted mind game.

'Thanks,' Caro said hesitantly.

'I hope it all goes well.' Again, there was a sincerity there. Maybe her fall from grace really had humbled her.

Caro gave her the closest thing she could muster to a smile.

They may have taken a baby step towards some kind of relationship, but that didn't mean Caro was suddenly going to tell her sister the truth.

There wasn't going to be a wedding. Nothing that had happened in the last hour had changed her mind. The very thought of putting on that dress and replicating the ceremony that had destroyed her mother's life still made spikes of anxiety shoot through her.

Now, she just had to go find Cammy and break his heart.

Sixteen

Seb

He was going to go straight to the next stop on his list for the day, but the need for a coffee convinced Seb otherwise. He checked his watch. Two o'clock. The check-in time at the hotel was three o'clock, but it would probably be worth chancing his arm in case the room was ready and they would let him in early. He could ditch his case, grab a coffee and then head back out again.

As he approached the hotel, the memories consumed him. He'd chosen it for this trip because it was across the road from the Kibble Palace. That's where Pearl had told him her niece was getting married. He had no idea how he was going to manage it, but at some point the plan was to go there and catch a glimpse of the bride. Of course, that wouldn't prove anything, but something inside him felt the need to do it anyway. He hadn't thought any further forward than that.

The other reason he'd chosen this hotel was because it was Juliet's favourite place to stay in Glasgow. They'd been here on all their previous visits, whether they were cosying up on wintery days or crossing the road to wander in the Botanic Gardens on summer afternoons. It was special to them. The fact that the wedding ceremony at the Kibble Palace, the glorious structure inside those gardens, felt significant to him. Almost like Juliet was leading him there. But why would she, after what he'd done to her?

He gingerly twisted his car up the ramps of the multi-storey car park, then descended the stairs and crossed the side road to the hotel, dodging the shopping trolleys left by shoppers at the supermarket next door. He knew there was a rear entrance, but he chose to walk round the corner to the main doors, which opened directly into the lobby. The assault of emotions as he faced the festive beauty of it all nearly slayed him. The gorgeous tree that almost reached the ceiling and sparkled with thousands of fairy lights. Gold and green tinsel garlands draped along the top of every surface. An orchestral version of 'We Three Kings' coming from the sound system. Bowls of ginger cookies on the reception desk for the arriving guests. Juliet would have loved this. She'd have giggled, and put her arm through his, and snuggled into his shoulder with the biggest grin on her face. The thought took his breath away for a moment, and only the arrival of a huge family behind him forced him to put one foot in front of the other and make his way forward to reception.

The girl behind the desk greeted him with a smile. Her badge identified her as Gemma, her Santa hat identified her as being in the festive spirit. 'Good afternoon, welcome to the West End Grand.'

'Thank you,' Seb replied automatically. Sometimes it was hard to appear normal. Would they speak to him with such warmth if they knew he was a killer? He pushed the thought away and tried to focus on the moment. 'I'm checking in today and I wondered if my room was ready? Seb Lloyd,' he added, putting his leather bag on the countertop and resting his hand on it. He needed to know it was safe.

Gemma typed on the keyboard for a few seconds, before looking back up. 'I'm so sorry. I'm afraid it won't be ready until 3 p.m. We can keep your luggage here though, if you'd like to have a drink in the bar while you're waiting.'

'No worries,' Seb answered, going for casual and friendly again. He'd known getting in early would be a long shot on the busiest week of the hotel's year. He wheeled his small trolley case forward. 'I'll just leave this with you and head back out.'

'Of course,' Gemma said, signalling a red-liveried concierge, who checked in Seb's case and gave him a ticket in return.

Okay, perhaps a quick coffee in the lounge and then he would go on to his next destination and revisit the memories that were waiting for him there.

He hadn't even reached the stairs to the lounge area when he heard a voice he recognised.

'Seb! Oh my goodness, isn't this a small world!'

Shit. He should have thought this through and realised that there was a possibility that Pearl would be staying here, given the close proximity to the wedding venue. He'd just assumed that she'd be staying with family in the city, but perhaps – other than her niece – she didn't have any other relatives in Glasgow.

'Pearl! It is indeed a small world,' he said, trying, as had become a habit over the last few months, to keep his voice as normal as possible.

Pearl, festive in a red sequined jumper and black trousers, leaned in to greet him with mutual kisses on both cheeks. 'You didn't say you were coming to Glasgow for Christmas,' she said, eyes wide with surprise.

'Last minute decision,' he explained. 'An invitation to meet up with some old friends.' A lie. But what else could he say? *I wanted to come and check out if the niece you told me about could be my daughter. Oh, and I'm on a mission to visit all the places that were special to my wife, the one I killed, before I finally fulfil my promise to scatter her ashes in the city she loved more than any other.*

She'd back away slowly and call security.

No, he had to bluff his way out of this one.

'What are you doing right now? You must come and meet my family! We're all in the restaurant having lunch with the lovely young man who is marrying our Caro.'

Right then, at that moment, if Seb had a choice between following Pearl and meeting the happy family or going into a war zone without protective armour, he'd choose the latter. He didn't do family gatherings. Especially happy ones that reminded him of everything he'd lost. God, he needed a drink. If it weren't for the fact that he needed a clear head for the things he had planned for today, he'd be on his way to the bar right now for a large Scotch.

Seb made a show of checking his watch. 'Ah, I'd have loved to, but I'm afraid I'm late to meet my friends. I'm just rushing out now.'

'That's such a shame!' Pearl wailed, and for a moment he felt a pang of guilt. She was a lovely woman and he was blatantly lying to her. He told himself it was for her own good. The last thing she needed was a maudlin widower in the mix of her happy family celebration. Still, it didn't seem to be dissuading her from her mission to get them all together. 'Listen, we're staying here and no doubt we'll all end up in the residents' bar after the wedding. Did I tell you it's just across the road at the Kibble Palace?' She went on without waiting for an answer. 'Anyway, it's at 7 p.m. so we'll probably be back here in the bar around midnight. Do stop by and join us.'

Seb let that thought run around his mind. Perhaps that would be the best way to meet the bride? But there was no guarantee that she'd be with the rest of the family. The newly-weds might head off on their honeymoon straight from the reception and then his chance would be gone. No, best to try to get a glimpse of her earlier in the evening. Seven o'clock. Across at the venue. If he went there earlier, he might catch sight of her as she arrived.

'I'll see you in the bar later then,' he answered, knowing that he had absolutely no intention of doing so. 'Anyway, I'd better be off. It was lovely to bump into you again, Pearl.'

'You too,' she said, giving him a warm hug. 'And see you again later!' she added.

He watched as she went off in the direction of the Ladies', and he made a split-second decision. He couldn't go to the lounge for a coffee now, in case she saw him there. Best to just head straight out, perhaps pop into one of the cafés on Byres Road, then do what he had to do before going across to the gardens later.

He crossed the lobby, opened the outside door and then paused to let a young woman with dark blonde hair, wearing a red duffle coat, rush in past him. She looked harassed, searching, breathing heavily as if she'd been running, perhaps to get out of the rain.

'Thank you,' she said gratefully.

He doubted she even heard his, 'No problem,' as she ran on past him, across the lobby in the direction of the restaurant. Probably late meeting someone for a lovely Christmas lunch. Another pang, this time of longing. Would he ever stop wishing that he'd see Juliet rushing towards him again? He closed his eyes for a moment, then shook the thought away and stepped outside. He had to keep going. Couldn't let himself crumble. Not yet.

The rain had subsided to a grey drizzle as he stepped out on to Byres Road. The street was packed now, many of the pedestrians sporting the harassed expressions of shoppers desperately trying to pick up the last essentials on the Friday before Christmas. It would be a dismal scene if it wasn't for the white twinkling Christmas lights, already illuminated, stretched high in the air across the street, and for the band of classical buskers, surrounded by a small crowd, playing East 17's 'Stay Another Day' on a selection of brass and string instruments. He assumed they were music students from one of the nearby colleges or universities. For a moment, he considered stopping to listen, but instead, he ducked into a coffee shop and ordered a cappuccino to go.

With the steaming cup in his hand, he walked a little further down Byres Road, turned right and went along Louden Terrace until he reached Kelvinside Hillhead Parish Church. Juliet had told him everything he knew about this building. Built in the late 1800s, it had a glorious curved frontage, and was modelled on the Sainte-Chapelle in Paris.

As a child, she would walk past it every day and marvel at its grandeur. It was her first and only choice of venue for their wedding, despite neither of them being particularly religious. It was special, she'd said. She felt a connection there.

Walking up the steps to the entrance, he breathed a sigh of relief when he saw that one of the doors lay open. He walked inside, immediately feeling small and insignificant under the grand curved wooden ceiling and the stunning stained glass windows that formed the top two thirds of every wall. It was as magnificent as he remembered.

There were a few people dotted around the church, and Seb took care to avoid them, slipping into an empty pew halfway up the aisle on the left-hand side. He wanted to rewind his mind to the day he declared that he would love her for eternity. In sickness and in health, for richer and poorer, he vowed to honour and protect her. On that day, he had no idea that he would break that promise so spectacularly.

He closed his eyes, trying desperately to form a vision of Juliet on that day, in her stunning but simple white floor length dress, under a Spanish-style veil that trailed to the floor. But he could only hold that image momentarily before it was pushed away, again and again, by another memory.

The morning Juliet died. She'd been wearing a white shift dress, her hair lightened at the front by the sun, so that tendrils of dark gold flowed between the chestnut waves. He'd been irritable, his mind consumed by the fact he was late for a meeting at work. It was rumoured that the management were going to announce that the club had a new owner, who, it was said, would undoubtedly clear out the existing team and bring in his own people. The prospect of having to find a new job, and move on yet again at the age of fifty-five, was filling him with anxiety. They were happy there. Settled. He was getting too old, he decided, to keep rebuilding their lives every few years in a new course, new city, new country.

'Are you ready yet?' he'd snapped, and Juliet had stared him down. He'd always loved that she was no pushover, but right at that moment, her glare irritated him even more. They rarely argued, but when they did, they were both as fiery as each other, so their clashes tended to flare quickly, then subside and be over with in minutes.

She only broke off the glare to pick up her bag, then she smiled at him with mock sweetness. 'I'm ready, your highness,' she'd quipped.

Seb had no time for the sarcasm. He reached out to lift the car keys from the worktop, when she swooped in and grabbed them first.

'What are you doing?' he'd said sharply.

'I'll drive,' she'd answered. 'You're way too wound up. I'll drive as far as the college, then when I get out, you can take over. It'll give you time to calm down.'

Refusing to go along with her plan, he'd sighed and took the keys from her hand. He didn't have time for this. Not today. He was driving. And they had to get going right now. 'Nonsense, I'm fine. Look, please, just get in the car and let's get going.'

'Seb Lloyd, don't you dare speak to me like that. I'm only going along with this because I need to get to work, otherwise I'd tell you where you could shove your bloody car keys.'

Even more wound up now, he'd stormed off, yanked the car door open and climbed in, tapping on the wheel in irritation while he waited for her to get in.

When she did, he'd immediately slammed the gearstick into first, put his foot on the accelerator and pressed.

She'd had no time to catch her breath. No time to fasten her seatbelt. And no time to scream as a van he hadn't even seen came hurtling towards them.

Seventeen

Josie

'Oh my word, you two are going to be the death of me!' Josie exclaimed. 'You can't spring surprises like this on a woman of my vintage. You'll give me a heart attack!'

Michael, her gorgeous son, chuckled and Josie knew that every woman within viewing distance would be swooning. Aye, she was biased, but he was a handsome big devil of a man. Well over six feet tall, he was fast approaching fifty, his dark hair now flecked with grey, but with his broad shoulders and chiselled jawline, he still looked like he'd just walked off the front of a knitting pattern.

Avril, her delightfully gobby daughter – a woman after her own heart – was the first to answer. 'I don't think so, Mother. We know you're indestructible and you'll outlive us all.'

The words almost took Josie's breath away. Until a few hours ago, she'd been pretty convinced of the same, would brush off the very thought of her own mortality with a defiant profanity and a rude gesture. Not now.

Thankfully, Avril was too busy hugging her to notice that Josie's legs wobbled slightly as a wave of reality sucked the life out of her. It took every ounce of strength left in her to force herself back to some show of normality.

'I absolutely will, and don't you be forgetting it,' she quipped, as they'd expect her to. 'Anyway, what are you two doing here? And, dear God, Avril, have you come as a Smurf, love?'

Avril rolled her eyes and flicked her bright blue hair off her shoulder. As a make-up artist who worked on TV and film sets, she never failed to make an impact, either with rainbow-shaded hair or dramatic cosmetics, or – as per her current look – both. A mass of cobalt waves fell to her shoulder blades and her blue and gold eyeshadow sparkled like glitter above the dramatic shading on the cheekbones of her porcelain face. Josie thought she was, as always, utterly spectacular. But she was an old-school West of Scotland mother, so she relayed this opinion in the form of teasing and entertaining barbs. And, as always, Avril, who was every bit as quick and sharp as her mother, responded in kind. 'I did, Ma. And good to see you're still dressing up as Andy Warhol,' she said, grinning, noting Josie's black polo neck, black trousers and short, chaotic white hair.

The two of them cackled as they resumed their hug, Josie swelling with emotion that she knew could overflow into tears at any moment. She wasn't having that; everyone would immediately know something was wrong. All their lives she'd been the strong, indomitable, flippant one and she couldn't let that change now.

'Right, you lot, much as I adore you all, I have duties today.'

That was rewarded with a group cheer, and for the first time Josie took in the rest of the assembled crowd. Cammy's parents, down from Perth. Caro's Aunt Pearl and her Uncle Bob. Their son Todd and his husband Jared. No Caro. Josie didn't know if she was relieved or disappointed. If she wasn't here, then where the hell was she? And was this the time to pull Cammy aside and ask him if he knew why his bride was bailing out of the wedding that was supposed to be happening in less than five hours? Probably not.

Okay, new plan. Where else would Caro go? Maybe she was back at the flat by now. Perhaps she'd had a walk, sorted her head out and all panic had been averted by her return. Her hopes rose for a second before plummeting again. No. If Caro had returned home, Val would have been straight on the phone to let Josie know.

A thought – maybe she'd gone to the wedding venue? Perhaps she was over there right now, checking everything out and calming her nerves? Yes! That made absolute sense. Or about as much sense as anything else that had happened today.

'Hang on, you can't just run out on us. Stay for lunch. Isn't that why you're here?' Cammy said, hugging her. 'I'll get them to set another place.'

'No!' Josie blurted, then saw by their expressions of surprise that she may have said that a little more forcefully than she intended. Bugger. She had to think on her feet. She had categorically told Cammy that she wouldn't be joining them for lunch because she'd be with Caro. What could she say that would explain why she was now standing in the middle of the flipping restaurant? 'I'm only... erm... here because all is going great over at Caro's. Yep, we're bang on schedule. So I decided to do my rounds and check that everything was okay with the booking I made for you lot here at the hotel. Next, I'm heading over to the Kibble Palace to check that's all set up and perfect too.'

Michael's low throaty laugh melted her soul. 'Ma, I think you've found your new vocation in life. Josie's Wedding Planning Service. It's not too late to start a whole new career.'

Oh, it is, son. Way, way too late. She didn't say that out loud, preferring to add it to all the other thoughts she didn't want to dwell on today.

Something, maybe the stress that was twisting her larynx, triggered a violent coughing bout that made Josie's eyes water as she bent forward in the hope of preventing it from cracking her ribs.

'Mother, you have to give up the fags,' Avril groaned, a familiar demand that she'd been churning out to Josie since she was about ten and learned about the evils of cigarettes in school. Every time, Josie answered with a glib comment, just as she did now.

'Aye, I will, ma love, as soon as I give up drinking, swearing and hoping Pierce Brosnan will track me down for a wild night on the town.'

Avril rolled her eyes in frustration, just as she'd been doing for decades. If there was a gold medal for showing disapproval of your mother's vices, that girl would have won it years ago.

She'd just managed to straighten up after the last cough escaped from her, when Cammy gave her another hug. 'I can't tell you how much I love you for this, Josie.'

'Sorry, Cammy' she quipped tartly, with just an edge of flirtation. Bugger, this trying to act normal lark was tougher than she thought, but she had to keep it going. 'It's too late to be declaring your feelings for me now. I don't succumb to married men and you'll be one of those by the end of the day. If you have feelings for me, you should have said so before now when there was still time for us.'

Everyone at the table was laughing now, including Pearl, who had just got out of her seat and gave Josie a quick cuddle as she passed. 'You're absolutely right, Josie,' she joked. 'But your loss is our Caro's gain. Just off to the loo. Will we get a chance to catch up later? I want to hear all your news.'

'Absolutely, Pearl. It's great to see you, pet, you're looking smashing,' Josie said, as Pearl nimbly headed off in the direction of the lobby.

Josie had a thought. Maybe she could go after Pearl, grab her while she was away from the rest of the guests and tell her about the Caro situation? Perhaps Pearl had some other insight into where her niece would go? It wasn't much of a plan, but it was a start.

Just as Pearl headed out of the room, another familiar face appeared in the restaurant doorway and made her way towards them. Actually 'made her way' was the understatement of the year. 'Sashayed like the goddess that she absolutely was' probably best described the newcomer's entrance. Despite Josie's devastation over her health, despite her current 'lost bride' fiasco, despite the fact that she was now going to have to keep a huge secret from her children for the whole of the rest of the day, she couldn't help the grin that crept across her bright red lips.

'Well, well, well, today is full of surprises,' Cammy bellowed, as he threw his arms around Stacey Summers.

'Ah, Stacey ma darlin', it's smashing to see you,' Josie said, meaning every word, as she wrapped the lass in a tight hug. Stacey's mum, Senga, had been one of Josie's best pals for years, and they'd all banded together to raise this girl, and Michael and Avril, and all the others that were born to members of their merry group of working mothers who juggled cleaning jobs, friendships and families.

'You get younger every time I see you, Aunt Josie,' Stacey chirped back. Although they weren't actually related, they'd been family forever and Stacey had called her Aunt Josie since she was a tiny mite.

Josie stretched back so that Stacey was at arm's length and she could see into her beautiful cobalt eyes. 'How are you doing, gorgeous?'

'I'm great, Aunt Josie. Life's good.'

Josie immediately tensed, her emotional alerts sending a warning signal to the ends of her nerves. Stacey looked stunning. Her smile was wide. She was saying the right things. But she'd known this lass since she was a babe in Senga's arms, and she could see when there was something not quite right with her. That big wide lip-glossed smile didn't reach her eyes. Och, what was wrong? Whatever it was, now wasn't the place or time to ask. She made a mental note to catch her later at the wedding. If there was going to be a bloody wedding! Time to get out of here and get back to searching for the runaway bride. Michael, Avril, and whatever was troubling Stacey, would need to wait until later.

'Right, you lot, it's been a slice of heaven, but I've got far more important things to do and people to see,' she announced, before delivering a round of kisses to everyone there. 'I love you all and I'll see you later,' were her parting words, before she charged back up the stairs to search for Pearl. She spotted her across the lobby, chatting to a tall, tanned bloke with grey hair. She couldn't see his face because he had his back to her, but she knew everyone on the wedding guest list and she was fairly sure he wasn't one of them. It was only a small wedding – about forty people in total. Actually, thirty-nine now that the bride wasn't coming.

Fuck it. Two choices. Storm over there and interrupt Pearl, then interrogate her for clues as to Caro's whereabouts. Or just bolt on over across the road to the Kibble Palace and hope that Caro was there.

She pulled out her phone and shot off a quick text to Val.

Any sign of the wandering bride?

Three little dots immediately started flickering on the screen, showing that Val was typing a response. Josie knew she might be in for a wait. Val's aptitude with modern technology was up there with her ability to get her Spanx on in less than five minutes – it rarely went well but it was frequently entertaining.

Her phone buzzed. Val.

No.

Succinct and straight to the point, yet it had still taken about twenty seconds and Val had probably broken two nails in the process of typing it.

Okay, interrupt Pearl or not?

Josie made an executive decision.

Not. She could see Pearl smiling and making conversation. There was no way she would be so laid back if she thought there was anything amiss.

Nope, there was nothing to be gained from worrying her. Instead, she crossed the lobby at warp speed and burst out on to the wet street outside. She dodged a group of buskers with brass instruments and strings and tried not to swear as she weaved around the random people that were blocking her path until she got to the pedestrian crossing that would hopefully get her across the road without being hit by one of the many vehicles navigating the busy four-way junction. 'Och, I could get hit by a bus tomorrow,' she'd always say, if anyone chided her for doing something dangerous, like her last parachute jump, or when she went water skiing on her seventieth birthday in Torremolinos, or when she climbed up on to a bar top, spraying a bottle of champagne to welcome the new millennium. The altercation with the bus didn't seem like such a terrible option right now. Over. Done with. No suffering. No lingering, waiting for the life to drain out of her.

I could get hit by a bus. The thought again. Then the pain. The grief. The fear of what was to come and how it would affect the people she loved, how it would drag everything out and make it so much worse for her and for them.

Josie glanced up at the pedestrian light. Red man. Do not walk.

Fuck it.

She stepped off the kerb. She waited. Waited longer. Nothing happened. No bloody bus.

Heart racing, she stepped back on to the pavement.

Those twisted Gods were interfering once again.

Well, sod them.

She'd be going soon, but first she had work to do, weddings to save, and then, she promised herself, she'd leave on her own terms, not theirs.

Eighteen

Stacey

She almost hadn't come. Mainly because her mother had threatened to grab her ankles and hang on until Stacey saw sense. In the end, Senga had thrown her arms up in despair and told Stacey to do 'whatever act of bloody foolishness' that she had to do.

'I'll be waiting here with a bottle of wine and a relationship counsellor to help you deal with rejection when you get back,' had been Senga's last words before Stacey had closed the door and made her way down the path to the waiting taxi.

She'd dressed carefully. A super-tight red pencil skirt that clung to every curve and ended below her knee, so it was both incredibly sexy and conservative at the same time. On top, she wore a black, long sleeved, off-the-shoulder bodysuit that showed off her tan, but again, wasn't tarty or provocative. Her coat was black, Jaeger, a beautifully cut wool blend that grazed her ankles, with enough padding in the shoulders to make reminiscent of a forties movie heroine. Her hair fell in glossy dark waves, her make-up was minimal: just a bit of mascara, a touch of smoky eyeliner and a nude lip. Classy, but with a hint of wow. That had been the look she was going for and she hoped she'd pulled it off.

On the way to the hotel, she'd changed her mind a hundred times. On the grand scale of bad ideas she'd ever had in her life, this one was pretty near the top. Number one on the list, however, was doing nothing after Cammy left LA, just waiting for him to realise he shouldn't have left and for him to remedy that by coming back to her. Definitely top spot on the stupid scale.

That's why she couldn't turn back now, couldn't stop herself. She had to see him, had to tell him why she'd just crossed an ocean to speak to him.

It was his laugh she heard first when she entered the restaurant, followed by his booming voice.

'Well, well, well, today is full of surprises,' Cammy bellowed, as she reached the table and he threw his arms around her. She flushed to a shade that she was pretty sure matched her skirt and half of the decorations in the room. Just being near him, seeing him after three years, her heart was thudding out of her chest. There had been a glimmer of hope that when she saw him she'd immediately realise that she felt differently, that the hype had been more than the depth of her longing for him. Now she knew that wasn't the case. Even the heat of his body as he held her was making her tremble. God, she loved him. Every single bit of him. She might have blurted something out right then and there, in front of a whole table of strangers and a few familiar faces, if she hadn't spotted a major fly in the marriage-disrupting ointment.

Aunt Josie. Someone she absolutely adored, and a woman who could sniff out suspicious behaviour a mile away.

Damn it.

Thankfully, Josie was in a hurry, so they just had a quick exchange before the older woman tore off out of the restaurant at a speed that absolutely was not normal for a woman of her age. Josie was a force of nature. Stacey didn't even want to contemplate what she would do to her when she found out why she was here. The thought made her shudder.

'Are you okay?' Cammy asked.

She wanted to answer with a casual smile, but her words seemed to have been swallowed by the fact that she could feel his hand resting gently on the small of her back and it was causing her brain to temporarily shut down. This was bloody ridiculous. She was a grown-ass woman who was acting like she was sixteen and in the presence of the hottest guy in school. *Get it together*, she warned her lovestruck inner teenager.

She almost wept with gratitude when Avril stepped forward and squeezed the life out of her. 'How are you, you old tart? Damn, you get uglier by the year. Terrible when people let themselves go like this.'

Even in her state of high anxiety, that made her chuckle.

Avril's brother, Michael, nudged his sister out of the way as he hugged her next. 'Ignore her. Jealousy has always been her biggest flaw. It's made her hair turn blue.'

Stacey was still laughing when Cammy pulled out the chair next to him and gestured to her to sit next to him. As soon as they were both seated, he made the introductions. 'Everyone, this is Stacey. Stacey, this is Caro's Uncle Bob.

That was his wife, Pearl, who nipped out to the loo a few minutes ago.'

Bob reached over to shake her hand.

'And this is Caro's cousin, Todd, and his husband, Jared,' he went on.

Todd was already out of his seat and leaning across the table, hand outstretched, his smile warm and welcoming. He was wearing beautifully cut jeans and a pale blue shirt, his blonde hair swept back off his face. 'Great to meet you.'

His partner, Jared, every bit as stylish in black jeans and a tight fitting grey Versace V-neck, followed suit, but then paused, as if something had just dawned on him. '*USA Speed Freaks*!' he exclaimed, in an accent that was clearly American or Canadian. Stacey still wasn't great at differentiating. 'You're Stacey!'

'I am,' Stacey said, grinning with gratitude for yet another diversion.

Jared wasn't holding back his delight. 'This is amazing, I love that show! I can't believe Caro never told us that she knew you!'

'Actually, they've never met,' Cammy interjected. 'Stacey and I have been friends for ever and we went off to LA together a million years ago. That makes me feel so old,' he groaned. 'Anyway, it was only after I left LA...' his eyes met Stacey's when he said this and she wasn't sure if she imagined some kind of significance to the way he said it, 'and came back to Scotland that I met Caro. You haven't been home since then, have you?'

Oh, how she wished she had. Preferably about a week before he met Caro, then maybe none of this would have happened.

'No, this is the first time,' she answered, trying not to make her regret obvious.

'I'm so glad you're here. I was totally shell-shocked when I saw Ida's tweet this morning. Why didn't you tell me you were coming?'

Stacey shrugged. Keeping up this level of nonchalance was excruciating.

Because I'm in love with you and didn't know if I'd have the courage to tell you.

'Because I didn't think I could make it.'

Then I decided that I couldn't live with myself if I didn't.

'Then I had a last minute break in filming.'

So I've come all this way to make a complete arse of myself.

'So I decided I couldn't miss seeing you walk down that aisle.'

Or stop it from happening.

Aaaaargh! The very thought made her squirm inside. She was never going to heaven. Never.

'Well, I couldn't be happier that you made it. I've missed you,' he said, putting his hand over hers. Anyone around the table would see it as a completely harmless gesture of affection, but only because they had no idea of the turmoil it was causing inside her. Hope. That's what it represented to Stacey. Hope.

Oblivious to the effect he was having on her, Cammy was now patting the pockets of the jacket that hung over his chair.

'Damn it, I've left my phone upstairs in my room. I'm just going to nip up for it.'

The words were out of Stacey's mouth before she'd even decided to say them. 'I'll come with you.' This was it. A sign. Foolish or not, she was going to get him alone, tell him the truth, make him understand how she felt about him.

'Eh, sure,' Cammy said, breezily as he rose from his chair and…

He paused, his whole face changing as he saw something behind her.

'Babe! What are you doing here?'

He was out of his seat again, arms outstretched, as a woman Stacey had only ever seen in pictures slowly, almost hesitantly, walked towards them.

Caro.

Something inside Stacey curled up and raised a surrender flag. This was the first time she'd actually seen her in the flesh and she could absolutely see why Cammy had fallen in love with her. This woman was completely make-up-free, yet she had a natural prettiness that just shone through. She was dressed in jeans and a jumper, with a pair of black biker boots and a bright red duffle coat. None of it should work, and yet there was something so warm, so fresh, about her that Stacey immediately felt like she'd tried too hard with her own outfit and wished she'd thrown on a pair of jeans and a sweater.

She was so busy analysing every second of the newcomer's arrival that she only now noticed the most crucial thing of all – Caro looked upset, worried, harassed.

She quickly went around the table, hugging everyone, but as Stacey watched her, she could see that it was the actions of someone who was going through the motions quickly so that she could get to the point of why she was there.

When she reached her, Stacey stood up. 'Hi, I'm Stacey. I've heard so much about you.'

I'm the woman who's in love with the man you're about to marry. I've travelled thousands of miles to be here and I'm planning on telling him before he says 'I do' to you. Sorry about that. I'm not usually that kind of girl. But… well… did I mention I was really sorry?

Stacey had never hated herself more than in that very moment.

Cammy couldn't take his eyes off his wife-to-be. 'I thought you said it was bad luck for us to see each other today, but, man, I'm glad you're here. Sit down, join us,' he said, smiling like this was the best thing that had happened to him all day. There it was. His love for this woman written all over his face.

Who had she been kidding?

He'd never looked at her like that. Not when they first met, not in the all the many years they'd known each other, not even when they were making love the night before he left California. He may have loved her back then, but seeing them together it was very clear that she had been replaced – make that surpassed – by the woman he was gazing at now.

Coming here had been a mistake, but thank God she'd seen this before she'd blurted out the truth to him. She would just wait until everyone was back in their seats and then she would make an excuse to leave and get out of here before she made a complete fool of herself. Decision made, she zoned back into the conversation between the bride and groom.

'No, I… I'm not staying. Can I just… erm… can I have a quick chat with you? In private?' Caro said.

Cammy looked a little confused, and everyone was staring at Caro now, bewilderment on all their faces.

'Just a couple of last minute things,' Caro blurted to the spectators around the table. 'I won't keep him for long.'

'You guys go ahead and eat. I'll catch up when I come back,' Cammy said breezily.

But Stacey was still watching Caro, and as she did so, she could feel her own eyes narrowing. There was something amiss. As Cammy lifted his room key off the table, and followed his fiancée out of the restaurant, Stacey had a feeling that it wasn't anything good.

'Would you like a menu, madam?' the waiter was asking her now.

Stay. Go. Stay. Go. Stay.

She turned and flashed him her Hollywood smile.

'Yes, I would, thank you.'

4 P.M. – 6 P.M.

Nineteen

Caro

An hour later, the rain was clinging to every strand of Caro's hair, making it stick to the side of her face, but she barely noticed. A sob escaped from her throat, and a woman at the pedestrian crossing beside her glanced up at her curiously. Caro put her head down and kept walking.

She walked. Just walked. One foot in front of the other. All the while, replaying the conversation she'd just had with the love of her life. What had she expected? That he would just say, 'Oh, darling, that's absolutely fine,' and then they'd jolly off into the sunset together?

If only it had played out that way.

The thing that almost broke her was that he'd looked so happy to see her when she'd walked into the restaurant. He was like a guy standing on a sun-kissed beach, thinking the approaching waves were beautiful, not realising that it was actually a tsunami that would destroy everything in its path.

She'd been grateful when an elderly couple had got into the lift with them, ruling out any chance of conversation until they reached his room. Inside, as soon as the door had closed behind her, he'd pulled her towards him and kissed her playfully. 'God, it is so good to see you. Did I mention how much I missed you last night?'

That, right there, was one of the many reasons that she loved Cammy Jones. He was funny, and loving, and he always found the joy in life. This was a guy who loved and lived in equal measure, who never let anything get him down for too long and who always wanted to make sure that everyone else was having a good time too. The night they'd met, in the middle of their first conversation, she'd got the phone call to say that her mum, who was desperately ill, had taken a turn for the worse. Without a second's hesitation, and despite the fact that Lila had just dumped him, Cammy had offered to drive her home, a three hour trip to Aberdeen. They hadn't made it in time, but he'd tried so hard to get her there. That's the kind of guy Cammy Jones was and she adored him. She wanted to spend the rest of her life with him. She just didn't want to marry him.

Back in the hotel room, it had taken him a few seconds to realise that she wasn't quite on the same page of excitement and glee. He'd pulled back, looked into her eyes, his expression questioning. 'Hey, what's up? Last minute hitch? Whatever it is, we can fix it. Josie's running this wedding like a military invasion.'

Caro had hesitated, too scared to say it, too scared not to.

'Please don't hate me,' she'd blurted, her eyes suddenly swimming with tears.

His whole demeanour had gone from joy to concern. 'Caro, what is it? Shit, what's happened?'

'I don't… I don't…' She couldn't say it. Couldn't get the words out. They were stuck somewhere between her brain and her gut, trapped by guilt and dread.

'Don't what?' he'd tried to help her.

In the end it had come out in one strangled gasp, with no spaces between the words. 'Idontwanttogetmarried.'

There was a pause as his brain rewound the outburst a few times, trying to decipher it.

'You don't want to get married?' he'd asked, incomprehension in every word.

Her tears were flowing then, as she shook her head.

'You don't want to marry me?' he'd asked again, for clarification, his skin paling a little, his eyes wide and troubled.

'I'm so sorry, Cammy. I love you. I really do. But I just can't do this. I feel like the whole thought of it is… choking me.'

He'd slumped down on the bed, elbows on his knees, his hands running through his hair as he tried to process this. After a few seconds, he'd looked up. 'I'm going to need more than that.'

She'd sat down on the edge of the grey velvet bucket chair facing the bed, unsure if it was by choice or because her legs had given way.

A hesitation. A mind-freeze. Then the words came.

'When you asked me to be your wife and I said yes, I meant it. I wanted that so much. But then… I know it doesn't make sense and I'm so, so sorry… but I started waking up with this feeling of dread in the middle of dreams where my mum is telling me not to get married. And I know that sounds nuts, but she was so in love with my dad and what did she get? Thirty years of waiting for him to walk in the door, then mourning him every time he left. And then, when she got sick and really needed him, he left her, and she died not even knowing that he'd lied to her every day of her life. That's what marriage gets you.'

'But—' he'd begun, but she'd cut him off.

Now that she was speaking, she needed to get it all out, get everything said and she couldn't stop until she was done. 'And I know you're going to say that you're nothing like him and what we have is completely different and I know that's true. I do. But I can't stop the panic that rises every time I think of actually walking down an aisle. My mind immediately goes to my mum and it takes away every shred of happiness that I should be feeling. I can't do it, Cammy. Why can't loving each other be enough? Why do we have to do the whole wedding thing? Can't we just be us and love each other without the contract?'

He'd taken this in, thought about it, paused for a moment to process it. 'We can,' he'd said, and her spirits soared. 'Caro, I love you, and I'll take a life with you in any way it comes. But marriage means something to me. My parents have been together for fifty years and they adore each other. I want that too. If you're saying that it's off the table, then I'll live with it. But it isn't what I want. I want to stand up in front of everyone we love and promise our lives to each other. If you don't love me enough...'

'It's nothing to do with how much I love you,' she'd cried.

He just wasn't getting it and she didn't blame him. It didn't make much sense to her either. All she knew was that she couldn't argue with the feeling that when Cammy made his vows to her, all she would hear in her head was her dad making those same vows to her mum. And every word had been a lie. He hadn't loved and cherished her. He hadn't stood by her until the end of time. He'd lied through his teeth.

She tried again to explain herself. 'I love you beyond words. I want to be with you. I just don't want to be married.'

'And you couldn't tell me this before now?'

'I'm sorry. I was trying so hard to make myself do it…'

She saw a flicker of hurt in his face as she said that.

'… And I thought maybe I could, but this morning I woke up and realised that no matter how much I love you, I can't walk up that aisle. I'm so, so sorry. Please don't hate me.'

He'd run his fingers through his hair again, always his subconscious habit when he was stressed or worried. 'Fuck, Josie will kill us,' he'd murmured, almost to himself. 'Does she know?'

Caro shrugged. 'I'm not sure. I told Val, so I'm guessing Josie will know by now.'

A look of understanding crossed his face. 'That's why she showed up here.'

'Josie was here? When?' she'd asked, realising that they were straying from the most crucial part of the conversation.

'About five minutes before you came in. I thought she was a bit frazzled, but I just put it down to the surprise of seeing Michael and Avril. It must have been because she was looking for you.'

Caro had nodded sadly, aware of the stress and disruption she was foisting on every single person that she loved. 'Oh

God, poor Josie. She's done so much for us. I hope she can forgive me. I'm so sorry, Cammy. Sorry about what I'm doing to you and to everyone else too.'

Two fresh tears ran down her cheeks and he'd reached forward and taken her hands.

'Don't cry. Please. It kills me.'

Sniffing, she'd wiped away the tears with the palms of her hands.

'You definitely still love me?' he'd asked, a sad smile on his lips.

She'd nodded. 'I do. I swear.'

He'd sighed. 'Okay.'

She'd seen that he was making a real effort to comprehend all this and, worse, trying to make her feel better, and it twisted that wrench of guilt just a little bit more.

'I'm trying to understand what you're saying, I really am. I think you lost your mum, then moved straight down here to be with me and maybe there just wasn't enough time to adjust, to grieve for her. I get that.'

'I love you,' she'd whispered.

Another sad smile from him. 'I just wished you'd realised before everyone we know and love made their way here today.'

All she could do was nod, biting her bottom lip to stop the avalanche of tears that was threatening to fall.

'Me too,' she'd finally managed to whisper.

'Do you want to tell people with me?' he'd asked gently.

She'd shaken her head, hearing the word 'coward' ringing inside her mind. She couldn't. She just couldn't.

He'd taken a deep breath and sat up a little straighter, some kind of decision made in his mind. 'Okay,' he'd said, with some kind of certainty. 'Look, I don't want this to be a complete disaster, and I'm not going to let everyone down when they've made such an effort to get here, so here's what I think we should do. I'm going to go ahead with the reception tonight. It's only a few hours from now and it's far too late to cancel everything. I'll tell people what's going on and then I'm going to let them know that we're having the party anyway.'

'Cammy, I can't.'

'I know,' he'd said. 'You don't have to. I'll come home tomorrow and we'll sort everything out, but tonight I'm going to be with everyone who's come here for us today. If you change your mind, you know where we will be. I hope you'll come, I really do. But if you don't, that's okay. We'll figure it out.'

Caro wasn't sure what she was feeling. Relief. Gratitude. Guilt. Sadness. Admiration for this incredible guy who was still putting other people before himself, even when she'd just dropped a bombshell on his world.

His face was ashen, his voice trembling, but still he was forcing himself to do the right thing. 'I should go back downstairs to our guests.'

Caro nodded. 'I need to go too. I'll try to find Josie, then I'll go back home and talk to Val and Jen and Chrissie. I just landed all this on them this morning. Did Josie say where she was going when she left here?'

'She said she was going over to the Kibble Palace to check on everything. I'm not sure now if that was even true, given that she was obviously just trying to hunt you down. She's probably still scouring the streets for you.' His words had been barely above a whisper and she could see he was struggling to process what was happening. He'd reached over, gently touched her face, and then they left the room, travelled back down to the lobby in silence. At the main door, he'd let her hand go. 'See you,' he'd said.

Caro couldn't even answer. She'd fled from the hotel, but instead of crossing over to the Botanic Gardens, she'd stopped and leaned against a wall, her heart breaking as a group of buskers sang Christmas songs only a few metres away.

'Blue Christmas'. 'Santa Claus Is Coming To Town'. 'All I Want For Christmas Is You'.

All I want for Christmas is to make this whole thing go away, she'd thought. She'd have given anything to press rewind to when it was just her and Cammy, no pressure, no fear, no looming wedding for her to let down everyone that she loved.

She wasn't sure how long she'd stood there, waiting until she thought her shaking legs would carry her, but it was a while before she stepped forward crossed the road.

Now, as she looked up and saw the huge dark green wrought-iron gates in front of her, every emotion swirled inside her. Love. Dread. Regret. Panic. There was also a gasp of wonder at the sheer beauty of the place. Every tree as far as she could see was bursting with fairy lights, like some kind of wonderland in a children's fairy tale.

The Botanic Gardens. A place she adored. Inside the garden walls was the building in which she'd planned to marry Cammy tonight. Right now, it was the last place she wanted to be, yet she had to look for Josie, to explain, to apologise.

The music, it sounded like a choir singing a classical piece that she couldn't name, got louder as she approached the entrance of the beautiful glass structure and she realised it was coming from speakers placed outside the foyer of the Kibble Palace. The name was a misnomer, conjuring up an image of a stone castle with turrets housing royalty. It was actually a huge glass house, with two domes (one large and one small) and a rotunda flanked by interlinked corridors and rooms, a truly magnificent testimony to architectural brilliance.

Inside the foyer, she saw the scene through a bride's eyes. It was perfection. Heart wrenching, devastating perfection. Josie had arranged for archways of white flowers, intertwined with Christmas holly, to line the main entrance and the doorway into the first area. She went through the entrance into the first hall, where a white circular iron fence bordered a large indoor pond, the whole space now bursting with red poinsettias Josie had shipped in because she knew how much Caro loved them. Another wave of guilt, of regret.

Four people in catering uniforms were opening boxes beside a table covered in a stunning silver and white draped fabric. Caro recognised it as one of the choices Josie had shown her weeks ago. There had been red silk covers, green taffeta runners, gold metallic fabrics, but this silver material, beautifully edged with embroidered white snowflakes, had been her favourite. Josie had made this happen. She'd done it all. And all Caro could do now was weep with sorrow and shame that she'd put everyone to all this trouble for nothing.

She wiped the tears away with the sleeve of her duffle coat, before approaching the staff that were now pulling glasses out of the boxes and polishing them before placing them on the table. The welcome drinks for the wedding tonight. This would all be so beautiful if it wasn't so tragic.

'Excuse me, but I'm looking for the lady who organised all this? Josie Cairney?'

Three of the team looked blank, but the other one, maybe the supervisor, spoke up.

'Do you mean the wedding planner? An older lady? White hair?'

Caro couldn't help thinking that Josie would take this guy out with a tea towel for calling her an 'older lady'.

'Yes!' Relief. 'Is she here?'

He was scanning the room quizzically now. 'She was here not long ago, checking that everything was the way she wanted it and that we were on schedule. But… I don't know where she went. I'm guessing she took off. No idea where.'

Damn. Bugger.

'Could she be in one of the other rooms?' The thought made Caro's insides twist. The other area they'd booked for the night was under the large dome, just down the wide corridor. She knew it would be set up with chairs for the ceremony and lined with tables that would later be laden with the food and the drink for the party they'd planned down to the last detail. One that she'd no longer be attending.

'I was just in the wedding room and there was no one there,' one of the waitresses offered.

Caro sagged with relief. She didn't want to go in there, didn't want to see the beauty that she was walking away from.

Josie must have gone, must have taken off back to Val and the others at the flat. And that's where she had to go now too.

She murmured her thanks and left the building, gasping for air as she stepped into the cold outside. What was she doing? How had it all come to this? Had she completely lost her mind?

She tried to take a step, but the thought of facing everyone sent a jolt of anxiety through her that rooted her feet to the ground. She couldn't do it. Not yet.

Instead of heading towards the park gates that she'd come in through only a few minutes ago, she walked along one of the other paths. Something in her soul needed to walk in the gardens, to sit in the tranquillity and block out the rest of the world before she went home and faced everyone.

She walked on, following the concrete path, until it came to a fork. She veered off to the right, to a beautiful little pagoda surrounded by oriental flowers that she couldn't name. It was breathtaking. But, most of all, it made her feel like she was the only person left in the world.

The wooden bench was dry when she sat on it and she loosened off the damp layers of her duffle coat, the wooden apex of the little roof protecting her from the drizzle. She laid her head against the wall behind her and closed her eyes. What the hell was she doing with her life? What was she thinking? Everything felt so wrong, yet she just didn't know how to fix it.

The irony was that she wanted to be alone, yet the loneliness was consuming her.

'I wish you were here, Mum,' she whispered. 'More than anything. I wish… I wish there was some way you could tell me if I'm making the biggest mistake of my life.'

Twenty

Seb

The church was almost silent, yet the noise in his head was deafening. The sound of the smash was as vivid in his mind now as it was back then. The bang, immediately followed by the sickening, brutal grind of twisting metal. His head thudded off the steering wheel in front of him, then a moment of blackness, then the screams, all his, because Juliet was silent, her body thrown forward and twisted, her limbs at odd angles, her neck snapped backwards, her face… oh God, her face. A mask of red, resting on the dashboard. Above it, a smear of blood coming downwards from the imprint on the smashed windscreen where her beautiful face had shattered the glass. Her eyes were open, staring at him, but seeing nothing. She was gone. He reached over, cradled her body, and he sobbed, begged her to come back to him, pleaded until the paramedics gently prised his fingers from her and carried him from the car.

A cough from one of the pews behind him brought Seb back to the present. Only then did he realise that his chest was sore, that his breaths were coming in short, sharp bursts, his ribcage constricting his lungs. This was why he'd drank way too much over the last six months. The only thing that made his muscles unclench was the second, maybe the third, glass of wine, that numbed the pain just enough to make it possible to carry on breathing.

Now, he needed his body to unravel itself with no alcoholic assistance and he wasn't sure it was possible. He put his hand on his brown leather bag, closed his eyes and spoke to her in his mind.

I'm so sorry, Juliet. I'm so, so sorry. He repeated it over and over again, until his pulse slowed and he could feel his ribs expand enough for him to breathe without physical pain. The emotional pain, he already knew, had no cure.

Around him, he could see that more people were arriving, beginning to fill the pews on both sides of the church. Some kind of service must be starting soon. For a second, he considered staying, but that would be a hypocritical act too far. If there was some higher power, he wanted no part of a God who would take his Juliet from him.

Slowly, he rose and, with apologies, climbed past the elderly couple who were now seated at the end of the row, nearest the aisle. Music began just as he made his way out of the wooden doors.

Outside, the sky was black and the rain had stopped now, letting the golden early moon illuminate the sky. He scanned the streets on either side of him, two stunning Victorian terraces, many of the windows bordered with coloured lights or lit by twinkling Christmas trees.

Another emotion, jealousy this time, and yes, bitterness too. All those families, all those people planning to spend the holidays with the ones they loved most. He was alone. And he deserved to be.

Enough. He couldn't do this any more.

He couldn't stand to watch the world turn without her.

It was pointless, and painful and there was no end to it.

He stumbled down the steps, not sure where he was headed. Actually, that wasn't true. He knew. He was going to go back to the hotel and check in, then tonight or tomorrow he would scatter Juliet's ashes, fulfilling his promise to her, then he would take the first plane back to Spain. There, he'd put his affairs in order and then... he couldn't think any further on than that. Not right now. One day at a time.

He began to walk back to the hotel, all thoughts of searching for Pearl's niece gone. He wasn't going to go to the wedding. He had no place there. What was the point? Even if she was his daughter, why would she want him? He had done the unimaginable, the unforgivable. He wasn't someone that a young woman would want as a father. He'd already destroyed one life and he didn't have it in him to cause any more pain or disruption. The truth was that he'd only been doing this for himself. Juliet was gone. His parents too. There was absolutely no one left in this world that he could call family. Maybe he was trying to fill that hole, find somewhere to tether his loneliness to.

He turned left and began to walk, ending up at a T-junction that he recognised. He turned right on to Great Western Road, knowing that it would take him back to his hotel.

The majestic terrace of the West End Grand was coming up on his right-hand side, when his eyes were drawn to the park across the road on his left. The Botanic Gardens.

The legendary landmark was bordered by trees, all of them glistening with white fairy lights. As always, his first thought was that Juliet would adore this view.

He'd changed his mind about going there tonight, but now, seeing this, he couldn't help but cross the road, oblivious to the beeps of the car horns, the drivers irate that he wasn't using the pedestrian crossing a hundred metres further up the road.

Step after step, he walked, hearing a faint sound that got louder as he got closer to the side gate of the gardens. Music. A choir. It sounded like it was coming from inside the gardens. He checked his watch: 5 p.m.. The wedding wasn't starting until seven o'clock, so he had time to go in, to wander, to see the places he and Juliet had visited so many times, then he would leave before the nuptials began.

An invisible force drew him in through the gate and along the concrete path, the moonlight reflecting off the glistening trees to light the way. He could see the glass and iron magnificence of the Kibble Palace ahead of him. The door at the main entrance was open, so Seb slipped inside, the familiarity of the building somehow comforting. He and Juliet would stand at the pond under the smaller dome for ages, watching the fish, taking in the tranquillity of the space. Now, a few people bustled around: a couple of bartenders – one male, one female – setting up a table with champagne glasses, presumably for the guests that would be arriving in an hour or so. They were laughing with two young men in waiter's uniforms, paying no attention to Seb at all.

A strange feeling of calm came over him. It was ironic. He'd sought solace in a church, only to have his insides eviscerated by guilt and regret, yet here, in the familiar surroundings of a place that Juliet loved, he felt a closeness to her that he'd been searching for all day. He could see her here, leaning over the railings, laughing as they gave ridiculous names to the more distinguishable fish. The vision of her was so alive, he felt like he could reach out and touch her.

A sob escaped his throat, making the young catering staff glance up at him. With as much nonchalance as he could muster, he coughed, hoping that covered up the outburst. He spotted a sign that said 'The Jones/Anderson Wedding' but he knew he didn't want to go there. Not now. Not any time. He'd caused enough suffering without laying his sins on a woman who was in the happiest time of her life. If she was his daughter, he told himself again, then the best thing he could do for her was to leave well alone.

Ignoring the wedding sign, he strolled through into the farthest section of the circular hall at the back of the building, away from the hustle and bustle of the catering staff. It was deserted and he guessed it wouldn't normally be open at this time on a Friday night. The area was dense with plants and vegetation, seats dotted along the edges of the glass walls. It was dim, the lighting switched off, but in the semi-darkness the faint glow from a huge statue of a nude male, crouched, every muscle of his body meticulously carved to perfection, his head resting in the crook of his arm, gave a glimmer of illumination. Sculpted by Edwin Roscoe Mullins, Seb knew it was called, 'Cain: My punishment is more than I can bear'. The arts had never evoked much emotion in him, but he had never related more to the pain he saw in front of him.

'Aye, they don't make them like that any more.' The raspy voice cut through the silence. A woman, standing against the wall to his left, her wry comment seamlessly transforming into a tortuous coughing fit.

Seb's eyes now adjusted to the darkness of the room, so he could see that she was older than him, maybe in her sixties, dressed all in black with a wild mop of white spiky hair. 'Are you okay? Can I get you some water?'

'No, I'm fine, son.'

Her words made him smile, so steeped in the West of Scotland culture he grew up in. That generation of women would say they were fine even if they were being swept down a hill by burning lava. And 'son'. Nothing to do with family. Just the catch-all term used either in affection or when reprimanding anyone younger than themselves.

'Aye, you sound fine,' he quipped back, and was rewarded with a loud cackle that immediately warmed him to this woman. On the scale of first impressions, she was up there at the top.

Another cough, then a long intake of breath before she spoke again, her tone almost wistful. 'Maybe not fine, right enough,' she conceded. 'In fact, today could quite safely be described as absolutely bollocks.'

'I thought I was having the monopoly on crap days,' he said, feeling a genuine desire to engage with this lady. Sometimes the people who were easiest to talk to were complete strangers.

'Oh no, son, I'm fairly sure that whatever you've got going on, mine will trump it.'

There was a silence as he pondered that for a moment before speaking, the semi-darkness almost feeling like a confessional. 'I was driving carelessly and crashed. My fault. My wife died. I've come back to Scotland to scatter her ashes.'

Seb felt a slap of shock, then the strangest thing. Relief. He'd said it. For the first time. To a woman he didn't know and would never see again. It was like picking a scab and feeling the pressure ease as the blood flowed out.

The woman spluttered as she spoke. 'Christ, could you not have gone with a loss on the stock market or some kind of suspicious rash?' After a pause, her tone changed, softer this time, compassion layering every word. 'Sorry! Sorry! I do that. I say inappropriate things at all the wrong times. I'm Josie. And I apologise, that was insensitive of me. I'm very sorry about your wife. That guilt must be a tough burden to bear.'

Seb felt tears spring to his eyes as her last comment showed that she'd read the situation with such insight. 'Thank you. I don't know why I just blurted that out. You're the first person I've ever said that to. I'm Seb, by the way.'

'Pleased to meet you, Seb. And I have some kind of superpower that makes people bare their soul to me. A woman in the post office queue yesterday told me she was shagging her next-door neighbour. He was called Cecil. Seriously, who has a wild affair with someone called Cecil? Nobody wants to shout that name out at the tickly bit.'

Seb's emotional pendulum immediately swung away from tears and towards affection. He liked this lady. This felt like the first real - yet bizarre – conversation he'd had in a long time.

'I see your point. So go on then…' he prompted. 'What made you think you'd win the "shit day" award?'

Josie's answer was delayed by another heaving cough, before she regained her voice. 'Lung cancer,' she said, absolutely matter-of-fact. 'Doctor told me this morning that even with treatment I won't have much longer. Och, it's a bastard, this life sometimes.'

Seb genuinely didn't know how to reply to that. This poor soul. Yet here she was, still standing. There was no right thing to say here, but he had the feeling that no matter what came out of his mouth, this wasn't the kind of woman who took offence. 'I don't know what to say.'

'Me neither, son.'

'Yeah, I sussed that out after the suspicious rash comment.'

That made her cackle, a gorgeous, raucous laugh that was so contagious he couldn't help but join her. He was laughing. Actually laughing. If someone had told him an hour ago how this detour would play out, he'd never have believed them.

'I think you win,' he conceded. 'I'm really sorry.'

'Aye, shit happens and then you die,' she said wistfully.

'Do you want to talk about it? My wife always said I was a pretty good listener. As long as there wasn't any golf on the TV.'

'Thanks, but there's no point. Talking about it will only waste time and that's something I'm running short on.'

He nodded, but he wasn't sure if she could see that in the semi-darkness. His curiosity carried on the conversation. 'Okay then – so am I allowed to ask why you're standing in the middle of a greenhouse in front of a naked statue?'

'My friends are getting married here tonight. Well, supposed to be. It's a long story. Anyway, the bride had taken cold feet and bolted, so I came here to look for her, but no luck. So instead of going back to face the world, I'm hiding in here until I'm ready to get back out and deal with the shitstorm that's waiting for me.'

Seb immediately put two and two together. Bloody hell. This was the last thing he expected. 'Caro is missing?'

Josie's head whipped around and her eyes narrowed with what looked like suspicion. 'You know Caro?'

'Er, no. Not, er, really. Not at all, actually. But, er, I know her aunt, Pearl. And… it's a long story too.'

'Well, I've got time to listen. Just don't make it too long in case I pop my clogs in the middle.'

Twenty-One

Josie

Josie's interest was piqued. She didn't get to the age she was at now without being able to detect underlying currents in what someone was saying and this bloke definitely had something else going on. There was something in the way he said Caro's name, then began to stutter as he lost his words. Poor bugger. It sounded like he'd had a rough time and Josie's innate desire to help people was kicking in. That, and a natural protectiveness over Caro. Right now, she wanted to kill her for running out on Cammy, but that aside, she wasn't going to let some stranger get near her friend if he was going to cause problems.

The man sighed and she knew that he was weighing up whether or not to confide in her any further. She also knew that best thing to do was to keep her mouth shut until he decided that he would. The CIA would be proud of her interrogation insight.

'You're, erm... You're... The thing is... you're going to think it's ridiculous...' he began.

Josie lost her powers of restraint and jumped right in. 'Oh, I hope so. I could do with a bit of ridiculous to cheer me up. Hang on, can we sit on that bench because these boots are the work of Satan and my feet are killing me?'

The light-hearted prompt seemed to be enough to make him talk. 'Sure,' he replied, following her a few feet to a wooden bench that was placed against one of the glass walls.

Once they were seated, he began speaking. 'I knew Caro's mum, Yvonne.'

Josie was even more interested now. Caro's mum had passed away right before Josie met her. Caro didn't talk about her too much and Josie respected that, choosing instead to mother her and keep an eye on her.

Josie was waiting for more, but Seb didn't seem to know where to go next. She decided to nudge him along. 'I don't want to hurry you, but I've only got about six months,' she said, with a gentle elbow poke in the side.

A street lamp outside the glass wall meant the light wasn't quite so dim here at the bench, and she could see that her jibe made him smile.

'I worked with Yvonne and her sister Pearl back in the eighties, but then we lost touch. I went off to travel the world and I never saw Yvonne again.'

Josie hoped the disappointment didn't show in her face. She'd been wanting something a little more interesting than that. Anyway, probably just as well. It was time to go, find Caro and get this bloody wedding back on track. Everything else could be dealt with tomorrow. Priorities. That's what she needed right now. Sitting here with this bloke wasn't one of them. She was about to interrupt him and make her excuses to leave when he went on…

'And then, last week, completely out of the blue, I met Pearl. We got talking and she mentioned that Yvonne had a daughter, Caro.'

Okay, interrupt him now. Time to go, she told herself.

'Oh, it's a small world. Anyway—'

'And that Caro was thirty-four,' he added.

Josie immediately detected that this was relevant, all thoughts of leaving instantly cancelled out by renewed curiosity.

'The thing is…' he paused, struggling with the words, and Josie had a feeling she was about to hear something else this guy had never said out loud. 'Yvonne and I, well we had a… *relationship*… just under thirty-five years ago.'

'Well, fuck me,' Josie gasped. 'So you could be her dad? Hang on, let me look at you.' She sparked up her lighter and held it perilously close to his face. 'Damn, hard to tell,' she groaned. 'Our Caro is a blonde, and she always said she looked like her mother.'

Thoughts ricocheted through Josie's mind, and for the first time all day, she could honestly say the biggest thing in her head wasn't this morning's meeting with the doctor. This was incredible. After all that lass's father had put her through and now there was another contender for the position? She'd only ever seen this kind of stuff on those programmes on telly, where they did DNA tests and there was a smug host who acted with fake sincerity while delivering the news.

Josie was thinking out loud. 'I don't know how she would feel about this. It would be an absolute bombshell in her life.'

'I promise that's not my intention. Actually, I don't even know what my intention was, but I promise I would never cause her any upset, especially on her wedding day. This will be a special day for her and her dad and I wouldn't spoil that.'

The snort was out before she could stop it, followed by, 'You know nothing about her, do you?'

'Nothing,' he admitted. 'One conversation with Pearl, that is it. And, to be honest, I'd actually decided to leave tomorrow without saying anything to her. I bottled out. Probably for the best, so please don't add me to your list of problems today.'

Josie let that sit as she considered her options. Caro's loathing of her father was no secret, and no wonder, given the terrible things that man did to her and her mum. However, that story was Caro's and Josie had no right to tell it, especially to a stranger. Even more so when that stranger may or may not have a cataclysmic effect on Caro's life. Therefore, for once in her many decades on this earth, Josie decided she was going to have to keep her gob shut. The very thought of that made her lips purse in outrage. It took her a minute to unclench them.

'Look, it's not my place to tell you all the things that poor girl has been through in her life…' Even in this light she saw his brow furrow in concern. 'But I want you to promise me you won't leave tomorrow. I'm staying over at the West End Grand across the road tonight—'

'I'm staying there too,' Seb interjected.

'Good. That makes everything easier. As I said, I'm not sure where Caro is right now. I'm hoping to find her and sort this out before the groom-to-be finds out that she's missing. Jesus wept, if the fucked lungs don't kill me, the bloody stress will.'

'Can I help?' he asked, sounding genuinely concerned.

'No, son. I'll track her down. But I know that one way or another, she'll want to meet you. What's your surname?'

'Lloyd,' he answered.

'Okay. Seb Lloyd. I'll find you at the hotel tomorrow morning and we'll hatch a plan.' A coughing bout interrupted her orders, immediately followed by the ringing of her phone. 'Shit, it's the groom,' she sighed, before her hopes rose. Maybe Caro had turned up, maybe she was there right now, and all was fine.

Come on, universe, throw me a fecking bone.

'Hello, handsome, how are you doing?' she said, with forced joviality.

'Josie, I've been trying to phone you for the last hour!'

Aw, bugger, he sounded like he was on a ledge and hanging by the fingertips. She had a quick glance at her screen. One bar. There must have been so little signal that his calls were going to answering machine.

'Erm, sorry, Cammy. I've got a shite signal here. Are you okay?' She already knew the answer, but hoped she was wrong. She wasn't.

'Caro has called it off. She's saying she can't go through with it.'

Fuck, he knew. Shit. Bugger. Fuck.

'How do you know that?' She tried to inject a bit of calmness she absolutely did not feel. This wasn't the time to tell him that she already knew about Caro bolting. They could do a post-mortem on the timeline later. All that mattered now was what happened from here on in.

'She came here. Says she can't go through with it. Says she needs some space. And I know you already know this and that's why you were here looking for her.'

Shit. Caught.

'Och, Cammy, I'm so sorry, I was hoping I'd find her and sort this and... Look, we can't give up. I'll track her down and—'

'No.' The word was steeped in weariness. 'I love you for trying – even the bit where you didn't tell me that I was getting jilted...'

Given the hint of teasing in his tone, she let that one pass.

'So I'm just going to let her be. Whatever is going on, I know she wouldn't be doing this if she could help it. I've told her we're going ahead with the reception though. I can't have everyone here and all of us sitting staring at each other. Christ, Josie, how am I going to do this?' For the first time, his voice cracked and she knew this had to be excruciating for him. 'I love her, Josie. All I care about is that she's okay.'

'She will be.' As she said it, Josie realised she had no idea if that was true or not. Shit, how had it come to this? She was the worst wedding planner in bloody history. Rule number one of successful nuptial organisation – make sure you have a bride and groom.

Cammy was still speaking. 'What am I going to say? How am I going to tell everyone?'

The cloying aroma of the plants that surrounded her stuck in her throat. Or perhaps that was just pure sorrow for this man that she loved like a son. Right, she was going to have to handle this and they needed a plan. First priority – support Cammy, and if he really did want to go ahead with the reception, she'd make sure it was organised and perfect. Second priority – sorting out the first priority would give her time to find Caro and make sure she was okay. Third priority – make sure this guy next to her didn't flee the country. Fourth priority – get through the day without crumbling into a heap and wailing about the unfairness of bloody life.

'Cammy, don't worry, ma darling, I'll take care of everything. If you're definitely going ahead with the reception, then I'd wait until everyone arrives at the Kibble for the ceremony before breaking the news. That way, you won't have to tell people at the hotel, and then tell the rest of the guests who are coming straight here. It also means no one will get all dramatic and decide to call it a day and go back home. No, wait until they're all here, then make one announcement and tell them the wedding is off, but we're going ahead with the party. It'll sting for a bit, but I honestly think it's the best way to handle it. It'll also give us from now until then to work out the best thing to say.'

'I feel so fricking helpless, Josie. I don't even care about the damn wedding now – I just want to be with her.'

'I know, and you will be, love. She obviously just needs a bit of time. Look, I'll get in touch with Val and update her and we'll all keep looking for Caro. I'm at the Kibble Palace right now and everything is set for tonight.'

'You're there now? She was coming over there to look for you and talk to you about it.'

'Shit. I'm hiding in a back bit where no one would find me. Well, almost no one.' Her gaze went to Seb, wide-eyed beside her. 'What was she wearing and I'll ask the staff if she's been here?'

'Her red duffle coat.'

The line was fuzzy and she didn't quite catch what he said. 'Her red duffle coat?'

'Yep.'

'Okay. I'll ask them if she's been here. If I've missed her, she's probably headed back to the flat. Anyway, you take care of things at your end, look after all the guests, and I'll find Caro. I know this sounds ridiculous but try not to worry. One day we'll look back on this and it'll all feel very different than it does now, son. We'll get through it.'

There was a slight hesitation in his reply and Josie wondered if he was wrestling a sob. It wouldn't surprise her. He was a strong guy, but he adored Caro and this must be slaying him.

'Thanks, Josie. I don't know what I'd do without you.'

A thought, that he'd soon find out what he'd do without her, flashed across her mind. She drowned it with a flippant attempt to console him by injecting a bit of levity into the situation. 'Yeah, wait and see if you say that when you open my bill.'

She hung up and sighed, which brought on a prolonged cough that sent shooting pains ricocheting around her chest. Only when they subsided did she speak, an edge of frustration in her tone.

'He knows that the wedding is off. Goddamn it.'

'I guessed that from your end of the conversation. Sorry, I'm not trying to involve myself in this, but if you need anything, please say. Can I help you look for her?'

Josie thought about it, but then shook her head. This wasn't the time to be adding a stranger – never mind a man who was possibly the bride's long lost father – into the messed up marital equation. She stood up, feeling an uncharacteristic ache in her bones as she did so. 'Thank you, but I'll be fine. He thinks she came over here to find me, so she might be here somewhere. Anyway, let me try to sort this mess out and I'll contact you via the hotel reception tomorrow morning.' She moved to leave, but then had a thought. 'The stuff I told you about my health – I haven't shared that with anyone yet, so let's be clear. Everything I told you is confidential and if you tell anyone I will hunt you down. And I'll respect your privacy too. Nothing you told me will be repeated.'

'Understood,' Seb agreed, and Josie could see a wry smile playing on his lips. 'I'll see you tomorrow. In the meantime, I hope you get tonight's plans back on track somehow.'

'Jesus, I hope so. Did I mention I'm too old for this shit?'

'You did. But somehow I think you can handle it.'

He was teasing her now, and she felt an affinity for him, an inherent instinct that she'd met someone whom she would come to know better. That thought pleased her. She just hoped she had enough time to do it.

'Right, much as I could sit here all night looking at that naked man over there…' she nodded towards the statue, 'I'm off.'

'I'll walk you out,' he offered.

In the foyer area, the staff were still setting up.

'Was there a woman in a red duffle coat here? She might have been looking for me?'

The supervisor broke off from staring at a glass he was holding up to the light. 'Yes! Not long ago. I'm sorry – we thought you'd gone.'

'Did she leave or is she still here?' Josie asked, hopes rising.

'She left.'

Hopes dashed.

'No worries. If she comes back, can you ask her to call Josie?'

The supervisor nodded and she made a mental to give his team a large tip. The place looked like a fairy tale. If only they had a bloody princess and a happy ending.

Seb followed her out to the exit. 'I just realised I passed a blonde woman in a red duffle coat at the hotel earlier. I held the door open for her. Bloody hell. That could have been her.'

'It could have been, Sherlock, but that's no use to me now. Too little too late. Story of my life. Anyway, what are you going to do now?'

'I'm just going to wander back through the gardens and over to the hotel. I'm glad I met you, Josie.'

'Likewise. Sometimes you just never know what's around the corner. Don't disappear until we've found out what's waiting there for you.'

As she left, Josie saw a change in the stranger's expression and thought it looked a little bit like hope.

Twenty-Two

Stacey

Stacey could feel a migraine coming on. Or maybe it was jet lag. Or perhaps just the fricking strain of sitting here for over an hour, making small talk and trying to act normal when the love of your life was away having a cosy chat to the woman he was getting hitched to in a few hours. This had been the longest lunch of her life. The plates had already been cleared and it was well after four o'clock by the time Cammy rejoined them and he seemed... odd. Tense.

'Bob said Caro popped in while I was at the loo? How was she?' Pearl asked, as soon as he pulled his chair out and sat down. 'I can't believe I missed her! I was hoping she'd come back to say hello.'

Cammy smiled, but Stacey could see that it was forced. Had he had a fight with Caro? Was there a problem? And did it make her a complete cow that she really hoped that was the case? She already knew the answer to that. No wonder her head was pounding. She deserved every bit of the pain. This wasn't the kind of shit she pulled. She was a good person. A decent human being. And yet now she was not only in denial about the fact that she already had a boyfriend back in the USA, but she was set on wrecking a marriage that hadn't even happened.

Yes, she told herself that she would just be giving him the facts, but the intent was there and she knew she was giving no thought to the consequences or the ramifications for anyone else. From everything she'd heard from others, Caro seemed like a good person, and if Cammy wanted to marry her, then she must be someone special. And Caro's family – her Aunt Pearl, Uncle Bob, and her cousin, Todd, and his husband, Jared – could not have been more welcoming to her since she'd turned up and joined them for lunch. Did she really want to stab them in the back? Especially when Cammy had so clearly moved on from whatever he felt about her when they were in LA. Fuck.

'She had to get back to do… er, bride things,' Cammy answered.

Wow, definitely something wrong. Stacey could hear it in his tone and see it in every contour of his face. There was clearly a problem, but this wasn't the time or place to ask him, not only because they were surrounded by family, but because he kept getting up every ten minutes and nipping out, using the excuse that he was trying to get hold of Josie. He'd come back in every time looking even more stressed than before.

No one else was paying too much attention to his emotional state, all engrossed in their own light-hearted conversations, so the lunch chat continued in a jovial fashion.

On any other day, Stacey knew she'd be loving this group and having a great time. Today, she just wanted them all to leave so that she could talk to Cammy alone.

When he returned from the fourth absence, citing another attempt to call Josie, Avril put down the spoon she was using to scoff her banoffee pie.

'Did you get her?' she asked Cammy, who shook his head in response. 'Nope, still going to voicemail.'

'She's bloody rubbish with that phone,' Avril sighed. 'We'd be better getting her a pigeon to send messages. Last week she sent me three texts – two were supposed to be for Val and the other one was entering a competition on *Good Morning Britain* to win a caravan. I mean, why the hell does she want a caravan? She won't stay anywhere on holiday unless it's got a minibar, a shagpile carpet and somebody bringing her hourly pina coladas.'

'Did Mum look okay to you?' Michael asked pensively, throwing the question out to Avril, her and Cammy.

Stacey thought about it. Actually, Josie had seemed different, a little weary, but Stacey hadn't seen her for a couple of years so she'd just put that down to the passage of time.

'Maybe a bit tired?' she'd offered.

Michael nodded. 'I thought the same. We forget what age she is sometimes. I'll have a chat later and see how she's doing.'

'Good luck with that,' Avril retorted. 'I tried to persuade her to let me install an alarm button in her house last year and she told me that if I went ahead, I'd be the one needing medical intervention to remove it from an orifice.'

That made Stacey laugh. Josie and her gang of pals, Senga included, were the kind of forces of nature who would never be tamed.

'I'll just go and try her again. Be two minutes,' Cammy said, getting to his feet. Stacey wanted to go after him, but decided that could look weird to the others round the table. Instead, she watched as Avril put her napkin down on her empty plate with a contented sigh. 'That was amazing. I think I need to go and lie down for an hour.' Avril checked her watch. 'We're leaving here at 6.30 p.m. then? The invitation said to be at across the road at seven. I'm guessing it's seven thirty for the "I do"s. That gives me an hour for a nap and an hour to make myself irresistibly gorgeous. Perfect.'

Stacey giggled at Avril's comment, but inside her stomach flipped at the mention of the 'I do's. Cammy was going to promise his life to someone else and if she wanted to have even a sliver of hope of changing that, she'd have to woman up and say something.

Cammy returned just as everyone was getting up and leaving the table in a flurry of hugs and joyful declarations of excitement about getting back together to witness the wedding. Stacey didn't share the sentiment. Not only that, but she felt at a loss as to what to do next. All the others at the table were going back to their rooms, Cammy was no doubt going to do the same, and she'd have no choice but to jump in a taxi and go home. Unless, of course...

'Stacey, what's your plan now?' he was asking her. It was as if he could read her mind.

To ask you if you're still in love with me. To tell you that I love you too and I'm ready now to make it work for us. To make you see that you're foolish to be marrying someone else and you should be with me.

Again, the unspoken thought that stayed in her head.

'Erm, nothing really,' she said out loud. 'Just head back home and get changed for tonight, I guess.'

The others interjected with hugs and goodbyes, so Cammy couldn't speak again until they were alone.

'Do you fancy coming upstairs for a coffee? Or something stronger?' he added, his words tense. He was also running his fingers through his hair, a gesture that did stirring things to her ovaries, but that she also knew was one of his habits when he was stressed. What the hell was going on here? Whatever it was; gift horse, mouth.

'Of course. Be good to catch up,' she said, trying to sound natural.

He didn't even seem to notice. In fact, she wasn't even sure that he was listening.

They squeezed into the lift with two sexy Santas and three elves, so conversation was impossible until they were on his floor. Even then, not a word was spoken until they'd gone along the corridor and into his room, his hand shaking as he took a couple of attempts to get the key card in the lock. If only it was trembling out of excitement at seeing her, but she knew him so well she could sense that this was about something much bigger than that.

As soon as they were inside, he leaned against the wall and she could see that he was on the edge. Something had definitely happened and it was nothing good. Had he changed his mind? Had he told Caro and she'd come here to persuade him to go ahead with it. Or was she...

Oh, shit, was she pregnant? If she was, then Stacey had no chance. Absolutely none. She'd concede defeat and back off quietly.

Cammy looked absolutely tortured as he shook his head and slid down the wall, until he was sitting on the floor.

Stacey tossed her coat on a nearby chair and sat on the bed directly in front of him.

'What's happened?' she blurted, unable to contain herself any longer. She had to know. He was such a good guy that if he'd changed his mind, this was exactly how she'd expect him to react. He'd feel terrible, be torn up with guilt.

'Caro doesn't want to marry me. She's called off the wedding. Says she can't do it.'

Stacey's heart stopped beating. Caro pulling out was the last thing she expected. Why, dear God, *why*, would anyone not want to marry this man? This was crazy. Unbelievable. Was there actually a possibility that this wedding wouldn't go ahead and it would be nothing to do with her? This wasn't the time to get her hopes up though. Bizarrely, his crushed demeanour was breaking her heart and all she wanted was to help him. This afternoon was definitely not playing out in any way that she could possibly have anticipated.

'Oh, Cammy, I'm so sorry. Why? I don't understand.'

'That makes two of us,' he said and there was a tinge of bitterness there.

Stacey got up, opened two beers from the minibar and handed one over. He took it without hesitation and she wondered if it reminded him of all the nights that they'd sat on Venice Beach, drinking Buds and putting the world to rights. She should have realised back then that they were meant to be together. It would have saved them so much time and heartache.

'Did she give a reason?' Stacey probed, not sure how to react. Nothing in her life had prepared her for this scenario. The man she loved had just been jilted on his wedding day. This kind of stuff only happened on TV soaps.

'She says she still loves me and wants to be with me, but it's the thought of the wedding. I think it's just all overwhelming her.'

'But why?'

He shrugged and Stacey realised there was so much she didn't know about his relationship with his fiancée.

'Her parents had a pretty screwed-up marriage and after her mum died she found out all kinds of stuff that was totally brutal. Her dad was a complete bastard – still is – and I think this is just bringing up all sorts of negative things for her.' He paused. 'Why the hell am I trying to explain this when I don't even understand it myself? I don't get it, I really don't. I'm not him. I love her, Stacey, and I'd never do anything to hurt her. She has to know that. Why doesn't she believe it?'

His declaration of love for someone else temporarily derailed her, but she pulled her thoughts back on track. 'I'm sure she does know it, deep down. But, you know, people do strange shit sometimes. They can be in love and not realise it. Or love someone so much it makes them do crazy things. Or they can take people for granted and not see what's right in front of them.' Every word was said in general terms, but the last sentence was loaded with meaning.

She waited, praying that he would get it, that it would strike some invisible chord and that he'd see what was right in front of him at this very minute.

Apparently not. He brushed right over it, with, 'I don't know what to do. She says she still loves me and wants to stay together, but...'

There was a 'but'. Stacey's heart soared.

'But if she doesn't trust me enough to marry me, what does that leave us with?'

He was looking at her with such heartbreaking earnestness that all she wanted to do was wrap her arms around him. 'I'm here,' she wanted to say, but he continued before she found the courage to speak.

'You know, after I left LA, and told you how I felt about you back then...'

Yes! He was bringing it up, but... shit, he was using the past tense.

'I was devastated. Gutted.'

Panic stunned her into silence. Her mouth wouldn't work, so she was completely incapable of joining the conversation.

'I thought I'd blown my chance of ever being happy. Then I met Lila and I can see now that I used her to take my mind off you. But Caro... I knew from the very first night that it was real. It was everything. What should I do, Stace?' he blurted.

Seriously? He was asking her to give him advice about his relationship, the one that she so desperately wanted to end, so that the two of them could be together? Cammy and Stacey. This was so, so messed up. And right here, right now, she had a choice. Fuel the fire, or be a friend. What she wanted to do versus what she should do.

'It's hard for me to answer that,' she said, going for honesty.

'Why?' He looked up at her now, genuinely curious. 'You've never been slow to give me advice before.'

'That was different, though,' she stuttered.

Oh God. Stop pushing. Just please stop, because if you don't, then I'll blurt out everything.

'How is it different?'

Shit! Don't say it. Do. Not. Say. It.

'Because back then, when I let you go, I didn't feel the way I do now.'

Twenty-Three

Website – www.itshouldhavebeenme.com

Members Discussion Forum

Responses to post by member, screen name NotOverYet:

Comments:

NotOverYet: @realitycheck Did you miss the bit where I said I couldn't care less about the haters? Blocked. For the others on here, it's two hours until the ceremony. Crunch time. I think I know what I'm going to say. Knowledge is power, isn't it? He just needs to know how I feel about him and after that? Who knows? But it's worth the risk. Like I said, I've got nothing to lose.

BethanySunshine: @NotOverYet You're so right! Every moment of every day I wish I'd done what you're going to do. I understand your heart and I support you. You must do this for all of us who didn't get their happy ending. #lionelrichie #endlesslove #dontwannaloseyou

JessieInAJam: @NotOverYet What are you trying to achieve? Do you honestly think he'll choose you? It's crazy. Please don't do it.

RealityCheck: What @JessieInAJam says. And, @ BethanySunshine, no wonder he fucked off if you kept talking in song lyrics. #patsycline #crazy

6 P.M. – 8 P.M.

Twenty-Four

Caro

Caro's eyes opened as she sensed a movement. She had no idea how long she'd been sitting there. The night was pitch-black, only the lights in the tree illuminating the area around her, the faint sound of a choir singing still playing in the background.

As her eyes adjusted, she saw a man coming towards where she sat in the pagoda. For a moment she thought it might be Cammy, that he might guess she was here. They'd once spent a whole day moving round each side of the pagoda to follow the sun. It was one of their favourite places.

But this wasn't Cammy. It was someone else, a stranger. A tall man, grey-haired, a brown leather bag over his shoulder and a face that was furrowed with worries.

It was probably time to go now. Val would be worried. Josie would be beside herself. The rain had stopped but the cold was beginning to permeate her duffle coat and the soles of her biker boots, despite the two pairs of socks underneath.

As her eyes locked on the new arrival's face, Caro heard a church bell somewhere nearby strike six o'clock.

Caro's first thought was curiosity as to why someone else was out here in this weather. Her second was that he could be some random serial killer. Her third was that this was the only path to the side gate – most people would use the other path, the one that led to the main gates – so she reckoned he'd just pass her by.

He almost did. He'd gone a couple of metres past her when he stopped, turned around.

Fuck. Serial killer.

'Sorry, I don't mean to scare you, but… red duffle coat.'

A serial killer with a thing for red duffle coats. What were the chances?

'Can I help you with something?' she asked, praying that this wouldn't be the opening scene in a *Crimewatch* reconstruction, while squinting at him, searching for any features that she recognised. She knew that most of the people in the gardens at this time would be here to work on the wedding. Was he perhaps one of the caterers? Or maybe a friend of Cammy's that she hadn't met yet? But it looked like he was leaving, so that didn't make sense. Probably just some local serial killer out for a walk.

Caro could see him taking a deep breath. Oh God, if there was a time to run, it was now. She reckoned she had a good twenty years on him, even if the cold meant she couldn't feel her feet.

'I don't want to freak you out altogether,' he said, 'but are you Caro?'

That shocked her. Serial killers didn't normally enquire as to the name of the victim. Maybe he was some kind of stalker instead. Frying pan. Fire.

'Yes, but how did you know that?'

'Your coat. I've just been speaking to a woman called Josie and she was looking for you. She said that's what you were wearing.'

Caro now had absolutely no idea what was going on.

'Josie is in there?' she gestured to the building in the distance. 'But I went in to find her and they said—'

'She was through at the very back. No one knew she was there so that's why they said she'd gone.'

Her cold bones ached as she jumped up. 'Aw, bollocks. I'll go catch her now. Thank you!'

'She's already left,' he blurted. 'She headed out the main gate when I came this way.'

Caro felt every bit of what energy she had left deflate from her body and she slumped back down on the seat. 'Okay, thanks. I've been trying to call her but it keeps going to voicemail. Bugger, I'm having the worst day.'

'That seems to be catching today,' he said, with a wry smile. 'I'm Seb.'

Caro lost all thoughts of a starring role on *Crimewatch*. This guy seemed nice.

'Pleased to meet you, Seb. Are you a friend of Josie's?'

'No. Well, not really. Kind of. It's a bit complicated.'

Caro had no idea what it was that suddenly made her want to hear his version of 'complicated'. Perhaps it was the fact that she'd been living in her own head all day. Or maybe she just needed a distraction from thinking the same problem through again and again, never reaching any kind of solution. Or it could be his kind face. He looked like the kind of guy who wouldn't judge. All she knew was that, right now, she was intrigued and wanted to hear what 'kind of' meant.

'Go on then – tell me what's complicated,' she said, before adding. 'It'll take my mind off my disaster of a day. Another complicated story,' she finished, sadness in every word.

'Well, for what it's worth, you've no idea how happy I am to meet you.'

'Really? Did Josie offer you a finder's fee for tracking me down? Only I wouldn't put that past her.'

He laughed, shaking his head as he sat down, an expression on his face that she couldn't read.

'I... I know your Aunt Pearl. We're old friends.'

'Oh God, Aunt Pearl. She's going to lose her mind today.' She realised that wouldn't make any sense to this guy, so she went on, 'Sorry. It's just that Aunt Pearl has come here for my wedding and I've called it off. I think my fiancé is probably in that hotel across the road breaking the news to her right now. That's why Josie is looking for me too.'

He exhaled. 'I need to come clean – she'd already told me that. I'm really sorry. Am I allowed to ask why you've called it off?'

Caro gazed at him again, eyes narrowing. 'You first. Didn't you say you had a story to tell?'

His smile was warm as he answered. 'Yep, but I think yours is a bit more urgent. Aunt Pearl's state of mind and Josie's wedding planning both depend on it.'

Caro felt a compelling urge to tell this man everything, to unburden herself of all the worries and stresses that were twisting her insides so that she could barely breathe.

'Tell me first how you know Aunt Pearl.'

'I worked at the same place as her many years ago. A golf club in Aberdeen. I… I hope this doesn't upset you, but I knew your mum too.'

It was so unexpected that what little breath she had in her lungs was now squeezed out of them.

'You knew my mum?' Her eyes filled again as she sought confirmation that she hadn't dreamt what he'd just said.

He nodded. 'I did. I'm so sorry – Pearl told me she passed away.'

That was all he said, but it was enough to break down every barrier and let the floodgates open.

'Yes,' Caro whispered. 'And I can't tell you how much I wish she was here now. I feel… lost without her.'

'Is that why you've cancelled the wedding?'

'No, it's just… Well, kind of. How well did you know her?'

'Pretty well back then, but it was a long time ago, before she married your dad. Won't he be able to help you sort things out?'

'He's the last person I want anywhere near me today,' she spat, surprising herself and this man sitting next to her with the viciousness of her words. She could see his confusion.

'I don't understand, you're not close?'

Caro shook her head. 'How much has Aunt Pearl told you about my father?'

'Nothing,' he said. 'I've literally had two conversations with Pearl in the last thirty-odd years, and one of them was outside the toilets in the hotel this morning. I'm really sorry for bringing him up. I didn't realise there was a problem, or I wouldn't have said anything.'

Caro felt terrible now. She'd made him visibly uncomfortable and he was probably trying to come up with an excuse to get away from her right now. Bugger. 'No, please… I shouldn't have said that. I don't usually do drama or bad feeling, but it's just… he's a sore subject and the reason I can't do this today. He's the reason I've just completely messed up my life and destroyed the man that I love.'

'How so?' he asked gently.

It was all Caro needed to go on. 'You sure you want to hear this?' She really hoped he said yes, because she needed to tell someone, to get it all off her chest.

'Absolutely,' he said, with palpable sincerity. She liked this man. It was a shame Pearl or her mum never mentioned him or kept in touch with him. He seemed like a good guy.

'Okay, but it's a mess. Don't say I didn't warn you.'

'I consider myself warned.'

'My mum had early-onset dementia…' That was the starting point. Before she could stop herself, she'd told him everything – her mum's illness, her dad's desertion, how she tracked him down, discovered his double life, met Cammy, and how this all led up to her meltdown this morning, how she just couldn't bring herself to walk in her mum's footsteps.

When she'd finished, he spoke softly. 'I'm so sorry you've had to go through all that. You must have been heartbroken.'

'Not by him,' Caro shot back. 'I didn't care that he'd lied to me, only that he'd lied to my mum. I hate him. But the problem is, I owe him too.' There it was. She'd said it. Much as it ripped her heart to shreds, she'd admitted it.

'I don't follow...'

'If my dad hadn't been such a bastard to my mum and me, then I'd never have met Cammy. I don't know how to explain it, but it feels like he's done me a favour. And I hate that. I don't want to benefit in any way from the man who treated my mother like that. If my dad hadn't been living a lie, and if my mum hadn't died, then we'd never have got together. Somehow, marrying him makes me feel like I'm betraying her all over again, getting joy out of the tragedy that was her whole life. Having this incredible ceremony and declaring my love for him while we drink and dance and give toasts to our happiness just feels wrong. Loving him is one thing, but celebrating our love without her here... I just can't do it.'

A gasping sob punctuated the last word, as she expressed the twisted feelings inside her. When it faded, a wave of embarrassment consumed her. Caro wasn't one for big outbursts of emotion and – friend of Aunt Pearl or not – she couldn't believe she'd just offloaded all this on a complete stranger. He was bound to be trying to figure out how he could escape from her as quickly as possible. The cold forgotten, her face burned with the mortification of it.

It seemed like ages before he said anything, but just as she was about to fill the silence with nervous ramblings of apology, he spoke.

'You could look at it that way,' he said, and Caro felt instant relief that he wasn't making up an imaginary dinner date and fleeing the scene. This was the most peaceful she'd felt all day, the only time the sirens in her head had stopped. She wasn't ready to go back to the real world and hear them again. 'Or you could look at it another way altogether.'

'What do you mean?' Caro couldn't explain why she felt comfortable with this man, but there was a connection there, an affinity, that was almost tangible. Perhaps because – her aunt and uncle aside – he was the first person she'd spoken to in a long time who actually knew her mum.

'Perhaps the world works in a different way. Your mum died the night that you met Cammy – maybe she had something to do with the fact that your relationship developed into love. Perhaps your mum made it happen that way, because maybe even after they're gone, the people who care about us can somehow guide us to the places we're meant to be in life and help us find new love, new happiness.'

'Do you honestly believe that?' Caro asked, trying desperately to process this alternative perspective. So what was he saying? That somehow her mum had influenced her relationship with Cammy and helped her find the love of her life?

He nodded slowly. 'I think I'm beginning to.'

This puzzled her. 'Why?'

He exhaled as his head fell into his hands. He stayed like that for several moments, as if he was deciding how to answer her question. When he lifted his head again, his face was a mask of... something. Worry? Pain?

'Because my wife died not long ago. And if I hadn't lost her, I wouldn't be here right now with you.'

Caro was baffled. 'I don't understand.'

Why would it be important that he was here now, with her, and why would his wife influence that? This was all getting way too weird. What was he trying to say?

'Sorry, I know that sounds crazy,' he said, reading her thoughts. 'But I think there are some things you should know...'

Twenty-Five

Seb

He couldn't tell her. Not here. Not now. And yet, he could never have anticipated having a moment like this with her, a time when it seemed like they were meant to meet and there was some higher reason for it.

Until a few days ago, he hadn't believed in destiny, or the afterlife, or anything like that. He was a man whose life was rooted in reality, and in things he could feel, see, hear and prove. Yet, as he was saying to Caro that perhaps there was some kind of inexplicable intervention in their lives, he knew he believed that now.

He just wasn't sure if Juliet had led him here to help him or to punish him. That would depend on the outcome. But for now, he knew that he had to help this woman in front of him, and if that meant baring his soul, then that's what he would do. For the second time tonight, he decided to tell his story – but this time it was to the person whom it affected most.

'My wife, Juliet, passed away in a car accident that was my fault. I killed her.' Seb heard Caro gasp when he said this, but he didn't look at her, knowing that if he did, he'd never get out everything else he wanted to say. 'I replay the moment in my head a thousand times a day. Every time I ask myself why I didn't wait until she'd put her seatbelt on, didn't look the other way, didn't see the van coming... So many questions. But, at the end of the day, the only answer to all those questions is that I killed my wife.'

'You couldn't have known...' Caro said gently. She didn't recoil as he'd feared, didn't call him a murderer or flee his presence. He could hear that there was no judgement there and he was grateful for it, although he didn't agree. He should have known. He should have been more careful. He should have taken care of his wife.

He took a breath, then carried on. 'My wife was Scottish, grew up just a mile away from here and although we lived abroad, we used to come to these gardens whenever we were back in Glasgow. We once made promises to each other that if either of us died, the other one would scatter their ashes in Scotland, somewhere that meant something to us.'

'That's so beautiful.' He could see the tears glistening in Caro's eyes. She sniffed and wiped them away. 'Sorry, I'm an emotional mess today.'

'Me too,' he said, making her smile. 'Anyway, for the last six months, I haven't been able to do it. I couldn't come back here, couldn't scatter her ashes, because I couldn't bear to say goodbye to her. I was so consumed by guilt and loss that I wanted to hang on to her and keep her with me.'

Her words soothed him. 'That's understandable. You'd had a terrible loss. It would be so hard to endure more.'

'That's true,' Seb agreed, 'but I was also racked with guilt because I wasn't keeping my promise to her. I just couldn't see a way forward. So I did nothing. I drank too much. I let my life slide by. To be honest, I hoped every single day that something would happen to me, then I could be with her, but I didn't have the courage to make that happen either.'

He heard Caro's sharp intake of breath. 'I'm glad you didn't.'

'Me too,' he said honestly, realising that for the first time in six months he meant it. 'Because then I met your Aunt Pearl.'

Caro's expression changed to one of curiosity and he knew this was the point of no return. It wasn't too late to gloss over the facts. Tell her. Or not. This was it.

'And my Aunt Pearl persuaded you to scatter your wife's ashes?'

'No, it's a bit more complicated than that. She told me your mum had passed away and then she told me about you.'

He was all in now. There was no credible way to backpedal from this.

'I still don't understand...'

'Please don't be freaked out by this. And I swear this isn't how or when I was going to tell you. But... your mum and I, we were more than friends.' He paused, unsure of his words. 'A brief fling' seemed tawdry. Undermined it. 'I was crazy about her for a long time, but she was in love with your dad. Then they split for a while and we...' he struggled again. 'We had a relationship. Just for a really short time, but it meant a lot to me. I was in love with her and I was gutted when she went back to your dad.'

'Wow. I didn't know she'd ever been with anyone other than him.'

A maelstrom of conflict was firing around his gut as he waited for her to say more, and he was flooded with relief when she did.

'I'm… glad. I don't know why, but it makes me happy that someone else loved her. Although, I just wish she hadn't gone back to my dad. He wasn't worthy of her. If she'd taken a different path, then she could have had such a better life. Although, I guess if she'd done that, I wouldn't be here.'

The words were out before he could stop them. 'Maybe you would be.'

She reeled like she'd been slapped. 'What do you mean?'

At that precise moment he saw that she'd caught on to what he was saying.

'Shit, I'm so sorry! I didn't mean to blurt it out…' he stammered.

'You might be my dad?' she whispered, searching his face for answers.

He leaned over, put his hand on hers, and, to his absolute relief, she didn't snatch it away. 'I honestly don't know. Your mum and I were only together for a short time. I left soon afterwards and I didn't even know your mum was pregnant or I swear I'd have stayed. I only discovered your existence when I bumped into Pearl again a couple of weeks ago. And when I counted back the dates… I had to… I had to come. I'm sorry,' he said again. 'The last thing I wanted was to upset you.'

'You might be my dad?' she repeated, still staring at him, clearly finding all this too much to take in. He took her direct gaze as a chance to search her face for any similarities or clues. He was disappointed when there was nothing obvious. The light wasn't great, but as far as he could see she didn't have his eyes or his nose. She was blonde, green-eyed and those cheekbones... now that he was up close and staring at her, he could see that she was Yvonne's double. But his daughter? He had no idea.

'I think the chances are unlikely, but it's a possibility. The timings match, but your mum went back to your dad straight after we'd been... together. I wish I could give you a definite answer, but there's no way of knowing without doing a DNA test.'

Her hand was still under his, her eyes wide with shock and bewilderment. 'And would you do that?'

'Of course! Caro, I've no idea whether I'm your dad or not, but over the last week I've done so much thinking about that possibility. You see, I never had children. Juliet and I met in our early forties and she was the only woman – other than your mum – that I was ever in love with. She was with me when I lost my parents, and I have no brothers or sisters. The thought that I could still have something, *someone* that I have a connection to – I can't tell you how much I'd love that to be the case. And the fact that the connection was to my first love, to Yvonne, you've no idea what that means to me. I don't want to get my hopes up, and I promise you that you only have to say the word and I'll walk away and I'll never bother you again, but this all brings me back to what I was saying earlier. I think Juliet brought me here. Or maybe Yvonne. Please don't think I've lost the plot, but I feel like I was meant to come here. I was meant to meet Pearl that night so that I'd find the reason I needed to come back to Scotland. And you're that reason.'

She didn't say anything at all to that.

He held the silence for a moment, then cracked, panic taking over.

'Have I completely freaked you out? Do you want to run? I'd understand, I promise. This is… a lot.'

She shook her head slowly. No, it feels… I'm not sure actually, how it feels. So what you're saying is that you think your late wife, or my mother, brought you here because you might be my dad and you were meant to meet me?'

'Okay, so if you say it like that, I'm fine with you calling some kind of emergency service,' he said, with a lightness that was infused with desperate hope that she wasn't about to run screaming for the exit. There was a long silence that he eventually broke. 'Is it too needy to ask what you're thinking?'

Another silence.

For so long…

That he almost forgot to breathe…

And then…

'I think I really hope it's true,' she began, speaking slowly and thoughtfully. 'Because if it is, it means that perhaps my mum brought you here for me right now too. Until ten minutes ago, I thought that I'd be letting my mum down by getting married. Somehow, the fact that you're here with your crazy theory… sorry, no offence…'

'None taken.'

'Makes me think that she knew this would happen and that you're here to make me see that I can't let his actions rule my life because he might not even be my dad. Does that make sense?'

'Absolutely none,' he answered honestly. 'But I get it, because when you lose someone, it changes you and it teaches you and you have to learn to be more open to a new way of life. Maybe all this has happened to teach us something.'

'You really might be my dad? Sorry, I keep saying that. I can't quite take it in.'

'Me neither. Is it wrong that I really, really hope I am?'

In fact, other than Juliet somehow coming back to him, he'd never wanted anything more.

'No, not wrong. Just... I still can't process this. You have no other children,' she said, a statement, not a question.

He shook his head. 'None.'

'So you're alone. I know how that feels.' There was such sadness in her voice that he felt a chip of his heart break off.

'Yes. Juliet and I hoped that kids might come along at the beginning, but it didn't happen. We were sad about it for a moment, but we accepted it. It was easier because we were so happy. The best day of my life was when I married her and I never felt we missed out on anything. Although now, I think she missed out on meeting you. I think you'd have liked each other very much.'

Another chip broke off as he realised that was true.

'I would have liked to have met her too. She sounds like a very special lady.'

Another pause, but there was no tension, just a gap as they both processed this.

Caro was the first to speak. 'What do we do now?'

Seb was honest. 'I hadn't really thought it all through. But maybe, if it's okay with you, then we could do one of those DNA tests and find out for sure? And then we could take it from there? What do you think?' He hoped that was the right answer to that question.

A noise distracted them before she could answer. He watched her shrink back into the wall of the pagoda as a crowd of people walked down the path and into the Palace. The trees and vegetation formed a semi-screen so that Seb and Caro were barely visible. None of them looked their way and he was glad.

'That's more people here to work at my wedding. We didn't call it off because Cammy said he was going to go ahead with the dinner and the party. He said it wasn't fair after our guests had made the effort to travel here for us.'

'He sounds like a good guy,' Seb said, meaning it, thinking that it took some class to follow through with a gathering in these circumstances.

'He is.'

Seb could see that she was thinking and decided not to interrupt.

After a few more seconds, she went on, 'I can't get what you said out of my head.'

'Which bit?' he asked, trying again to keep his tone light.

'Maybe my mum sent you. And if she did, then I know that she's here with me. You know, much as I hated my dad, I always knew that my mum loved me and wanted me to be happy.'

'I'm sure she did. Yvonne was always the one who was looking out for everyone else. She had a big heart.'

'She did. And I think that maybe it would be breaking if she could see me now, causing such pain to someone I love.'

'Caro, you have to do what's right for you. It doesn't matter what your dad…' he struggled to say the word, hoping that it was an outdated description, 'or your mum or anyone else thinks. If you've found the right person, the one that you absolutely know you want to wake up next to every day, then that's all that matters. If you don't want to get married, that's absolutely fine too. You can live your life any way you please. But don't let the actions of other people be the reason that you walk away. Trust your heart.'

As soon as he finished, he wondered if he'd overstepped. Who was he to give advice? His own life was a disaster. He definitely wasn't qualified.

'I think you're right,' she said, before she suddenly jumped to her feet.

Seb felt his stomach churn. He had gone too far. He'd scared her off.

He stood up too, but it seemed like a lifetime before she turned to look at him again.

'You know, for a non-father, you're not bad at this stuff.'

He could see she was teasing him and he liked it so much it brought on another pang of longing. He so wanted to get to know this woman better. Her 'father' was a fool if he couldn't see how great she was.

'Really? I'm thinking I need work, but I'm hoping to get the chance to improve.' Seb meant every word.

'Would you like some practice?' There was a hint of apprehension in her voice.

'Absolutely. I just don't know where to start.'

She held out her hand. 'I think I know the answer to that.'

Twenty-Six

Josie

'Somebody pour me a tequila. It's for medicinal purposes,' Josie bellowed as she burst back into Cammy and Caro's flat. Which, ironically, still contained neither Caro nor Cammy. Life would be so much fecking easier if it did.

'Oh, thank God!' Val greeted her arrival with a shrill exclamation of relief. 'We've been worried sick! Did you find Caro? WHAT THE BUGGERING HELL IS HAPPENING?'

'Somebody pour a tequila for Val too. She's hysterical,' Josie bellowed as she trooped past her friend and straight into the kitchen. Chrissie was sitting at the table, looking a lot more human than she did this morning, and Jen, equally recovered from her hangover, was already on her feet and pouring Mexico's finest refreshment into two glasses. Both women had obviously heeded Josie's command to continue as if all was still on track. Their make-up and hair were done, and they even had slides of flowers holding their curls back over their left ears. They scrubbed up pretty nicely for two women that looked like they'd been dragged through a bush and doused in margaritas only a few hours before.

Val came in behind her and stood, hands on hips, in the doorway. 'Has anyone ever told you that your powers of communication are shite? We've been beside ourselves waiting for news all day.'

Josie rolled her eyes. 'Does Jack Bauer's pal phone him for hourly chats when he's saving the world in 24? Or that sexy Thor one—'

'Chris Hemsworth...' Jen interjected.

'Aye, him. Is he getting texts every hour demanding updates or does he just get on with looking entirely shaggable while hitting folk with a mallet?' She was too busy knocking back the tequila to listen to Val's answer. She put the glass back on the table and raised her eyes to Jen, signalling for a refill. What a bloody day. She kept wishing she would wake up, realise that she was under her duvet and this had all been a bad dream.

The second tequila set off her cough, delaying her response to Val even further. Her pal's face was now almost the colour of the red tinsel draped from the top of the kitchen cupboards.

'First of all, how's Caro? Did you find her?' Jen asked. 'I'm not refilling your glass again until we know.' That Jen was a smart cookie. She always knew how to hit the soft spot.

Josie sighed. 'Okay, here's where we're at. I didn't find Caro. I've no idea where the poor lass is, but I know she's okay because she went to see Cammy this afternoon. She told him the wedding's off and then bolted again – we thought she'd come back here, but obviously she hasn't?'

The blank looks on their faces confirmed that assumption.

'Och, my heart goes out to her. I honestly don't know what's going on with her. I just wish she could have spoken to us,' she said, with genuine sympathy, before adding, 'However, that doesn't take away from the fact that I may boot her arse for worrying us all sick.'

Val was sitting at the table now, downing the remnants of her first tequila. 'How's Cammy? He must be in bits.'

'He is. I don't think he knows if he's coming or going, but he's decided to go ahead with the reception tonight. It's going to be more drowning of the sorrows than celebration, but at least we'll be there to support him. He's a good man, that one.' Josie meant every word. Cammy Jones was one of her favourite people on this earth and he deserved happiness. She just hoped that even if Caro didn't want to marry him, then at least they could still find a way to get past this and make things work. She truly believed they belonged together.

Jen squirmed and turned a tad grey while putting the top back on the tequila bottle. Perhaps the hangover hadn't completely subsided after all. 'So, what's the plan then? I've never been a bridesmaid when there's no bride before.'

Josie shrugged. 'We get changed pronto and we head straight back over to the Kibble Palace. We surround Cammy with love and get him through tonight. And if we can track down Caro, we make sure she knows we love her too. That's all we can do, isn't it? Feck, Jen, pour me another one. Being a paragon of wisdom and kindness is making me thirsty.'

The truth? She could do with another drink because what she wasn't telling Jen, Chrissie or Val was that she had an alternative motive for supporting Cammy's decision to go ahead with the reception tonight. If they weren't going to the venue, where they'd be surrounded with friends and family, then no doubt she'd spend the evening with Michael and Avril and she didn't trust herself not to blurt out her prognosis. No, she was too vulnerable right now. Better to be in a crowd tonight to give her a chance to process what had happened and come to terms with it herself. She'd then tell Michael and Avril, and everyone else, when she was ready – maybe in a couple of weeks, so that it wouldn't spoil their Christmas and New Year. There would be enough time for misery and fussing later.

She picked up the fresh drink and stood up. 'So, ladies, let's get the glad rags on and get back over there. Val, did you cancel the wedding car?'

'No, I didn't...'

With perfect timing, the door buzzer rang. Chrissie picked up the kitchen intercom. 'Hello?' She listened for a moment before covering the handset. 'That's the car downstairs.'

Josie felt a glimmer of satisfaction. She'd organised every detail of this wedding and it was all going exactly to plan. Except for the whole missing bride thing. 'Great. Tell them we'll be ten minutes.'

Chrissie did as she was told, then hung up.

'Right, you three, ten minutes to get ready and get down there.'

In the end, they did it in eight. They clambered into the wedding car, feeling faintly ridiculous that the four of them were being transported to a non-wedding in the back of a vintage Rolls-Royce.

'Will you stop waving to people,' Val chided Josie, as they moved slowly through the packed streets of the West End.

'Och, it'll make their day. I bet every one of them goes home and tells folk that they saw the Queen, Helen Mirren or Keith Richards. Depends how close a look they got.'

The other three were still laughing when the car pulled up outside the West End Grand. In the lobby, the rest of the guests were already assembling, ready to walk across the road to the Kibble Palace. Josie prepared to greet them with solemn condolences and supportive solidarity. That went right out the window as soon as Avril saw her.

'Mother! If the Rolling Stones need a groupie, I reckon the gig is yours.'

Josie took two things from that comment. Number one, Avril seemed perfectly jovial and not like someone who'd just found out that the wedding they'd travelled to was off. Cammy must have taken her advice and decided to tell all the guests together when they got to the venue. Wise move. It meant they'd be more inclined to stay to cheer him up and to make sure all that food and drink didn't go to waste. And number two, Josie had been wearing leather trousers on special occasions for most of her daughter's life, so she wasn't sure why they were now worthy of comment.

She ignored the dig, and focused on the first observation. 'You're not too old for me to ground you, madam,' she quipped to her daughter, before grabbing Val's hand and whispering out of the side of her mouth. 'They still don't know about Caro. Don't say a word.'

Just at that, the lift doors opened and out came Cammy in the suit that Josie had helped him pick out for the wedding. He was so handsome, it almost broke her heart. The suit was a deep navy, with a white shirt and an emerald green tie, picked to fit with the Christmas theme of the wedding and to match the shade of the bridesmaid's dresses. His hair was in its usual style, swept back from his face, falling to the nape of his neck. Only the most observant would realise that his five o'clock shadow and the frown lines between his eyes suggested that all was not well with the groom.

While beaming welcoming, 'nothing wrong here' smiles to the rest of the congregated guests, she made her way over to him, then waylaid him into a corner. 'I'm glad you haven't told them,' she hissed.

'I couldn't,' he blurted helplessly. 'I didn't know what to say. You're right about telling them when we get there. You know, after a couple of drinks. If I tell them now, half of them will bail out and go to bed and Caro's Aunt Pearl will have me pinned against a wall demanding answers. And then I'll have to repeat the bad news to everyone who's going straight to the reception. It'll be even more of a nightmare than this already is.'

'You impress the crap out of me sometimes, Cammy Jones. I mean, not too often. But every now and then.' Teasing him was her very own way of expressing her love for him and they both knew it.

'That's good because, erm, I need a favour. If I freeze when I'm telling everyone it's off, will you help me out?'

Her love for him swelled as she could see how exhausted and stressed he was.

'Of course I will, my darlin'. How are you holding up? Have you heard from her?'

He looked crestfallen. 'Not since she was here. Have you? Did you find her?'

Josie shook her head. 'No. I'm sorry, Cammy. I wish I could tell you different. But she was definitely at the Kibble Palace after she left here, so at least we know that she's okay.'

'I keep telling myself that's all that matters. I don't know how this happened though. And I don't know what to think, Josie. I love her, but...'

'Don't be giving me any "buts" right now, love. Let's just get through tonight and we'll see how everything pans out tomorrow. Tonight, whatever you need Val and me to do, just say. Preferably to Val, because I'm way too old and knackered for all this drama.' It was said in jest, in an attempt to make him smile, but there was a whole load of truth in there. 'I swear you're going to owe me an internal organ after this night.' A thought came to her and she couldn't resist adding, 'Preferably a lung.'

'It's yours,' Cammy replied, not realising there was any significance in the joke. His grateful expression melted her heart and she leaned over and hugged him.

'I'm sorry this is happening to you, son, I really am. You don't deserve it. You're one of the good ones.'

He paused. 'Josie, you're scaring the crap out of me. You haven't been this nice to me since I got booted in the bollocks by a shoplifter trying to steal three pairs of Armani boxers in 2008.'

'Aye, well don't get used to it. Your next display of affection is scheduled for 2029. Once every ten years should keep you humble.' In her mind, she used her steel toe-capped, leather stilettoes to kick away the thought that she wouldn't be around then.

It was his turn to hug her now. 'Thanks Josie. And if I forget to tell you later when I'm drunk and weeping into my beer, I love you.'

She was quite unprepared for the massive boulder that lodged in her throat at that exact moment. Or for the realisation that it was just as well she was not longer for this world because she was getting sentimental in her old age.

'Yeah, well, you're still my third favourite man,' she said. It was an old private joke that she repeated to him often – telling him that Michael was top of her list because she'd given birth to him. And Pierce Brosnan was next, because she wanted to have sex with him before she... It was tough to finish that line now. Before she died. Well, she was going to have to get a move on with that one. 'Right, come on then. Let's get everyone over there. At least none of the booze and food will go to waste. We'll tell them after the hors d'oeuvres. Let everyone enjoy them first because they cost a bloody fortune.'

Josie shot a psychic message to Val, Jen and Chrissie, all of whom she could see were mingling and making small talk with the others. Act normal, it said. We're not rocking the boat yet.

Val nodded, instinctively understanding her best friend's telepathy.

Thankfully, the rain had stopped, allowing them all to cross the road and get to the venue dry in just a couple of minutes. Inside, there were a handful of other guests, including – oh, what a sight for sore fecking eyes – Senga and the rest of the Manky Scrubbers, the merry band of cleaners who'd been her friends for decades.

'Senga, ma love!' Josie roared. 'You're the very best thing I've seen in ages. Or at least since I gave up porn.'

Sanga collapsed into giggles and squeezed the older woman tightly. It was only when she was wrapped in her arms, her mouth right up at Josie's ear that she whispered, 'Josie, is everything okay with this wedding?'

Josie froze, pulled back, then tugged Senga over to the side of the foyer, out of earshot of everyone else. 'What makes you ask that?' Did Senga know where Caro was? Did she have some insight into what was going on, some clue that would help them understand?

'Because our Stacey… aw, bugger. Never mind.'

Josie caught Senga's glance going to her daughter, who had just entered the room, looking absolutely sensational in a pale blush dress that hugged every curve, her dark hair tumbling in waves down her back, her flawless face bearing more than a little resemblance to a young Catherine Zeta-Jones.

Josie and Senga both watched wordlessly as Stacey, oblivious to their presence, made a beeline for Cammy. As soon as he saw her, he pulled her to one side and whispered in her ear, as if they were in cahoots about something, Josie thought. The way she looked at him, the absolute adoration in her eyes, was plain for anyone watching to see.

'Feck, she's in love with him?' Josie whispered to Senga.

Her friend nodded. 'And, Josie, I'm so sorry, but I think she might have done something that will throw that poor boy's life into turmoil.'

Josie closed her eyes, sighed, then opened them and raised them heavenwards. Someone up there was definitely having a laugh.

Her beady gaze trained on Stacey and Cammy again, as she let go of Senga's hand and started to make her way towards them.

Problem number 2343 of the day. And right now, she didn't have a solution.

Twenty-Seven

Stacey

As soon as Stacey entered the reception room, her pulse quickened. It was beyond exquisite. The guests walked through the entrance foyer, collecting a crystal flute of champagne from the uniformed waiting staff, the aroma of fresh flowers preparing everyone for what came next. She was directed through to a stunning flower-lined conservatory, with about twenty white wooden chairs on either side of an emerald green carpet, each chair adorned with a trellis of blooms that stretched from one side of each row to the other. There were already many guests here, but before she could scan the faces, her gaze fell on the most important one. Cammy's eyes met hers and she experienced such a rush of longing it almost unsteadied her. He looked exactly how she'd always imagined he would on his wedding day. The impeccable suit, the handsome face, the hair falling sexily over his dark lashes. The only thing missing from the picture was the reflection of herself, dressed in white, holding flowers and wearing something borrowed and blue.

He made a beeline for her and pulled her to one side. 'Thank God you're here,' he blurted. 'I need to make the announcement, but I'm bricking it. I don't know where to start. Josie said she'll help me, but the reality is, it has to come from me.'

'Do you want me to do it?' She wanted to take that back as soon as she'd said it. What was she thinking? Of course she didn't want to stand up there and announce to a room full of people that the wedding was off. Her acting skills weren't great, so it would be too easy for people to read her true feelings. Plus, there was every chance that Senga would ground her until she was fifty for getting involved.

Thankfully, he shook his head. 'No, it should be me. And I will. I just wanted to wait until everyone was here, because we owe it to them to still put on a party. Or a wake. RIP my wedding. And, Stacey, about this afternoon...'

She clenched her teeth together to stop herself responding. This afternoon. Thank God it was chilly in here because thinking back on it was making her face burn. Her mind pressed rewind to just a couple of hours ago, to the conversation they'd had in his hotel room.

'Because back then, when I let you go, I didn't feel the way I do now,' she'd said, her eyes locked on his, hoping against hope that he'd realise, that he wouldn't make her say it.

'What do you mean?' he'd asked, completely clueless. Damn it! He was making this way too difficult. If he'd given her just one clue that he knew, one hint that there was something there, one gesture that made her think that he was aware of something more between them, then she'd have blurted everything out. Instead she'd had to test the water, take it gently, because the last thing she wanted to do was make it worse.

'I don't know,' she'd said, a white lie. 'I guess I was just a bit more naïve and thought that everyone fell into their happy ever after. I didn't realise that sometimes you have to go after it, work for it, that sometimes people realise what they want at different times.'

Come on, Cammy, see me. Hear what I'm saying.

'So you're saying that I need to work for this? That I should make Caro change her mind? That she'll want to get married at some point in the future?'

If her head had been near a wall she'd have been banging it right about then.

'No! I mean…' Oh, fuck. She'd realised she was just going to have to be a little more explicit, lead him down the path, leave breadcrumbs. 'I just mean that sometimes it's not a given that everything works out the way it should. Sometimes you need to make things happen. Take for example…' She'd paused, her internal voices clashing. One was opting for silence and the other was screaming, *Say it. Say it!* '… when you told me you loved me that last night in LA.'

His head had snapped up in surprise.

Keep going. Keeping bloody going.

'I guess what I mean is that if we were meant to be together, then I would have realised at some point between then and now that I loved you too, and I'd have come after you, no matter what the cost. And you'd still believe now that we were meant to be together too.'

Say something that will give me hope. Tell me you sometimes wonder, tell me you settled for someone else because you couldn't have me.

'We never did talk about that, did we?' The frown eased in his brow for the first time since they'd entered the room.

'No.' One word, then the inner voice opting for silence won out that time. *Let him talk.*

The next few seconds felt like a week, until a sad, rueful smile crossed his face.

'I wanted to come back. Every day for the next couple of months, I thought about jumping on a plane and doing one of those *An Officer and a Gentleman* moments where Richard Gere sweeps Debra Winger off her feet...'

It was one of her favourite movies and they'd watched it together more times than she could count.

'Why didn't you?' She'd found it hard to get the words past the strangle knot in her throat.

He'd shrugged.

Please say that you regret it, that you should have done it...

'Because I'd probably have pulled my back out and then Jax would have beaten me to a pulp.' It was obvious to her that he was using flippancy to cover a more meaningful thought.

'Probably true,' she'd joked back, trying to stay on the same page, knowing that the truth would follow. With Cammy, it always did.

Another week-long silence, before he finally spoke again. 'I guess I knew that you weren't interested in me that way. We'd been friends for so long and nothing had ever happened... I knew you didn't want me like that.'

In her mind, she was formulating what to say next.

I want you now.

I wish you had come back.

It's not too late.

I love you. I just didn't realise it then.

Maybe Caro cancelling the wedding is because we were meant to be together.

Did I mention I love you?

Before she could get any of those words out, he'd gone on.

'The thing is, I knew that if I came back, then you'd blow me out of the water...'

I wouldn't have. I promise.

'And that would have killed our friendship. I couldn't do that because you matter too much to me. I've loved you since the minute I met you, Stacey Summers...'

Yes!

'You're the sister I never had.'

No! Oh, don't. Not the 'sister' thing.

'And I couldn't do anything that would jeopardise that. Besides...' he'd switched to flippancy again, 'I'm glad I didn't fuck it up, because you'd have blocked me for being some crazy weird needy stalker and then you wouldn't be here with me now and I'm so, so fucking glad that you are.'

Stacey's heart had sunk. Oh, the irony. He was saying all the things she'd have wanted him to say if she didn't have feelings for him: that one night of passion hadn't wrecked their relationship, that he loved her too much to risk it, that he needed her here now. Fantastic. Great. All good. Except... she was in love with him and wanted him to feel the same, to come to his senses, to realise that this, right here, was an opportunity for them to do what they should have done three years ago.

It was time to correct him and speak her truth.

But she couldn't.

'Me too,' she'd said, inwardly cursing her cowardice while desperately trying to hold back the tears and be the bloody sister that he thought she was.

Game over. If, even in his jilted state, he still didn't realise that he was almost marrying the wrong woman, then she was only going to push him away by telling him. Caro wasn't his second choice – she was the one he'd been meant to be with all along.

That stung. Really, truly stung. She could almost hear Senga's voice saying, 'Suck it up, love – what did you expect? And what are you going to do now?'

Good question. She loved him – but what he needed today was his best friend. And that was who she was going to be.

For now.

'So...' she'd said, with a renewed energy and strength that she definitely wasn't feeling. 'What's the plan? What do you need me to do?'

Please make it involve being naked.

Enough!

She'd switched off her internal thoughts. Speculation was over. It was done. Time for self-preservation and moving forward.

Beer finished, she'd taken another two from the minibar, handing one to Cammy.

'I don't have a plan,' he'd admitted. 'I'm just going to carry on, go over to the venue, tell everyone, and then get drunk with all my friends and family at my non-wedding. Christ, it'll be awful, but it's the only thing I can do. May as well make the most of it, eh? Fucked if I know what

I'm going to say, though. I'll have to wing it. I don't have any choice.'

Somehow, the fact that he was being so stoic and thoughtful made her love him even more – and made her want to shake Caro for doing this to him.

In her dreams, he'd confessed that he loved her and they'd spent the afternoon engaged in wild passion and giving thanks that they'd realised in time. In reality? He'd gone for a shower, and she'd headed home for a quick change of clothes, then gone straight to the beautiful glass wedding venue, where she stood beside him now, a tiny glimmer of hope still flickering.

'And Stacey, about this afternoon…' Cammy was saying. She reached down and instinctively took his hand, something they'd done as friends a thousand times over the years. 'Thank you,' he went on. 'I needed a pal and I'm so glad it was you.'

Jesus, he was killing her here.

'Any time,' she said, squeezing his fingers. 'When are you going to tell everyone?'

'Soon. I can't bear to hear another person say congratulations. I'm hoping that Josie—'

'Did I hear you call my name, oh master?' Josie's booming, husky voice made her jump. She was like a bloody ninja, sneaking up like that.

Stacey instinctively let go of Cammy's hand and experienced a wave of guilt, even though she'd done absolutely nothing wrong. Not. A. Thing. Although, the way Josie was looking at her with an all-knowing gaze of suspicion made her wonder if she'd been reading her mind. Then, out of the corner of her eye, she caught her mother staring over, looking fearful. Bugger. Her mum must have said something to Josie and sent her careering over here. Well, she wasn't fifteen any more. Josie couldn't ground her or chide her for impure thoughts.

She met the older woman's steely glare… and crumbled on the inside. Who was she kidding? Stacey could be sixty and one sideways look from Josie would still make her throw up her hands in surrender.

Of course, Cammy was completely oblivious to any undercurrent and too busy fretting to notice that she'd suddenly gone a bit red around the neck. He pulled at the collar of his shirt as if it were strangling him. 'I did, Josie. I was just saying to Stacey that I'm going to tell everyone soon. Either that or start drinking, get wrecked and hope they guess it's off when Caro doesn't make an appearance.'

Josie nodded with sage wisdom. 'That sounds like the kind of plan I can get on board with. I'll track us down a bottle of Jack Daniels and two straws.'

Stacey knew how much the older woman loved Cammy and another wave of regret tugged at her soul. They could be one big dysfunctional non-related family here if only she'd got in there with this man first. Instead, she'd let someone else take him. Or not, as the absence of a bride would seem to suggest.

'But before we drink our feelings away, I've been thinking you should probably let Pearl and Bob know first, before you make the announcement to everyone else. Just have a quiet word in their ear,' Josie suggested. 'And probably let the celebrant go too. With a bit of luck, he'll only charge by the hour and you might get some money back.'

'Yeah, good idea,' he agreed, yet he didn't move.

Josie was the first one to realise why. 'You're still hoping she'll turn up, aren't you?'

Cammy exhaled, his expression desperate. 'I don't know. I'm just... I know she's not coming, yet I still can't quite believe it. I just want her to walk in that door right now and tell me it was all a big mistake.'

Stacey could see the sympathy in Josie's eyes. 'It's not going to happen, son.'

'I know, but there's nothing like hope, eh?'

With that, he hugged them both and went off in search of Pearl and Bob and the humanist celebrant they'd booked for the night.

Josie, meanwhile, put her arm through Stacey's.

'You okay there, ma darlin'?' she asked, like the mistress of interrogation that she was.

Stacey contemplated revealing all. Josie had been there for every problem in her life, every worry, every mistake. However, this wasn't one that she wanted to share yet. Not today.

'I'm fine, Josie.'

'Okay, love, I'm glad to hear it,' was the loaded reply.

Just at that, her phone buzzed and, with her free hand, she pulled it from her clutch purse.

A text. Jax.

Where the fuck are you? Need to talk to you now. Call me.

She slipped it back into her bag, no intention of doing as he asked. Jax was a problem for another day. Right now she had as much as she could deal with.

'Do you need to reply to that?' Josie asked.

Stacey knew it was a test. 'No, it's fine. It's Jax. I'll buzz him later.'

Fail. Josie absolutely had the measure of what was happening here. Like a scene from the *Godfather* (another of her favourite films), the older woman reached up and kissed her on the cheek. Christ, she could get whacked at any moment.

'Okay, my darlin',' Josie said. 'You know where I am if you need to talk. Can't be easy coming back here and finding everyone has changed, moved on with their lives.'

There was a weight to her carefully chosen words, one that sat between care, concern, love and a subtle warning: *People have moved on. Cammy has moved on. I know what you're thinking, but don't do it.*

With that, Josie went off to mingle, leaving Stacey standing surrounded by beautiful flowers and regrets.

But then, as she took a sip of champagne, Cammy's parting words echoed in her mind: *There's nothing like hope, eh?*

Twenty-Eight

Website – www.itshouldhavebeenme.com

Members Discussion Forum

Responses to post by member, screen name NotOverYet:

Comments:

NotOverYet: Last chance to tell him. Here goes.

JessieInAJam: Damn, if this is really going down, I want ring side tickets.

Bethany Sunshine: I'm sending love vibes into the universe for you. Please, please, keep us updated. I need to know how this works out. #asgeorgebensonsays #nevergiveuponagoodthing

MIstressNumberOne: Sheeeeeiiiiiitttttt. New to the party but loving this. Popcorn ready. Can't wait to see how this plays out.

8 P.M. – 10 P.M.

Twenty-Nine

Caro

'Can you go as fast as you can, please?' Caro begged the taxi driver.

The driver glanced in his rear view mirror so he could catch a glimpse of her as he nodded.

'Don't you worry, pet, we'll get you there. What time does it start?'

Caro checked her watch. 'An hour ago.'

She could see his eyes widen in the mirror. 'Ah, right. I've always wanted to be like those blokes in *Fast and Furious*. Let's hope all the coppers are out at their Christmas party,' he said with a chuckle, before putting his foot down on the accelerator. 'I had a Santa, two reindeer and a flashing penguin this morning, but this might just be my favourite fare of the day.'

Caro knew that this would be his top story to share over his Christmas Day dinner next week and every Christmas until the end of time.

The taxi had picked them up an hour ago on Great Western Road, outside the Botanic Gardens. She'd given the driver her address and told him it was a rush job and that she wanted him to wait at the other end and bring them back to the same place. 'Not a bother, pet,' he'd assured her, pleasantly. 'Makes a change from the drunk suits I've been picking up all day. Last bloke had been tanking the wine at a lunch that lasted six hours. Sorry if it still smells a bit dodgy back there.'

'No, it's fine. Thank you. I really appreciate you being so nice.'

Desperately trying to calm her anxiety, she'd leaned back in her seat and smiled at the man beside her, feeling like the day had just been elevated to a whole new level of unexpected. Her dad? Or rather, potentially her dad? She still couldn't quite take it in, but she was going with it. Everything he'd said was completely bonkers and shocking and incomprehensible, yet, somehow, it all made sense, because she was choosing to believe that her mum had – by some power of divine intervention – sent this man here today to help her, to change her mind, to make her see that she had to grab on to Cammy and love him. And that meant marrying him.

'Are you okay?' Seb – she couldn't think of him as Dad until she knew for sure – had asked.

Without warning, a chuckle had escaped her. 'I know I shouldn't be, but somehow, I am. This is… crazy. All of it. You. The wedding. I'm so grateful that we met, though. What scares me is that you could have left tomorrow and I'd never have known…'

'Caro, you know I'm not sure. There's only a small chance.'

'I get that,' she'd said, knowing it was true. 'But no matter what, you've changed my life today and I'm so, so thankful.'

'Me too,' Seb had told her. 'No matter what happens, I'm glad that I was here today to see this.'

His words had sparked a thought, and she'd snatched her phone out of her pocket. She'd been so busy changing her mind and processing all this that she hadn't let Cammy know she was coming. She could have nipped into the hotel to see him first, or told someone at the Kibble Palace to let him know, or called Josie, or done a million different things, but in her mind, she'd just wanted to get back to her flat and do what she had to do.

'I'll just call Cammy and tell him that I'm coming…' she'd pulled her phone out of her pocket and checked the screen. Shit. Out of charge. And she couldn't even use Seb's phone because she didn't know Cammy's number off the top of her head. She really was a rubbish fiancée. All she could do now was hope that he'd waited, and that there was still a relationship there to salvage. Cammy had said he understood and they'd sort it out, but this must have hurt him. She just prayed he would forgive her. 'Aaargh, my stomach is flipping here,' she'd admitted. 'Tell me more about you. Anything at all. I just need you to make the time pass faster so I can get back there and make this right.'

Over the next twenty minutes, he'd told her more about his life with Juliet. How they'd met, where he'd proposed to her, what their wedding had been like, and her heart had ached for him. His love for his wife oozed from every pore and she couldn't imagine the pain that he must be in. And the guilt. Not that she blamed him for a second. It had clearly been a horrendous, devastating accident. Still, how would anyone ever get over something like that? No matter what any DNA test showed, she knew that she would do everything she could to help him.

'Just here!' she'd said urgently, as they drew into her street, and then she'd held on to the door handle as the taxi driver swooped into a space right outside the flat. She could see it was in darkness. Bugger, she'd missed them. They must have crossed paths. They'd either be at the hotel now, or already over at the Kibble Palace. 'Okay, if you wouldn't mind waiting? I'll be about ten minutes.'

'No problem at all, pet, but I have to keep the meter running – are you okay with that?'

'Of course! I'll be as quick as I can!'

'Do you want me to wait here or come with you?' She could see that Seb was a bit embarrassed, unsure what to do. They'd gone from strangers to being together and invested in each other's lives in the length of time other people took to buy a pint of milk.

'Please come! I might need help with the dress.'

He took his cue from her, and followed as she'd raced upstairs.

Please be there, please be there, she'd prayed, as she thrust the key in the lock, swung the door open and...

It was still there. Directly in front of her. Hanging in a white bag, with the gold emblem that Caro recognised as her friend Claire's dress design company logo, was her wedding gown. For a moment she'd been worried that Claire would have taken it back to her studio after Caro had run out this morning.

'Yes!' she'd squealed, before snatching it off the door and heading to her room. 'I'll be two minutes. There was a headdress of flowers in the kitchen this morning – it's the door straight ahead – can you have a look and see if it's still there, please?'

Just a few minutes later, they'd met back in the hall. 'Here you go – it was where you said it would be.'

'Brilliant, thanks!' Caro had taken it and plonked it on her head. When she'd been planning her wedding accessories, she'd decided against a veil, opting for a slim ring of Christmas flowers – white, green and silver – instead. It was much more her style. Natural. No fuss. Simple. Her dress was similarly understated. Cut from stunning winter white matt satin, it was off the shoulder, and skimmed her body to the waist, before flaring to the floor. Elegant. Classy. She'd loved it from the moment Claire had shown her the first design. The wonderful thing about having a friend design your dress was that they knew exactly what you wanted. It would have been such a waste if it never saw the outside of the garment hanger.

'You look beautiful,' Seb had told her, and she could hear the emotion in his voice. Dad or not, she felt an incredible feeling of warmth towards him and – even more inexplicably – an absolute reversal in her feelings about the wedding. It was as if he'd wiped away all her doubts and fears. It was difficult to explain all the reasons why. It was the way that he spoke of his love for his wife. It was the fact that she now knew that her mother had been loved by someone other than the father she hated. But most of all it was his feeling that both Juliet and her mum had led them to this point, to this meeting, and if that was true, then it was because her mum was sending her a message. Be happy. Live and love. It's ok. I'm with you.

'Can you zip me up please?'

'My pleasure.' Caro was sure his eyes were glistening. DNA or not, with the care and honesty he'd shown her today, he'd already been more of a father to her than her own dad had ever been.

'Two secs, just let me call...' She'd grabbed her home phone and pressed speed dial 1. Cammy. It went straight to voicemail. Damn! She had to let him know she was coming. Speed dial 2. Josie. Voicemail. Bugger! If they were already in the reception, they might have their phones off. Or perhaps the signal wasn't great there. Either way, she didn't have time to call everyone she knew. 'Okay, let's go,' she'd gushed, grinning with genuine happiness, as they bolted back down the stairs.

They were already at the bottom when she'd realised she was still wearing her biker boots under the dress. Bugger it. No-one would care. Cammy didn't think she was going to make it tonight so she felt he'd come to terms with the fact that it was only her sparkly white shoes that didn't turn up.

'Naw, pet, you've got to be joking me!' the taxi driver had bellowed, with a huge guffaw as she climbed back into the cab. 'You said you were in a rush to get back to a wedding, but you didn't mention it was yer own! Ach, this is brilliant. I bloody love ma job sometimes.'

'I knew there was something I forgot to mention,' she'd giggled.

'Brilliant. Bloody brilliant,' he'd repeated, speeding away from the kerb.

'Bugger, I've left my phone at the flat. I put it on charge and completely forgot about it. I wanted to keep trying to contact Cammy. What if he's told them the wedding is off and they've all gone home?'

Seb had put his hand on hers. 'Didn't you say he was going to go ahead with the reception as planned?'

Caro bit her bottom lip. 'Yes, but… oh, damn it, I don't know. This morning I didn't want this wedding to happen and now there's nothing I want more. I think maybe Cammy was getting a lucky escape.' Her anxiety was back up to full throttle again.

'He's going to be there, all your guests will be too, and this is all going to work out. You're going to be the most beautiful bride in boots ever.' Seb's calmness began to rub off on her.

He was right. It was going to be fine. Absolutely. Positively. Wasn't it?

As requested, the driver had kept his foot to the floor the whole way back, and now they were screeching into the kerb.

Caro checked out the clock on his dashboard. 8.05 p.m.

An hour late. Damn it.

'Here you go, folks. Botanic Gardens. And I managed to get us here without a flashing blue light pouncing on us. That must be a sign from the gods.'

'Thank you so much. Do you want to come in for a glass of something?' Caro asked him. It seemed only fair given that he might just have saved the day.

'Ach, I'd love to, but it's the Friday before Christmas. Big earner. You have a great night though, pet. Me and the missus have been married for thirty years and I can definitely recommend it. Although, I'm not sure she'd have said the same if she'd had to bail me out for speeding tonight.'

Caro leaned forward and gave him an impromptu hug. 'She's a lucky woman.'

'Aye, I tell her that often,' he joked.

Seb was leaning forward now too. 'How much do I owe you?'

'Bugger! I didn't even bring my purse!' Caro exclaimed, mortified. She'd been this guy's maybe/almost/possibly daughter for a whole two hours and already she was costing him money. This was beyond embarrassing.

Fortunately, Seb seemed to find it amusing. 'Don't be daft. If this works out, I owe a whole load of child support payments,' he quipped. 'How much, pal?' he asked the driver again, only for the man in the front to shake his head.

'Nothing, mate. Call it my wedding present to you,' he said to Caro. 'And also, I'll put this in the memoirs I'm going to write one day and I'll make a million. At least, that's what I tell the wife.'

'You're amazing,' Caro said, clambering out, feeling so grateful. In a day of highs and lows, this was near the top of the scale. 'Thank you. And Merry Christmas!'

'Merry Christmas to you too, pet, and good luck.'

With that, and a roar of the engine, he was off. Caro made a note to track him down when all this was done and send him a bottle of something. She exhaled. *Please be there. Please be there.* She turned to Seb, who was standing beside her on the pavement now, holding up his hand for her to take. She accepted it gratefully.

'Are you ready to do this?' he asked.

Caro nodded.

'Then let's go.'

As they broke into a run, she held on to him with one hand, while clutching her headdress to her head with the other.

As they tore through the gates, she realised that it was all quiet. There was no music, no noise except the sound of their feet splashing in the puddles.

After everything that had happened today was she too late for her own wedding?

Thirty

Seb

Seb just hoped, more than anything, that Juliet was looking down on him right now. If she was, she'd be laughing her head off at him, jogging through the Botanic Gardens at night, illuminated only by thousands of fairy lights on the trees around them, a bride on his arm, his shoes soggy with rain.

They'd once got caught in a storm in Bali, and they'd run along the beach, laughing, arms thrown wide, as sheets of rain pummelled their T-shirts and shorts. Juliet had grabbed him and they'd danced along the sands, giggling as they did so. It was one of his favourite memories. And Seb had a feeling that – no matter how the question of his paternity was answered – this would be another moment that he'd love to relive until the end of time.

'There's no music. Oh God, they've all gone home,' Caro wailed and he could hear the panic in her voice, but he refused to believe they were too late. After everything that had happened today, every meeting, every conversation, every tear that had been shed, he had to keep thinking that it had all been for this purpose, to bring this gorgeous woman here tonight and to help her get her happy ever after.

With his free hand, he clenched his brown leather bag to his side.

Stay with us, Juliet, he said silently. He had to believe that she would.

They turned a corner and the Kibble Palace came into view, the structure glowing against the black December sky. Caro was right – there was no music.

Come on, Juliet, don't let us down.

They ran on: thirty metres, twenty metres, fifteen... a shadow in front of them suddenly became a figure walking along the path in their direction A tall man in a striking grey suit and long coat, a fedora on his head.

Caro spotted him too and stopped suddenly, the action almost pulling his shoulder out of its socket. 'Mr Naismith,' she gasped, out of breath.

The elderly man didn't hide his surprise. 'Well, Caro! This is a surprise. Cammy just told me that...' Seb could hear the Jamaican lilt in his voice, before he paused, glanced at Seb, obviously not wishing to be indiscreet.

'Mr Naismith, this is...'

Seb could see she was struggling to define him, so he stepped in. 'I'm Seb. I'm a friend of Caro's family.'

'Thanks Seb,' she said gratefully, before going on, 'Mr Naismith is the celebrant who is officiating at our wedding.' Introductions over, she addressed Mr Naismith again. 'Were you about to tell me that Cammy said the wedding was off?'

'I was, dear. And I must say, I was sorry to hear that. You're such a lovely couple. It would have been my pleasure to marry you.' He peered at Caro, as if his eyesight wasn't the best, and then his whole demeanour changed, presumably when he realised that she was wearing a wedding dress. 'Unless… was he mistaken, dear?'

'No!' Caro blurted. 'At least, not completely. I had… cold feet, but I've come to my senses. Am I too late? Has everyone gone home? I can't hear anything…'

Seb registered the increasing panic in her voice again and he held his breath, waiting for the old man's answer. When it came, Seb felt his spirits soar.

'Everyone's still in there. Cammy took me to one side to tell me and he said he was going to make an announcement shortly. I'm guessing that's why he turned off the music. Damn loud, so it was. All that modern stuff. Nothing wrong with a classical tune, if you ask me.'

There was still time. Seb watched the relief flood Caro's face and for the first time since he met her, her shoulders dropped down from a stressed position.

He decided to step in. 'Mr Naismith, I'm very sorry for the confusion. Would you be willing to come back in with us and conduct the ceremony after all?'

The elder man nodded immediately. 'Of course! Although, I might make a comment about your punctuality, dear,' he warned Caro, but there was a warmth there. Seb loved old blokes like this. Eccentric characters. He'd met loads of them on the golf course over the years and they were always entertaining.

'Then we would be very grateful if you would come with us,' Seb told him, before turning to Caro. 'Are you okay? Still ready to do this?'

'Absolutely! Let's go. Mr Naismith, we're going to run, so that I can try to stop Cammy before he tells the world what I've done. Is that okay?'

'Of course, dear. I'll catch up with you. A glass of red would help quench the thirst when I get there,' he teased.

'It'll be waiting for you,' Seb assured him, before taking Caro's hand again and sprinting the remaining distance into the building.

A waiter was just inside the door, topping up champagne glasses on a tray. He looked up at them with undisguised curiosity, but Seb didn't have time to explain.

'This way!' Caro steered him through the foyer. As they moved, they could hear the buzz of conversation getting louder. Suddenly, a man's voice cut through the noise.

'Excuse me everyone, can I have your attention please?'

'Shit, that's Cammy,' Caro groaned breathlessly.

As Seb and Caro reached the entrance to the reception area, the noise subsided. Seb immediately scoped the situation. In a landscape that looked like a stunning winter wonderland of whites, silvers and emerald greens were about forty people, all with their backs to them. Over to the right, he could see Pearl, tears streaming down her face, as she held her husband Bob's hand. It didn't take a genius to work out that they already knew there was a problem. In front of the guests, one man stood facing his audience, discomfort and sadness in every sinew of his face and body. He began to speak again...

'I'm so sorry to have kept you waiting,' he said. 'I guess you've noticed that Caro isn't here tonight...'

'Oh God, what am I going to do? I can't just run in there and—'

She didn't even finish the sentence. Something in Seb, an urge to help her, to fix this, to make it right, took over and he heard himself saying, 'Stay here, I'll be right back. Don't worry. Just stay out of sight for a minute.' As he nudged her backwards, Caro's chin dropped, but before she could object, Seb walked forward and cleared his throat loudly.

Cammy stopped talking and glanced up at him, as a few of the guests turned to see who had taken Cammy's attention.

'Cammy, sorry to interrupt, but can I have a quick word with you?' Seb raised his voice so he could be heard at the other end of the room.

Cammy's eyes narrowed in puzzlement and Seb could see that he was completely confused as to what was going on.

Come on, he willed him. *Just go with me here.*

'Sorry, you are...?' It was a question, but one that was rapidly answered by his very own, recently acquainted, guardian angel, a woman so sharp that as soon as she spotted Seb, she obviously sussed that he would only interrupt proceedings if he had something to bring to the party. Preferably a bride.

Josie immediately stepped forward. 'Seb! Great to see you,' she gushed, obviously trying to act like this was the most natural thing in the world in front of the assembled congregation. 'Cammy, love, this is my pal, Seb. He just needs a quick word. Come on then,' she beckoned. 'Don't take all day.' Her tone made it perfectly clear to Cammy and everyone else that resistance would be futile. 'Sorry about the interruption, folks. Jean...' she gestured to a group of women who were all gathered together in the corner, 'can you get the music back on and get Senga up to do Beyoncé. You'll no' need to ask her twice.'

Jean and Senga immediately sprang into action, much to the amusement of everyone else. Even Pearl had stopped crying and was now staring at Seb in shock, trying to suss out why he was there and what was going on. Bob handed her another glass of champagne.

A determined Josie and a bewildered Cammy were now heading towards him, and he backed out into the foyer, just as Mr Naismith, the celebrant, arrived and went past him into the room, heading for his position at the top of the aisle. Seb just prayed that they weren't being too optimistic. Would Cammy still want to go ahead with this after everything he'd been through today? It must have shaken him to the core and it would be understandable if his confidence in his relationship was rattled.

He knew the answer to that question as soon as Cammy reached him, then glanced over his shoulder and saw Caro. He took in her wide-eyed hope, her tentative smile and her wedding dress. Thankfully, his gaze didn't reach the boots. Not that it would have mattered. Seb could see from the relief, the surprise and the pure adoration on his face that he adored this woman.

Seb and Josie, meanwhile, met each other's eyes and she gave him a cheeky smile and a wink of approval.

'Caro, I thought...' Cammy began.

'I'm so sorry,' she cried at the same time. 'I was an idiot. I don't know what happened to me, I was just...' she stopped, and Seb could see that she was struggling to find the right words.

'It doesn't matter,' Cammy said, going to her, wrapping her in his arms, pulling her head against his shoulder. 'God, I love you. I just care that you're here now. Are you sure you want to do this?'

'Totally! Are you sure you still want to marry me?'

His smile was splitting his face. 'Never more.'

Seb felt Josie nudging him.

'You did good,' she murmured.

Cammy must have heard it because he broke off from his embrace and turned to Seb. 'I'm sorry, I don't know who you are, do I?'

Seb held out his hand in introduction. 'I'm Seb Lloyd. I was a friend of Caro's mum a long time ago. I thought I'd gatecrash the wedding. I hope you don't mind.'

'Mate, you brought her here. You could limbo down that aisle naked and I wouldn't mind.'

'I'd buy tickets for that,' Josie quipped, deadpan.

'There's so much more and I need to explain it, but can we get married first?' Caro begged.

'Yes!' Cammy exclaimed. 'I'll just go and let Mr Naismith know and check he's ready. Josie, can you sort out the music please? Senga is singing "All The Single Ladies". Oh dear God.'

With that he was off, Josie right behind him, leaving Seb staring at Caro, with what he knew was a daft, emotional grin on his face.

Caro took his hand. 'You know, I truly hope my mum and your wife are sitting up there together somewhere, with a big box of popcorn and a glass of champagne, watching this.'

That conjured up a wonderful image in his mind. 'I love that thought. They'll be passing the tissues between them. My Juliet always cries at weddings.'

'My mum did too,' she said, laughing, before her expression softened to something more serious. 'Can I ask you something?'

Seb nodded. 'Anything.' It was true. There was nothing, absolutely nothing that he wouldn't give her if he could.

Her beautiful green eyes, the exact same shade as her mother's, met his. 'I was just going to walk down the aisle on my own. How would you feel about giving me away?'

Cammy appeared back in the doorway. 'Eh, hate to hurry this up,' he teased, grinning. Seb could already see why Caro loved this guy. 'But could we get a move on? I'd like to marry my fiancée before she changes her mind again.'

The three of them were still laughing when the music began. Cammy darted ahead of them so he could be at the end of the aisle to greet his bride.

As Caro and Seb, arm in arm, took their first steps into the flower-decked room, neither of them noticed that, in the shadows behind them, there was a woman who had been listening to every word they'd said.

Thirty-One

Josie

The exertion of making her way back to her seat set Josie off on a coughing fit that was, thankfully, drowned out by the strains of Texas singing 'So In Love With You.' Cammy had told her that it had been their only choice of song, one that summed up exactly how they felt about each other.

Now, as Caro slowly glided up the aisle on Seb's arm, Josie could feel the words having a strange effect on her. There was moisture in her eyes, a lump in her throat… Jesus wept, she was getting sentimental. If this was another symptom of this bastard disease, she'd be raging. She sniffed and stood up straighter, pulling her shoulders back. She'd spent seven decades on this planet being tough and stoic and she wasn't going to bloody fall apart now.

Bugger, she was tired though. Bone-weary exhausted. In some ways, she was grateful for all the drama today, because it had taken her mind off this morning's news, and off the fact that she was so knackered that all she wanted to do was climb under a duvet. Not that she'd give in to that. No. The minute you stopped, that's when that bastard death got you – but at the same time, the thought of a long, lingering weakening of her body and mind made her shiver.

'Are you okay, Ma?' Michael, standing next to her, asked, slipping his arm around her shoulders and squeezing her, sharing both his body heat and his love. On the other side of her, Avril pressed her hand into her mother's. She'd got lucky with these two and she adored the very bones of them. They both had their own lives and no longer needed her – Michael in Italy with his wife, Mel and their children, and Avril in London – but at the same time, they knew she would walk through fire for them.

'I'm fine, son. Been a long day, that's all.'

If he thought she didn't spot the look that Michael gave his sister over the top of Josie's head, he would be wrong. She might have cancer, but it didn't affect her powers of observation. The concerned expression on his face made her stomach churn. This was what she had ahead of her. She had been ferociously independent her whole life, always the toughest person in every room, and now she was going to have to let other people take care of her, worry about her, talk about her like she wasn't there. The thought of that made her want to punch a wall. No. She wasn't doing it. She'd deal with this disease on her terms, no one else's.

Caro was at the front of the aisle now, and the music was fading out. Josie felt her heart melt as Cammy leaned over and kissed his bride, jumping the gun somewhat, but his happiness was irrepressible. The guests laughed at his obvious glee, unaware of the emotional turmoil that had led up to it today, then they all sat down, much to her relief. Her legs, like the rest of her, were exhausted.

'Ladies and gentlemen, bride and groom and Josie...' Mr Naismith began, causing the guests to laugh, as he explained, 'She says she's writing my cheque, so I had to give her a special mention.'

Cammy and Caro chuckled, as she knew they would. It was exactly the kind of icebreaker she'd wanted, perfect for setting the tone that the happy couple had hoped for. Informal. Relaxed. Funny. Intimate. The epitome of both their personalities. Or at least, it usually was – Caro had definitely given them all a fright today, poor lass.

'We're all here today to celebrate the wedding of Cammy and Caro. Now, for those of you who don't know, I'm a humanist celebrant, and I've been asked by Cammy and Caro to celebrate their wedding in a way that they felt best illustrated their love for each other.'

Josie watched Mr Naismith take a plaid scarf from his pocket.

'Caro, Cammy, if you could both put one hand out in front of you...'

They did as they were beckoned. The celebrant then placed Caro's hand, palm down, on top of Cammy's and tied the scarf around them.

'This is an old tradition known as handfasting. By tying your hands together, it signifies your connection and the love that you have for each other.'

'Bondage,' Avril whispered in her mother's ear. 'That malarkey is one step away from a safe word.'

The giggle rose from Josie's gut and caught in her throat, causing yet another coughing fit. She kicked Avril's ankle in punishment. That bloody lassie had been coming out with outrageous things since she told her nursery teacher that her roots needed doing. God, she made her laugh though.

And Michael, well, he impressed her every day of his life. A sudden thought - how would they react to her dying?

She stopped, unable to even contemplate that word. She rephrased it in her mind. How would they react to her no longer being here? She let the thought ruminate for a little while, the answer forming as she did so. She honestly believed that the two of them would be okay. They were strong, and much as she knew they loved her, they had other priorities now. Michael had his children to worry about. Her granddaughters from his first marriage, Abrielle and Josefina were teenagers now, and with his second wife, Mel, he had little Harrison and another one on the way. Michael had already shown that he was an incredible dad – hands on and interested, loving all those kids more than life. Avril, on the other hand, had never wanted children, and that was fine too. She was living with Eric, an actor who felt the same way, and Josie loved their life balance of career, adventure, travel and a huge friendship group. They worked hard and partied hard. Not a bad way to live their lives. Josie respected the fact that she lived life on her own terms. Hadn't Josie done the same? After the kids' father had bailed out when they were still in primary school, she'd decided that she'd never live with another man. Instead she'd had many relationships over the years, keeping them for as long as they made her happy. Nothing serious, no commitment, just fun while it lasted. It had suited her perfectly.

Her eyes drifted to the person who would face the biggest hole when she was gone. In the front row sat Val, her husband Don, and Jen and Chrissie, the two worst bridesmaids ever. She and Val spoke several times every day, and met up most days too. They were a dynamic duo, co-conspirators and partners in crime. They'd been inseparable for over a decade, and they'd faced some tough things in life – the hardest being the death of Val's daughter, Dee, who was mown down in the street by a drugged-up driver. Even now, Val still found it difficult to talk about, but they'd got through it by filling their lives with waifs, strays and people who needed them – and by God, they knew how to laugh.

What would Val do now? Sure, she had her husband, Don, but lovely as he was, he was the strong, silent type, who liked a quiet life – the opposite of Josie and Val. Her death… *Leaving,* she corrected herself, would leave a huge gap in Val's life and that thought devastated her, almost as much as the knowledge that there was absolutely nothing she could do about it, except try to prepare her friend over the next few months. What she'd give to be able to turn back the clock, to live this lifetime again. For all its ups and downs, most of it had been absolutely bloody brilliant. Given her time again, she wouldn't change a thing – except the ending.

At the front of the room, Mr Naismith went on to talk about Cammy and Caro and how their relationship had grown, and their hopes and dreams for the future.

The future. She felt a pang of pain as she realised that she'd probably never see their children, or their next home, or even celebrate their first anniversary with them. She wouldn't see them grow older together. Maybe it was the heat in the room, but she'd suddenly gone from shivering, to feeling woozy.

Every single person she loved was here… and the next time they congregated it would probably be at her funeral. If she hadn't already been sitting down, that thought would have been enough to make her fall to the floor.

There was a comfort though, in knowing that Cammy and Caro were sorted, that they'd made it this far and they had each other now. Although, she suspected that the same couldn't be said for Stacey. She scanned the room, searching for the woman whom she'd loved since she was a little girl. She had a good heart, Stacey did, and Josie was pretty sure it had been broken today. All she could do was make sure that she spoke to her tomorrow and then checked in on her regularly… Although, where was she? Had this all been too much for her? It couldn't have been easy to watch the man she loved marry someone else. Senga would help her through it, though. If anyone knew heartbreak, it was Senga. She'd lost two husbands, and she was still standing. That took a special kind of strength.

'Caro…' Cammy was saying now, as he gazed into his bride's eyes. 'I have loved you since the first day I met you. You're my heart, my soul and my best friend. I can't wait to see what life brings us, and no matter what it is, all I care about is that I'll be by your side.'

Aw, for feck's sake. This was going to end her, it really was. They hadn't shared their vows with her in the run-up to the ceremony, because they both said they were going to wing it on the day. Even if Cammy Jones had spent a month preparing them, he couldn't have said anything more perfect. She sniffed again, causing another glance of note to travel between Michael and Avril.

'Cammy, from the first night I met you, I knew you were everything. You've shown me a kind of happiness that I never knew existed and I can't wait to go through this life beside you, because that's the only place I'll ever want to be.'

Only the very churlish would point out that she wasn't feeling that way this morning when she did a runner. Josie made a mental note to tease her about that later. Churlish had always been her specialty.

They were repeating all the 'honour and cherish, in sickness and health' stuff now, both of them grinning from ear to ear. Almost done. Then the buffet would come out and they could all go and eat, drink and dance until midnight, and then she could go to bed, knowing that her job was done. She'd somehow, despite curve balls no one could have anticipated, managed to pull off this wonderful celebration of Cammy and Caro's love.

'I always dread this bit,' Mr Naismith was joking now. 'So I'll say it quickly and get it out of the way.' He cleared his throat and then spoke like a vinyl record that had been speeded up a notch. 'If anyone knows of any reason why these two people should not be joined in marriage, please speak now or forever hold your peace.' There was a moment's hesitation, before his face broke into a smile, and he began, 'Excellent. Therefore—'

It was the screeching of a chair moving along the floor that Josie heard first. Then the rustling of a person moving, of clothes rearranging as the wearer went from sitting to standing. Then the voice, weak at first, gaining strength as it went on.

'I do,' it said. 'Cammy shouldn't be marrying her, it should be me.'

Thirty-Two

Stacey

The bride had turned up. The minute that guy had interrupted Cammy's announcement, Stacey's heart had seized, because she'd just known what was about to happen. Sure enough, the music started and the next thing, Cammy was back in position and Caro was waltzing up the aisle, and the two of them were grinning at each other, all that drama over the bride's no-show suddenly washed away and Stacey's hopes of being with him drowned in the wake.

Stacey had thought about slipping out but had decided to see it through. She'd sat next to Jared and Todd, directly behind Josie (a deliberate choice so that she'd be out of Josie's inquisitive eyeline) and across the aisle from her mum, who kept glancing in her direction, with an expression that Stacey knew was somewhere between concern, sympathy and fear that Stacey would make a show of herself.

Stacey kept her eyes front and centre, resigned to enduring the pain of every word. Her mother and Josie would be furious if she sneaked out, and if she left, Cammy might guess what had been right there in front of him all day – she was in love with him. He was just too dazzled by Caro to see it.

Caro. It was impossible to dislike her. She was beautiful, in a natural, understated way, and if her dress was anything to go by, she didn't need drama and glitz. Although, the footwear was an interesting choice.

The buzz of her phone cut through her thoughts, and for a second she thought about surreptitiously fishing in her bag for the device and checking out who was contacting her. In the end, she decided against it. It was probably Jax, and he would just be doling out more pleas for her to contact him. She was dreading their next conversation, with his inevitable demands for explanations, so she was up for avoiding it for as long as possible.

Cammy was saying his vows now, and Stacey closed her eyes, imagining he was saying them to her. 'In sickness and in health, until death do us part.'

She'd have taken that deal. Still would.

She zoned back into what was happening at the front of the room as the celebrant continued to speak. 'If anyone knows of any reason why these two people should not be joined in marriage, please speak now or forever hold your peace.'

Stacey closed her eyes, heart thudding, objections firing around her mind, screaming to be heard.

Suddenly another voice rang out loud and clear. 'I do,' it was saying. 'Cammy shouldn't be marrying her, it should be me.'

Stacey snapped her head up so fast she almost gave herself whiplash, her stomach clenching in fear. Had she said that out loud? Had she? Oh, holy fuck, her mum would kill her. But, hang on, nobody was looking at her. Even Josie, sitting in the seat directly in front of her, was now swivelling her head from side to side like a submarine periscope searching for a lethal enemy. If it were Stacey who'd blurted out the objection, Josie would have instantly whipped round and given her the stare of doom, undoubtedly followed by some kind of threat involving a staple gun and a gag.

No, she wasn't the culprit here.

Her eyes went to Cammy's face, and she saw that both the bride and groom had turned to look back down the aisle, in the direction of the entrance, and they were locked in a stare-out with a woman that Stacey recognised from photos that were taken a long time ago.

Cammy's photos. The ones that used to be plastered all over his Instagram account, about six months after he returned from LA. In fact, Stacey had followed this person on Instagram too, and tortured herself by looking at the endless daily snaps of her with Cammy, first thing in the morning, last thing at night, all glammed up and out partying, dressed in a power suit at work, walking the dog, putting on her make-up, blowing kisses to her followers. She was one of the most prolific social media users that Stacey had ever known, portraying a perfect, glamorous, gifted life... right up until it was no longer perfect.

This was...

Stacey looked at Caro for confirmation and saw recognition etched on the bride's expression as she stared at the interloper.

This was Lila. Caro's sister. Half-sister actually. Cammy's ex-girlfriend, the one who'd cheated on him and then dumped him and run off with a football player from the French national team on the night that Cammy and Caro met.

Stacey could see why Lila had managed to bag a high-profile famous face. The woman was truly stunning. Not in the same understated way as Caro, but in a sexy, vampy, pouty, I-know-I'm-gorgeous style that oozed confidence and entitlement.

Stacey racked her brain for some kind of explanation as to what was going on here. In all the calls and emails she'd shared with Cammy over the last couple of years, she couldn't remember him mentioning Lila at all since he'd met Caro, other than to say that Lila and Caro shared a dad but couldn't be more different. That aside, he'd completely moved on.

Obviously, Lila hadn't moved on quite so quickly.

You could hear a pin drop in the room, every single person now wide-eyed and stunned as they watched the drama unfold.

'Lila, what are you doing here?' Caro asked, and Stacey had to give her credit – there was no malice or fury there, just a calm, reasoned question.

'You know what I'm doing here,' Lila bit back. 'He only went with you because he thought I was no longer interested, but he was wrong.'

Cammy was having none of it. 'Lila, that's not why I'm with Caro. Look, please, you've made your point... there's nothing else to say, other than it's you who's got all this wrong. I want to be with Caro.'

'You know that's not true,' she fired at him.

Oh, bollocks, this wasn't going to end well. Stacey wasn't sure if she felt sorry for Lila or not. On the one hand, she could understand those feelings and the loss that Lila must be carrying inside now that she'd realised she'd made a mistake in letting Cammy go. It was like looking in a mirror. But, on the other hand… she'd had the strength and the decency not to storm his bloody wedding and humiliate herself by fighting for his love. Lila, it would seem, had no such restraint.

In the seat in front of Stacey, Josie was getting to her feet now, obviously deciding that as chief wedding planner, this was another glitch to be ironed out. But she hadn't even reached a standing position, when Stacey shot up. There was no way she was letting Aunt Josie deal with this and equally no way she would allow this idiot to ruin Cammy's wedding. If Stacey couldn't have him, there was no bloody way that Lila was swooping in. Not that either of them stood a chance over the beautiful bride standing at the end of the aisle holding her soon-to-be-husband's hand.

Stacey climbed over Jared, then Todd, both of them transfixed by the drama, and reached Lila in just a few seconds.

'Lila, can I have a word outside?' she asked, taking her lead from Caro's calm handling of the situation.

Lila stared into her face with completely undisguised contempt. 'Why?' she spat, peering at Stacey's face. A flicker of recognition clearly registered, because she went on, 'You're Stacey! I remember you.'

Stacey nodded, trying to stay neutral and keep the situation under control. When Cammy and Lila had been together, she'd chatted to her a few times when she was on FaceTime to Cammy. Stacey had always found her distant and offhand, but she'd assumed something was just getting lost in cyberspace. Now she could see that it was because Lila was a whole bag of self-centred narcissism.

'I remember you too,' Stacey said, still calm, feeling the eyes of everyone in the room burning into her back.

'Stace, are you okay?' Cammy shouted.

Stacey didn't even turn around, just raised her hand in confirmation. 'Yep, I've got this. Just talk among yourselves.'

Lila was looking her up and down now. 'You know, I used to worry that he had a thing for you, but I guess not. He obviously prefers plain.'

'Okay, that's it. Come on,' Stacey challenged her, before grabbing her hand, spinning her around and marching her right out of the wedding area.

As they went, she saw Lila reach over and grab a mobile phone that had been sitting on a tall plinth just behind them. As Lila picked it up, Stacey could see that the screen was illuminated. What the hell was going on here?

Out in the foyer, Stacey closed the door behind them, so that it was just her and Lila in the room.

Suddenly, it opened again, and Josie popped her head out.

'You all right, Stacey?'

'I am, Aunt Josie. Don't worry. Go back in and tell them to carry on.'

Josie switched her gaze to the other woman. 'You know, Lila, I never did like you and tonight you just showed everyone why. Caro is so much more than you'll ever be.'

Lila's face cracked into a slow, calculating grin of malice. 'Yeah, I never liked you much either.'

'I'd be offended if you did,' Josie retorted with pitch-perfect superiority and Stacey was reminded – not that she needed to be – of just what a class act Josie was and had always been.

Another head appeared in the doorway now, and Stacey reacted to that one too. 'It's okay, Ma – everything's fine.'

'Need some back-up there, darling?' Senga asked.

'Nope, I've got this.' Stacey assured her. 'Carry on with the wedding. I'll come back in once I've put the trash out.'

Senga and Josie were still grinning when the door closed behind them. 'She'll be fine,' she heard her mum tell Josie. 'Ten bloody years I took her to those Taekwondo classes.'

Stacey zeroed back in on Lila. She expected the other woman to be hysterical, frantic, emotional, crying, but she was none of those things. Instead, she was now tapping the screen on her mobile phone, completely disconnected from Stacey's presence.

And that's when it dawned.

Stacey grabbed the phone and, for the first time, Lila looked panicked.

'You are fricking unbelievable,' Stacey yelled, as she stared at the screen and saw a frozen image of herself, reaching over to grab the phone just a second ago. That must have been the point that Lila pressed 'stop'. 'You were recording all of this?' Stacey exclaimed, hearing a clinking sound in her head as more nuggets of realisation dropped in. 'Holy shit, this wasn't about Cammy at all. This was some kind of messed up publicity stunt?'

Lila had the cheek, the absolute audacity, to look pleased with herself as she snatched her phone back. It took every single ounce of restraint and discipline Stacey possessed not to slap her.

Lila went on the offensive. 'Don't you fucking dare judge me. Have you any idea what I've been through? I was humiliated, dumped, completely ruined by that cheating fucking footballer. I became a laughing stock. All those "likes", all the attention, it all turned to shit. Do you know what it's like to have all those people turn on you, make fun of you?'

Stacey remembered seeing news of it at the time. It had caused a bit of an internet sensation – the gorgeous blonde who'd run off with Jean Pascal, the captain of the French national squad, star striker for Paris St Germain, Gallic equivalent of David Beckham, only to be dumped by him a month later when he took off with a Victoria's Secret Angel with forty-four inch legs. Stacey remembered details like that. 'So you do this? I don't get it.'

Lila shrugged. 'For two years I've been nobody. Tonight, I'm everywhere...' she checked her phone. 'Over ten thousand people were watching that live. It helps that I'd been teasing it all day, putting my plans on loads of forums, whipping up some interest and hype. And when it gets retweeted and shared it'll go viral.'

'So you'd rather be famous for being a tit than be nobody?' Stacey asked. In LA, she'd known so many young women – and men – like this. They'd do anything for exposure, whether it was immoral, illegal or just plain embarrassing. To them, all that mattered was the attention, the profile, the controversy. Their egos fed off it, and it became like the oxygen they needed to survive. The sad thing was, that in this time of inane worship for the zero-talented, there were people who got the reality shows, the fame and the adulation they craved. Lila couldn't care less about Cammy. All she wanted was the fame.

And ten thousand viewers was a pretty solid start.

'You really are a sad cow, you realise that, don't you?'

Lila shrugged, a self-satisfied grin on her face. The device in her hand was beeping like a Morse Code signal now. 'Yep, but one whose phone is ringing off the hook.'

Stacey gestured to the door. 'Well, you'd better piss off and answer your public.'

With a toss of her hair extensions, Lila strutted towards the exit, her Louboutins carrying her to a whole new life of notoriety. What. A. Horror.

Stacey felt a vibration against her body and wondered if she was having a heart attack, but no. It was coming from the bag that had been clenched under her arm the whole time. Sighing, she decided to check it. May as well see what Jax had to say to her and get it over with.

Still buzzing. More buzzing. Damn, he must be on a total rant now. Finally locating the phone, she pulled it out and glanced at the screen, taking a moment to understand what she saw there. Yes, there were a couple of notifications of messages from Jax over the last hour or so, but that wasn't what was causing the frenzy of activity now.

Beep. Beep. Beep. The notifications from Twitter and Instagram were firing up on the screen at one second intervals. Stacey clicked on her Twitter app and saw the explanation right there. A video clip, the still image showing that it had obviously been taken from Lila's live recording, had been retweeted by someone who had tagged her in it and now it had... Holy crap, 4408 likes, 4410, 4422...

The number was increasing faster than she could read it. The comments and the shares were growing too. What the hell…?

Heart pounding, she clicked on the video.

There she was, standing with one hand on her hip, clutch bag under the other arm, her body language screaming defiance and strength as she said to some unseen person in the background. 'Nope, I've got this. Carry on with the wedding. I'll come back in once I've put the trash out.'

More tweets. More comments. Every one of them with the hashtag #putthetrashout.

The phone buzzed again, an incoming call this time. Jax. It was time to stop putting this off. She pressed accept and put the phone to her ear.

'Hi.'

There was a very slight delay as the international phone line connected, before she heard Jax's voice, urgent, hyper, gushing. 'Stacey, I'm sorry, babe.'

Damn. Something was clearly wrong. What had happened now? As she listened, she walked through the foyer area to the exit and stood in the doorway, embracing the blast of cold air that assaulted her.

'It wasn't what it looked like. I've got no idea who she is. I'd never met her before. She's nobody.' The words came out in a tumbled rush that Stacey struggled to understand.

'Who's nobody?'

'That chick, babe. It was a set-up.'

Two things registered. One, he was sounding very like a man who had messed up and was desperately trying to cover it up. And two, Jax was way too experienced and media-savvy to get caught in a set-up. If he'd done something wrong, it was through choice or bad judgement.

Stacey felt every synapse of her brain shutting down. She had no time for this. None. She'd had enough drama today to last a lifetime and, right now, she had no appetite for any more. She pressed the red button to end the call. Whatever it was, she'd deal with it. But right now she had her best friend's wedding to attend.

10 P.M. – MIDNIGHT

Thirty-Three

Caro

'I love you, Cammy Jones,' Caro whispered, as they slow-danced, despite the fact that the ceilidh hour had given way to pop classics, and Robbie William's 'Let Me Entertain You' was blaring from the speakers. When Josie had sent out the invitations, she'd asked every guest to RSVP with their two favourite songs, and she'd made up the playlist for this section of the night from their suggestions. The result was crazily eclectic and brilliantly entertaining, because every time a song came on, someone shouted 'That's mine!' and dragged everyone around them up to the area that had been commandeered for dancing. Caro had no idea who'd chosen Mr Williams, but her money was on Val – she'd almost got arrested for trying to bluff her way into Take That's hotel back in the day.

'Are you sure?' Cammy joked, a cheeky twinkle in his eye. 'Because, you know, if you change your mind again, the lawyers' fees are going to be expensive.'

He was amazing, this man. She'd absolutely devastated him today, put him through a wringer of pain and confusion, and yet, here he was, forgiving her, joking with her, just glad they'd made it in the end. All he cared about was how much they loved each other – and even in her darkest moments over the last few days, she'd never doubted how she felt about him.

'Well, not really,' she teased. 'You do come with a lot of baggage. That ex-girlfriend of yours is something else.' It was going to take time to process Lila's stunt – the poor cow – but that was for another day. She wasn't going to let it pour even a sliver of shade on their day. Right now, Cammy's laughter was contagious and her cheeks were beginning to hurt. Lila wasn't taking that away from them.

'Come here, I want to kiss your face off,' Cammy said, leading her over to a quiet corner at the side of the dance floor, where he proceeded to do as he'd promised. This was everything. Nothing could spoil this moment.

Except... Josie swanned by, rolling her eyes as she spotted them. 'Urgh, you get one day, ONE DAY for all that public displays of affection nonsense. If I see you two doing that tomorrow, I'm going to batter you with my handbag.'

'You should come with a health warning,' Cammy told her. 'May explode when placed near instances of high-grade sentimentality.'

'Urgh, I'd ban it all.' Josie shivered, but Caro knew she didn't mean a word of it. On the outside, Josie was hard as nails, but on the inside? Pure mush.

'Josie, we can't thank you enough for everything you did to organise today. It's been amazing.'

Josie pursed her lips in faux despair. 'Aye, every wedding needs a vanishing bride, a long-lost father and a psycho ex-girlfriend trying to hijack the ceremony.'

Caro had briefly filled a shocked Cammy in on the possibility that Seb was her dad. He'd been delighted for her. That's the kind of man he was – one who rolled with the punches. That's why she wasn't surprised that he was taking a pragmatic approach to Josie's recap of the events so far. 'Well, it certainly won't be one that anyone forgets in a hurry. I'd rather be memorable than easily forgotten.'

'That's the story of my life, son,' Josie replied. 'The story of my life.'

Caro thought she saw a tinge of uncharacteristic emotion in her friend as she said that and felt a wave of self-reproach. Had they given Josie too much stress? Too much to deal with? Not just in the run-up to the wedding, but today, when everything seemed like it could fall apart? It was so easy to forget Josie had strutted into her seventies, but actually, as Caro watched her darling friend, Josie looked more tired than she'd ever seen her.

As if she could read her mind, Josie put her hand on Caro's. 'If we're doing all that PDA shite, then I'm going to get one in too. Thank you for letting me be a part of this wedding today. I loved every minute of putting it together, and you've no idea how much all of it, even the drama, has kept me going. I'm the happiest woman alive to see you both like this. You're two of my favourite people in the world and I'm so happy you found each other. I love you both.' She paused, as if it was too hard for her to continue, and Caro instinctively reached over and hugged her tight. To her surprise, she thought she heard Josie sniff. Just as she was about to ask her if she was okay, Josie shrugged her off with a wry grin. 'However, if you tell anyone that I came out with all this mushy stuff, I'll hunt you down. Do we understand each other?'

Caro's aching cheeks got another workout. 'Indeed we do. We love you, Josie, you know that, don't you?'

Josie rolled her eyes. 'Aye, all right, pet, you're going too far now, I need a drink.' And with that, and a loud, husky cackle of a laugh, she danced off, hands in the air, towards Val, who was swinging her hips on the dance floor.

'If I ever leave you, it'll be for her,' Cammy said, watching her go.

'Same goes for me, to be honest,' Caro shot back. 'Anyway, where were we? I think you were declaring undying love for me. Or were we talking about my delightful sister?'

'You know, Stacey said Lila recorded the whole thing. It wasn't an attempt to get me back because she wants to be with me, it was a publicity stunt to get attention.'

'Seriously?' Caro found it impossible to take this in. 'You know, I always thought that Lila had it better than me. I mean, my dad pretty much ignored me all of my life, and yet, Lila was always gushing about him on social media, saying how much he loved her. I'm starting to wonder if that's actually true. She seems so messed up, so desperate for some kind of validation. I spoke to her earlier today and she looked terrible. Nothing at all like she did tonight. She said she'd lost her job, that she was back living with her mum and dad, and that basically the world had turned its back on her. That must have been so tough to deal with.'

'I think you're being too kind to her.'

'Maybe,' Caro shrugged. 'But I think at some point soon I should try to talk to her…' She caught sight of Seb and watched as he made a beeline for Josie. 'Whether she's actually my half-sister or not. Maybe she just needs a friend. I mean, look what we've got here. I love every single person in this room and they love us too. I don't think Lila has that. She doesn't seem to have anyone at all…'

'Because if she did, they'd be telling her to get a grip and stop acting like a self-obsessed maniac?' Cammy interjected, his face a picture of innocence.

Caro pushed him, laughing. 'Not exactly the point I was making.'

'I know. And I get what you're saying, but when I knew Lila, she wasn't interested in friends. Or in anyone but herself. It just took me a while to see that.'

Once again, Caro thought how difficult it was to believe that Cammy and Lila had been a couple. They were such opposites in every way. He once admitted that he'd got caught up in the glamour and excitement of Lila's life, and that he'd been at a point when he'd just returned from LA and didn't really know where he belonged. Caro figured it was just a collision of two people who saw something in each other that they needed at the time. She was just grateful that Lila had sabotaged it in time for Cammy to come to his senses.

The music changed and the opening bars of Tina Turner's 'Proud Mary' blared from the speakers, causing a roar of appreciation from the dance floor.

'That's mine!' Josie cried, before a coughing fit made her cling on to Val for a minute. Caro made a mental note to get her one of those books on stopping smoking for Christmas. She'd also buy herself body armour for the inevitable moment when Josie realised what it was and hit her with it. On the dance floor, she'd made a recovery, and now she was sashaying towards Cammy, arms outstretched. 'Come on, son, you know it's our favourite! Try and keep up.'

They both knew that resistance was futile, so Cammy allowed himself to be dragged on to the dance floor and thrust into the middle of Josie's pals, all of them whooping and cheering at his moves.

Caro felt the surge of joy start at her toes and explode in her chest. What had she been thinking this morning? It was simply impossible to love anyone more than she loved Cammy Jones. Her husband.

Happy, joyful, bursting with gratitude, she nipped out to the loo, then, on the way back, took a detour to the main door. She just needed to see the stars for a moment.

Eyes heavenwards, she smiled. 'Thanks, Mum,' she whispered. 'I've no idea how you did it, but that was a master stroke today. I need you to know that I'm happy. So, so happy, Mum. In fact, the only thing missing from my life is you. But I hope I'm making you proud. I've found a good man and he loves me back. Oh, and I met Seb today. Did you know how he felt about you? I don't even want to think what would have happened if you'd chosen him back then and I'd grown up with him as my dad. Hopefully it's not too late for us to make that right. I love you, Mum. I hope you're smiling up there.'

A sense of peace descended as she turned and headed back down the glass corridor towards the room containing her whole world. She was almost there when Seb came out of the door, meeting her in the hallway.

'You know, you've got some pretty special friends in there,' he said. 'But I think I've pulled several muscles and Proud Mary may have done my back in.'

Caro giggled. 'Yep, I saw Josie and Val throwing you around the dance floor. And was that Senga you were doing the Macarena with? She's got muscles like a race horse.'

He laughed, but then it turned to something more solemn. 'I explained everything to your Aunt Pearl too and she was surprised but lovely – says she'd be over the moon if it works out for us. Today has been quite a day,' he said. 'I would never have believed it would turn out this way.'

'Me neither. I was just outside having a chat to my mum and I told her how great it was.'

He acted like this was a perfectly normal and rational comment. 'I hope you told her I send my love.'

'I did. I think she's glad you're here,' Caro replied, grinning, before noticing something she'd wondered about. 'Can I ask you something?'

'Anything.'

'Your bag,' she gestured to the brown leather bag over his shoulder. 'It hasn't left your side all day, even when you were dancing,' she said. 'You know no one's going to steal it, right?'

Seb sighed, and she could see his forehead crease into a frown of worry. 'I don't know how to say this without sounding like the kind of complete weirdo that you'll definitely want to have removed from your wedding.'

Caro's whole body deflated. 'Och, bugger. My existing dad is a sociopathic, rude, lying, cheating dick, and now his possible replacement is carrying… what? Drugs? Guns? Please tell me it's a stamp collection and nothing illegal.'

Seb leaned against the iron window frame behind him. 'Please don't be freaked out.'

'Porn? PLEASE DO NOT LET THERE BE PORN AT MY WEDDING.'

'No, no! It's...' he paused. 'Okay, please understand, I just flew here this morning, and also understand that I haven't had a chance to go back to the hotel and check into my room. The day has kind of got away from me – in the best possible way, of course.'

Caro processed what he was saying, her mind flashing back to earlier, to his conversation about coming here to keep his promise to Juliet. Juliet. Juliet. The word went round in circles in her head until...

'Oh, my goodness. It's... *Juliet's ashes*?'

Thirty-Four

Seb

Seb cursed himself for his stupidity. He immediately put his hands up. 'I'm so sorry. It wasn't deliberate and I'd never have brought her to your wedding, but it just… happened. I've had her with me all day, on some kind of pilgrimage, I guess. I wanted to revisit all the places she loved, and then scatter her ashes somewhere with meaning. I just didn't find the right moment, and then you came along and… I know it sounds so weird. Are you totally horrified? I wouldn't blame you at all.'

Shit! For the first time in months, he'd had a glimmer of happiness today, a shred of hope that there could be something in his future other than regret and loss, and now he'd messed it up. He should have made some excuse and gone to the hotel to put his bag in the room, but there had just never seemed like the right time and now he'd upset this lovely young woman on the day of her w—

'No,' Caro said, calmly. And she wasn't backing away with a look of fear on her face, so he took that as a good sign. 'In fact, I think it's really sweet and beautiful. In a weird kind of way, obviously.'

'Obviously,' he agreed.

'And I get it, to be honest. I scattered my mum's ashes on a beach that I knew she loved. It gave me comfort to know that she'd been so happy there. Have you found the right place yet?'

He decided to be completely honest. 'Okay, if the ashes in my bag didn't freak you out, this one might.'

'I'm ready,' she said, and he appreciated her calm pragmatism. He'd had real feelings for her mum, but Yvonne was flighty, a bit bohemian almost. Caro had a quiet, down to earth strength that he found completely enchanting.

'All day I've been thinking that I'd know when the time was right, and now I feel it is. I think I'd like to scatter them here, in the gardens. We never came to Glasgow without coming here because she adored it. We spent so many afternoons lying on a blanket on the grass, just reading, talking...' He could feel the tears starting to pool on his lower eyelids and he blinked them back. 'It was special to her, to us both. And no matter whether I'm your dad or not, it also has even more meaning because I met you here and because this has been – without question – one of the most special nights of my life. The fact that you got married here today... well, Juliet would have loved that. Maybe this, whether we're related or not, is a connection between us.'

He stopped speaking, partly because the emotion was squeezing the life out of him and partly because he was scared that he'd pushed too far. There should be a process to this relationship. They'd met, now they should establish if they actually were related, and then they could gradually work on getting to know each other and building a friendship. He and Caro seemed to have jumped several steps, and now he was asking her to take a leap of faith that would seem crazy to most people. He was about to backpedal, to come up with another plan, when she spoke.

'I think that's a beautiful idea. You know, if you loved Juliet like this in life, then she was a very lucky woman. I hope I'm your daughter, I really do. But if I'm not, then please know that I think you're really special and I'd still like to get to know you.'

Waves and waves of gratitude almost floored him. For the last six months, he'd felt completely alone, his loneliness a gnawing ache that no painkiller, not even the one that came at the bottom of a bottle, could cure.

Before he could tell her that, the doors to the wedding area slammed open behind him and out came a conga line led by Caro's friend Val, with Josie bringing up the rear. There were party blowers, streamers, and brilliantly out-of-tune voices singing at the top of their lungs as it passed them. Val grabbed Caro and tucked her in behind her. Seb stepped back just in time to avoid the same fate, laughing as they passed him and trailed off down the corridor. He had no idea where they would end up, but they'd have a great time getting there.

'Jesus, if I wasn't already dying, that lot would kill me,' Josie barked, and only then did he see that she'd left the line and was standing a couple of metres away, hands on knees, her words punctuated with a cough that made him wince.

'Can I get you anything? Water? Wine?'

That made her laugh. 'Nah, I'm fine. But this trying to act normal is exhausting stuff.'

'I know all about that,' he said, 'and you're right. Look, there's a seat over there, fancy a breather?'

'An iron lung and a big shot of drugs would be my preferred choice, but if it's all you're offering...' She took his hand and let him lead her over to a bench halfway down the glass corridor.

'How are you doing?' he asked, 'and don't be trying to fob me off with some glib answer.'

'Nothing involving meaningless sex during my career as a groupie in the seventies then?'

A gale of laughter overtook his attempts to be serious. 'No, but those are definitely stories we can revisit in the future.'

She grinned but didn't speak for a moment, too busy prising off her boots and giving her feet a rub. 'My poor feet are killing me,' she groaned. 'I really hope the afterlife has sussed out comfortable shoes that still make the calves look good.'

'I'm pretty sure it's top of their list,' he assured her. Okay, so she wanted to keep this light and away from the serious stuff they were talking about earlier. That was completely understandable. He just wanted to let her know that he was around if she needed to vent. Not that he knew her well, but he could already sense that Josie wasn't someone who leaned on others for support. They'd already discovered that sometimes it was easier to lay out your worries on a stranger and he was happily volunteering for the job.

'Been some day for both of us, eh?' she said. 'Well done on getting Caro here. How did she take the news?'

'Better than I could ever have imagined. What about you? Managed to talk to anyone?'

He knew that he didn't have to explain what he was referring to and he wasn't surprised when she shook her head.

'You know, I've had the best night,' she said, with a sigh that had hints of both joy and sadness. 'At five o'clock today, I was bone-weary, exhausted to my very core. Then tonight, I come here, and I feel rougher than a badger's arse. But then something happens when I'm around the people in there. Every single one of them means something to me."

He let her talk, worried that if he even made a sound, she'd clam up and be back to that stoic woman he'd watched all night.

'Before I knew it, my energy was back and my fecked-up lungs were cutting me enough slack to enjoy myself. That's what life is to me. Those people. And I've had them for all these years. I think I'm luckier than anyone else I know.' It was almost like she was talking to herself now. 'So I've decided I don't want any fuss and drama and I'm not going to drag this out. And I'm telling you this on the agreement that if you repeat a word of it, I'll shoot you.'

'Understood,' he said.

'I'm going to refuse treatment. It was my first instinct this morning and I still feel the same way. The doctors said it would buy me a few more months at best, but what would they be like? All sympathetic looks and everyone tiptoeing around me. I couldn't bloody stand it. So I won't. And I'm not going to tell anyone until I absolutely have to either. My life is amazing, and I want to keep it just the way it is for a while longer. I'll tell them eventually, but only when I'm ready. Or maybe I'll get away with not telling them at all. Jesus, I could still get run over by a bus tomorrow. What's the point of us all living in fear and worry when we can be completely bloody oblivious?'

She had a point. There was no silver lining to Juliet's death at all. Every single thing about it had been horrific, but it had been instant, she hadn't suffered and he hadn't had to watch her in pain. Standing by while someone you love was in agony had to be the most painful thing anyone could go through. He understood that she didn't want the people in her life to endure that.

'I'm in no position to give anyone advice,' he said. 'I still look at my life and wonder how it went so wrong. The only thing I would say, though, is make sure your secrets don't isolate you. If they do, if you're staying away from people because you don't want them to see you at your most vulnerable, then you're doing them – and you – a disservice. You need them, and they'll want to help you.'

She took that on board and he could see she was thinking about it.

'I understand what you're saying, and I'll be careful not to do that, but until the time comes that there's no choice but to tell them, I'm going to keep this to myself and enjoy my life exactly as it is. I had a thought today that I might not see some of the people here again. That was a punch to the soul, that was. So my mission over the next wee while is to make sure that everyone in my life knows exactly how I feel about them, because that way when the worst happens...' Her words tailed off, but it didn't matter. She didn't have to say them. He'd known Josie for no more than a few hours – hell, he didn't even know her surname – but there were very few people he'd admired more.

The sounds of feet, of singing, of hooters and laughter went from being a distant rumble to an ever-increasing warning of a party approaching.

'Aw bugger, I was just getting the feeling back in my feet,' she groaned, with a twinkle in her eye, leaning down to pull her boots back on.

She'd just succeeded when the conga line reached them, and Stacey's mum, Senga, reached out and pulled Josie in, then spun around and, in a nimble move, pulled herself out of the line and plonked herself down on the seat that Josie had just vacated.

'I'm going to need a chiropractor tomorrow if I keep this up,' she chuckled. 'I'm way too old for this level of exertion.'

'If that's true, then I'm doomed, because we're almost the same age,' Seb joked. Like Josie, and everyone else he'd met tonight, she spoke to him like an old friend, and strangely, that's how he'd felt all night in their company. He'd been chatting to Senga at the buffet table earlier and he'd refused to believe that she was Stacey's mother. And much as that sounded like the cheesiest line ever, he'd been absolutely genuine. They looked like sisters, and even then, sisters that were close in age. Senga had made him chuckle when she'd explained that she'd had Stacey when she was in her early twenties and she used "a shit-load of moisturiser."

There was a companionable silence for a few moments before Senga spoke again.

'I hope you don't mind, but Josie mentioned that you recently lost your wife.'

Hearing that still took his breath away, like it was some kind of shock that he was hearing for the first time. He'd no idea when that would stop.

'You know, I lost my husband a couple of years ago and I thought the world had ended. I wanted so much more than we got. I guess you can relate to that.'

He nodded, not trusting himself to speak.

'Anyway, I just wanted to say that I understand where you are because I've been there. And I survived. You will too.'

'Thank you,' he croaked, truly touched by her kindness.

She jumped to her feet. 'Right then, better get back in there and make sure Josie hasn't set the place on fire. She was asking the barman for flaming sambucas earlier and he was off to google how to make them. Youngsters these days. They've lost all of life's vital skills. You coming?'

Seb weighed up his options. Stay here, contemplate life, sit in his sadness, or give himself a chance to laugh, to feel something other than sorrow, for the first time in a long time.

He stood up and let her lead the way.

Thirty-Five

Josie

'Just a heads up – Michael wants to put you in an old folks' home,' Avril announced, before tossing back a flaming sambuca shot that held every possibility of setting her hair extensions alight.

Josie turned to glare at him like a python, right before it unhinged its jaw and swallowed its prey.

'I do not! Why would you say that?' he stuttered, outraged at the suggestion.

Josie's head spun again, this time to see her daughter giving her brother an evil smile.

'Because you've always been the favourite and I wanted a glimpse of what that was like, just for a second. Ah, it felt great.' She dissolved into a raucous laugh, and Josie couldn't help but join in. This bloody lass was outrageous, but she wouldn't change a single thing about her. Except perhaps Avril's often repeated allegation that Michael was Josie's favourite. It wasn't true, but Avril got much mileage out of toying with them.

Having them here tonight had been the best surprise she could have wished for. They'd both said that they couldn't make it – Michael because his wife Mel was too pregnant to fly, and Avril because she was supposed to be on location with the TV show she was working on. Josie had already learned that Mel had insisted that Michael come alone, and Avril's shoot had been postponed because the leading man was suffering with complications from a dodgy liposuction op. Apparently he hadn't appreciated Avril's suggestion that he'd have had better results if he'd let her do it with Dettox spray and a Dyson.

'I promise you, Ma, when you're past it, we won't put you anywhere with rules. Or without a bar. We know it wouldn't end well,' Michael teased her.

'No, it would not, son. I'm glad we have an understanding.'

He took a sip of his beer and Josie's maternal signals began to tingle. He had something on his mind. The pulse that was throbbing on the side of that big handsome face of his gave it away.

'Right, out with it. What's the problem?'

'Nothing! There's no problem…' he blustered, just as he always had when Avril had misbehaved as a child and he was trying to cover up for her. He was naturally inclined to stick to the rules, so she'd had very little trouble with him, but his sister? Josie would never need a DNA test to prove that Avril was her child.

'He thinks you're getting on a bit and we should install cameras and panic buttons in your house and buy you a Zimmer.'

Michael glared at her in amused exasperation. 'I swear

to God, I'm going to put gaffer tape on your gob while you sleep.'

'Don't you worry, son, I've got this,' Josie assured him, before rounding on Avril, who was trying her best to assimilate something approaching an innocent face.

Needless to say, she was failing miserably, so she gave up and instead, went for a snarky, 'Told you he was the favourite.'

Josie pursed her lips. 'Avril Cairney, you're not too old for me to wipe the floor with you. Now what's going on?'

Avril sighed. 'Okay, okay! We're just a bit… worried about you.'

'And why would that be?' she challenged. Josie could feel a burning sensation creeping up her neck. Did they know? Had someone told them? The only person she'd confided in was Seb and if he'd blabbed, then so help her she would…

'Ma, you're in your seventies, you smoke twenty fags a day and you drink like a sailor. This shouldn't be a newsflash.' As always, Avril went straight to the crux of the matter, while Michael chimed in to try to soften the blow.

'We know you're completely bloody indestructible, Ma, but we're allowed to worry about you.'

For some inexplicable reason, Josie found herself getting angry. 'Well, you can stop that right now. You two are my children and it's my job to worry about you, not the other way around. Do you hear me?'

Their chastened expressions – even Avril looked mortified – pulled her up short and she realised she may have added a bit more vehemence than intended. Christ, she was an emotional mess today. She also knew that her anger was misdirected. She was fucking furious at this bastard disease, not at these two gems sitting in front of her. Bugger, she was an old fool sometimes.

'Look, I'm fine. I promise you. But you know, all I want is for you two and your families to have great lives. If I need you to worry about me, then I'll let you know. Okay?'

Both of them nodded, like two teenagers that had just been given a lecture about under-age drinking. Talking of which... Josie signalled the waiter for another round of flaming sambucas, then adjusted her tone back to light-hearted and as normal as she could possibly make it.

'Right, so tell me, how long are you staying and what's the plan?'

'I need to head back tomorrow,' Michael said. 'But I got a later flight. I thought we could have lunch and catch up?'

'That sounds great, ma darlin'.' It did. She could keep the pretence going for one more day, and it would be worth it to spend every moment she could with him. 'What about you, love?' she asked Avril.

'Same. In fact, I think our flights are at around the same time. I was planning on joining you two for lunch, unless you want to be alone with the favourite, of course,' she teased. Josie didn't even rise to it, so Avril went on. 'Sorry I couldn't stay for Christmas, Ma. I tried to wangle a few more days, but the director is a sadist and wants us there for some kind of bonding shite while the main man waits for his infected wounds to heal. Daft tosser. Honestly, half the female population of the country fancies him and they've got no idea that he's about as smart as my hair straighteners. Every time I think of spending three months on set in a remote African safari with this guy, a million more of my brain cells top themselves.'

Josie was happy to let her witter, while she tried to steady her heart and keep her composure. Christmas. The very mention of it.

'Are you sure you don't want to fly over with me tomorrow and spend Christmas with us? You know that Mel and the kids would love to see you. And it'll be a while until we can get back again. We'll need to wait a couple of months until the little one is old enough to fly.'

She thought about that for a moment, but just knew she couldn't do it. It was one thing being exhausted and trying to deal with this thing here, where she could lock herself in the house and get a few hours' reprieve, but it would be another thing being in someone else's house, especially with the kids there and Mel being so heavily pregnant. Josie would want to pull her weight and take care of everyone, and it would frustrate her until the ends of the earth that she couldn't do it.

'Och, thanks for the offer, love, but you know I like to have Christmas in my own house. I've already arranged to have the whole gang over for post-dinner drinks and our Jean has been practising her karaoke number for months.'

That was all true. Josie's house on Christmas night had been an annual fixture in the diary for years. Everyone was welcome – sometimes there were six of them and sometimes there were twenty, but every year they had a great time.

Michael understood that. 'Okay, Ma, but you know we'll be thinking about you, don't you?'

Avril tutted. 'No wonder she likes you better – you've got all the lines. I don't stand a chance, do I?'

'Absolutely not,' he replied with a wink. 'Watch and learn.'

Josie laughed, all anger and trepidation gone now, replaced with gratitude that these two lovely human beings were her legacy. More than that, as she watched them tease each other and giggle together, she knew that they'd always have the kind of bond that would sustain them when she... when she was no longer here. They'd be fine, these two.

'Right, listen up, because I'm only going to say this once,' she heard herself say. Mother of God, her mouth was on an emotional roll again. She'd laid a whole heap of sentimentality on Cammy and Caro earlier and now it was Michael and Avril's turn. 'I love every last bit of the two of you. I couldn't be prouder that I somehow managed to squeeze you out of my lady bits.'

'Urgh, you had me right up until lady bits,' Avril groaned.

'But we need to get something straight. I'm getting old and I'm not always going to be here.' Michael went to interrupt her, but she put her hand up to stop him. 'No, son, let me say this. I want you to know that the both of you are everything I could ever have hoped that you would be. Although, you're a bit extra with that gob of yours, Avril,' she quipped.

'I try,' Avril conceded, as if it was some kind of honour. 'By the way, Mother, you should drink sambucas more often – they're bringing out the touchy-feely stuff in you.' She switched her gaze to Michael. 'She'll be chanting and embracing her inner goddess next.'

Josie grinned, shaking her head. Like her, Avril wasn't one for public displays or declarations of affection. Well, on this occasion, she'd just have to suck it up, because there was a belter coming.

'The two of you make me prouder than I could ever have imagined. Michael, son, you're an incredible dad, and I'm in awe of the family and the life that you've built for yourself. I know that you'll take care of Mel and the kids and they will grow up to be so grateful that you are their dad, just like I'm so grateful that you're my son.'

For once, Avril didn't jump in with a cheeky one liner. Michael, meanwhile, was grinning at her with that bashful expression he'd always had when anyone paid him a compliment. He was almost fifty, but to her, he was still that kid she'd held when he came out screaming on the floor of the chippy in the High Street. She'd been sure she had time to stop for a fish supper on her way to the hospital.

'Thanks, Ma,' he said now. 'However I've turned out is all down to you.'

'Aaargh!' Avril threw her hands up in despair. 'See what I mean about the suave lines!'

Josie ignored her outrage. 'And you, ma darlin,' she said to her, 'you are extraordinary. You're funny, you're beautiful – apart from that bloody awful hair dye. Has anyone told you that Smurfs are no longer in fashion? Anyway, you're also the quickest, smartest person I've ever known. I love your honesty, your individuality and your boldness. Under that smart mouth and brusque exterior, I know you've got the biggest heart. And you make me laugh more than anyone else on this planet. I think you're bloody magnificent.'

'Yasssss!' Avril cackled, punching the air, before enveloping Josie in a hug and squeezing her so tightly

Josie feared her knackered lungs would give up the ghost. Eventually, she released her. 'We love you, Mum,' Avril said, serious for once. Josie was grateful that it didn't last long. 'I've no idea what brought all this on, but if it's because you've won the lottery and you're about to bugger off to the Bahamas without us I'll be raging.'

'I'd never do that!' Josie assured her. 'I'm more of a Marbella kind of chick. I'll send you a postcard.'

'That one's mine!' Avril screeched suddenly, as Stevie Wonder's 'Superstition' filled the room. 'I asked Cammy to add it to the list for me,' she explained as she jumped up, grabbed her mother's hand and led her to the dance floor. Michael followed behind them and Val, already busting out her trademark hip shimmy, joined them on the floor.

Josie felt a weight partially lift from her shoulders. She'd said what she needed to say. No matter what happened after this, the kids would always remember the night that she told them exactly how she felt about them.

Another two people off the list.

But there were still a couple more to go. And the last one was going to be the toughest.

Thirty-Six

Stacey

'Aunt Josie, I'm going to go on out and get some fresh air. I'll wait for you at the door.'

'Okay, ma love, I'll be right there. There are a few people who are not coming back to the hotel that I still need to say goodbye to.'

Stacey cast a glance over at her mum, Senga, deep in conversation with Seb. He was a bit of a mystery, this complete stranger who had only recently discovered that he might be Caro's dad, but so far today, he'd been pretty impressive. He'd mingled, he'd chatted to people, and he hadn't argued when Senga and Josie had taken turns to whisk him around the room in a particularly energetic Gay Gordons.

In fact, everyone had put the early glitches to one side, and they'd all danced, drank and celebrated in true style. Even her. All in all, it had been a good night, as far as watching the love of your life marry someone else goes.

She wandered back out to the front, to where she'd been standing when she'd dropped Jax's call earlier that evening. She hadn't been able to deal with it then. Now, her emotional reserves had been topped back up by a combination of champagne, laughter and the company of at least half a dozen people she loved. She'd missed this. She just hadn't realised how much until tonight.

In a moment of insight, she wondered if that had contributed to how she felt about Cammy. Was he that connection with home, that security blanket that she'd missed so much more when he was gone because she felt cast adrift, disconnected from her roots?

She'd never been romantically attracted to him when they both lived in Glasgow back in the early years. Sure, she'd thought he was good-looking and he was one of her favourite people to hang out with, but that was as far as it had gone. Until now, she'd thought it was spending the night with him in LA and his declarations of love that had changed her feelings towards him, made her realise what she felt for him and showed her what they could have, but perhaps that wasn't it. Maybe it was him leaving and cutting the constant tie to her home that had skewed her affection for him and twisted it into something else.

Whatever it was, it was done. Over. Time to move on. And she knew that her relationship with Cammy wasn't the only one she felt that way about. She'd planned to leave whatever issue was brewing with Jax until tomorrow, but now she felt an urgent need to deal with it and to get it out of the way. It was time for some honesty, and putting it off until tomorrow would just give her another day of drama that she had no energy for. No, may as well be done with it now.

She pulled her phone from her bag and switched it on, then watched as it sprung to life in a disco of beeps, buzzes and flashing lights. Holy shit, the stuff with Lila must still be going viral.

Flicking it on to silent, so she could concentrate on the call, she brought up Jax's number and dialled.

'Stace! What the fuck is going on?' he roared, and she could hear the stress and anxiety in his voice. Whatever the problem was, it hadn't sorted itself out then.

'Sorry, my battery died and I didn't have a charger. I only just got it fired up again.' One more white lie was hardly going to be a deal breaker. 'Anyway, what's up?'

'You honestly don't know? Oh fuck, Stace, I'm freaking out here.'

Good to see that despite the fact that this drama seemed to affect her, all he was concerned about was how he was feeling.

'Look, take a deep breath and tell me what's happened.'

'I fucked up, Stace. I know I did. But she preyed on me, man.'

Stacey suspected that a whole team of his PR people had done exactly what they were paid to do, and grovelled to the star, diverting all blame for something that she'd hazard a guess was his bloody fault.

'TMZ got the pictures. They're everywhere.'

'Hang on a minute,' she said, sighing, before taking the phone away from her ear and pressing her Twitter icon for the second time tonight. This time, she ignored the zillion notifications and typed 'Jax Green' in the search box. The reason for his panic immediately flashed up on the feeds of countless celebrity websites. TMZ had him as a headline, as he'd said. So did Radar Online, the *Daily Mirror*, the *Sun*, Perez Hilton and at least a dozen other showbiz sites. He wasn't exaggerating when he said it was everywhere. Great. Two big viral episodes in the social media world tonight and she was connected to both of them, despite wanting nothing but a quiet life.

She scrolled through the search results. Every single one of them used a variation of the same picture – a shot of Jax Green, naked, on a hotel or apartment balcony, cigarette in one hand, bottle of Jack Daniel's in the other, his penis inserted in a female who was bent over in front of him, grasping the balcony rail for support, an expression of orgasmic ecstasy on her cosmetically enhanced face. It said something that Stacey's first thought was relief that this woman was blonde and could in no way be mistaken for her. Her second thought was that, from his oblivious abandon, Jax obviously had absolutely no idea that someone was in proximity to the building with a long lens camera. Given that it was taken at – she checked the time of the posts and knew they'd have gone up almost instantly – 4 a.m., she could hazard a guess that he was wasted and that his decisions had been sponsored by his buddy in the picture, Jack Daniel's.

Slowly, she returned the phone to her ear. 'What a fuck-up,' she said, but with something approaching weariness, not anger.

'Babe, I'm sorry, I—'

Time to cut right through all of this. 'Jax, it's fine. Don't worry.'

'Seriously? My agent is saying that if I release a statement saying I'm admitting myself to a clinic for sex addiction, we can make this go away.'

'That sounds like a plan, Jax,' she offered, still speaking like this guy was a casual bystander as opposed to the lover who had shared her life for the last few years.

'Babe, I knew you'd be okay, I knew we'd handle this—'

'Jax, we're not handling it. Look, I don't want to get into this on the phone, but it's over. If we're honest, we've both known it for a long time. I'll do whatever you want me to do, and I'll support you in whatever way you need, but as friends. I think that's all we've really been for a long time anyway.'

As she was saying it, she knew it was true. They'd been a convenience, a great PR story, and she'd loved him. Not in the all-consuming, breathless way that she'd loved Cammy, but they'd had good times and she regretted nothing. Apart from, perhaps, the photos of him banging someone else on a balcony. Although, as Lila had just proved, no exposure was bad exposure in this world.

More than anything, though, she knew she had no right to be upset with him because she wasn't exactly teetering on the moral high ground here.

There was a silence on the other end of the phone and she knew he was weighing up his options. Arguing with her now wouldn't serve any purpose – he needed her on side.

'You'll walk into the clinic with me, show it's amicable?'

'I will. Look, I'll be home in a few days and we'll sort it out. Try to stay out of trouble until then.'

'Yeah, yeah...'

By the sound of his distracted voice, she could tell that his mind was already working out how to spin this. She also knew that he'd be sitting in a room right now with his agent, his manager, and at least a couple of executives that specialised in damage limitation. This wasn't the break-up of a loving relationship – it was more the end of a cordial but worn-out business arrangement. And the lack of emotion from all concerned showed that to be true.

'Okay, thanks, Stacey. We'll work it out.'

'We will. See ya, Jax.'

Hanging up, Stacey realised she felt nothing but relief. It was done. All of this – Jax, Cammy – was over. The outcome hadn't been the one she'd hoped for, but she was still in one piece, still standing and it could be worse... she could be Lila.

'Jesus, you'll get your fecking death of cold out here.' As always, she heard Josie before she saw her. Josie slipped her arm through hers and they began to walk. 'You did good today, sweetheart,' Josie said, and Stacey knew exactly what she was referring to. It wasn't just the way she'd dealt with Lila, but the fact that she hadn't confessed all, that she'd let Cammy go. 'You know, your mum would like you around a bit more. She misses you,' Josie went on, as they exited the gardens and stopped at the traffic lights, waiting to cross over to their hotel.

'I miss her too. And you, of course,' Stacey teased. 'But only when you're not pissed off with me.'

Josie's low, throaty cackle warmed Stacey's heart and made her smile.

Maybe there was something in what she was saying, though. She'd been based in LA for so long that the homesickness had subsided, but it still wasn't home. Home was here, with these incredible women who made her laugh, supported her and surrounded her with love. Perhaps it was time to start putting the feelers out for work here, and look at splitting her time between the two countries. After her new-found fame tonight, she'd probably be in a better position than ever to land something on this side of the Atlantic. The irony was unmissable. She'd slogged for years to make a name for herself, and Lila had just raised that bar to unprecedented levels in a matter of seconds.

Only when they reached the warmth of the hotel lobby and joined Val, Michael and Avril, who were waiting there for them, did Stacey let Josie's arm go. 'I'll think about that, Aunt Josie. It's not the worst idea you've ever had.'

'Naw, pet, that was the night in Acapulco with Keith Richards, but the less said about that the better.' With another cackle, Josie hugged her. 'You know, Stacey, Cammy wasn't the one for you. The right man is out there, love. You just haven't met him yet, but he'll come along when it's the right time. You mark my words. In the meantime, you just live your best life, do you hear me?'

'I will. I promise.'

Another hug. 'I love you, pet. More than words. I hope you know that.'

She did. And she also marvelled at the powers of the flaming sambuca, because her beloved Josie was never this sentimental.

'I know, Aunt Josie. I love you too.'

They'd held each other for a moment, before Josie let out a familiar war cry. 'Right, who's for heading to the bar?'

'I'll catch up,' Stacey said, needing a minute to catch her breath. Her phone was still buzzing like a game of

Operation being played by four drunk medical students. As she went to switch it off, she glanced at the screen and saw a notification with a name that sparked her curiosity.

Instagram message from Zac Benson. The guy from the plane?

> Great to meet you today. If you fancy showing a weary traveller around Glasgow, give me a call. PS: Still awake – any tips for dealing with jet lag?

Above the message was a picture of Zac, his head on a pillow, eyes wide open, a crooked but hopelessly endearing smile. It took her a moment to realise she was grinning. Her first instinct was to close the message, but she paused. All the others were in the bar, and she knew the party would be in full swing and would last for hours. If ever there was a great introduction to her homeland, this was it. Of course, this thought had nothing to do with the fact that he was gorgeous, keen and seemed like the perfect distraction to take her mind off her disastrous love life.

Decision made, her red manicured fingernails flew across the screen.

> I believe the best cure is to meet a tour guide in the bar at the West End Grand Hotel.

A pause. No reply. He'd probably fallen asleep. Oh, well. That pretty much summed up her bloody day.

Ping.

> Thank you for the medical advice. When should I embark

on this course of treatment?

That made her smile again. She liked this guy's style.

Immediately.

Another pause. Had she gone too far? Was he really going to get out of his bed in the middle of the night and come and meet a woman he'd only ever shared a packet of peanuts with on a plane?

On my way.

Yes, he was.

Thirty-Seven

Website – www.itshouldhavebeenme.com

Members Discussion Forum

Responses to post by member, screen name NotOverYet:

Comments:

BethanySunshine: OMFG! Have you guys seen all the stuff on Twitter? Lila (@NotOverYet – that's her real name) did it and she live recorded the whole thing. It's everywhere. Didn't work though. Some hard-faced cow marched her out of there and the bloke went ahead and married the other woman. But what an inspiration she is. @NotOverYet, we worship you! #EnriqueIglesias #Hero

RealityCheck: Are you fricking kidding me? She's a complete embarrassment! Why would she do that? She had no back-up plan and none of it came off as sincere. I adore my ex, but come on, are we not past the days when we'd humiliate ourselves for some dude? Incidentally, if her ex ever reads this? Think you did the right thing pal. #notoveryet #notinmyname #muppet

SATURDAY 21 DECEMBER

MIDNIGHT – 8 A.M.

Thirty-Eight

Caro

Caro sat on a chair at an empty table and scanned the room. Streamers were draped from light fittings, glasses littered the surfaces, there were plates, party poppers, favours, napkins and, rather worryingly, a set of false teeth on the table by the door. She put that one down to Cammy's dad. It wasn't the first time he'd popped out his gnashers after a long night of partying.

Other than the dental issue, she decided she'd never seen a more beautiful vision of chaos. It had been the perfect party, if you excluded the bit where her nightmare of a sister turned up and made a play for her husband. All in the name of publicity, of course. Caro couldn't even find it in herself to be angry. Lila's life was hers to live, but Caro wouldn't want it for all the clicks and likes in the world.

Four of the staff that Josie had hired for the night came into the room now, all armed with black plastic bags. Cammy had slipped them all a generous tip that had more than doubled their wages for the night, so they were discussing which club they were going to hit as soon as they'd cleared up and clocked off. Caro remembered those single days of random clubs and parties, and she'd loved them, but she wouldn't trade them for what she had now.

The door opened again and she automatically smiled, expecting to see Cammy walking through it. He'd nipped out to make sure that everyone who wasn't staying across the road at the hotel had managed to get taxis at the gate. That's the kind of guy her husband was. Her husband. That sounded so perfect. What had she been thinking this morning? The truth was that she'd been so tied up in knots about her mum and dad – or the man she'd believed to be her dad – that she hadn't been thinking at all. She'd been panicking and mourning the fact that her mother wasn't there with her and somehow that had manifested itself in a need to run. Well, Cammy Jones had better brace himself because she was never running again.

'Hey,' she said, 'What took you so long?' The last word stuck in mid-air as she saw that it wasn't Cammy. In fact, it was as far from Cammy as you could possibly get.

Jack Anderson, the man she'd always called 'Dad', stood there, scanning the room, then fixed his gaze when it fell on Caro. She got some sense of satisfaction over the fact that he didn't seem to know what to say to her. He'd been her father for thirty-four years and they were like strangers now. Actually, they always had been, even in the times when they were living under the same roof and he decided to grace them with his presence.

She decided to give him somewhere to start. 'You're a bit late for the wedding.'

'I see that,' he said, unnecessarily.

'So you're here because…?' She was dying to know. Had he come to some kind of epiphany and realised how terribly he'd behaved? Did he want to make it up to her? Had he come to apologise, to beg her forgiveness, or even to explain why he'd spent thirty-odd years lying to her and her mum? Too late, chum. Too late.

'I'm looking for Lila.'

Caro almost laughed at the predictability of it. Of course he was. His other daughter. The one who'd come here earlier with the intention of turning her sister's wedding into a cheap publicity stunt.

'Well, you missed her. She bailed out right after she stood up in the middle of the ceremony and told my husband he was making a mistake marrying me.'

'Yeah, I saw that,' he said, almost casually. Christ, he had a cheek. But then, audacity had always been something that came naturally to him. 'Thing is, we haven't seen Lila since then and haven't been able to contact her. She's not answering her phone and Louise—'

'Your other wife, the one that's not my mum and not dead…' Caro piped in. It wasn't in her nature to be malicious, but she couldn't seem to help herself. It was so unfair that he was here, this vile, uncaring liar, when her lovely mum, who would have revelled in every minute of today, wasn't with them.

He didn't even acknowledge her interruption. 'Louise is frantic with worry. She's out in the car. We've been searching everywhere we could think of for her. This is the last place that we know for sure she was at because of… you know, the video.'

Even now, he couldn't ask her how she was, what had happened, if everything was okay. He couldn't even apologise on Lila's behalf. He was truly disgusting. But the last six hours had been the most incredible in Caro's life and she wasn't going to let the appearance of Jack Anderson destroy her happiness. She just wanted him gone.

'Well, she's not here. She shouldn't be hard to find though.'

'How's that?' he asked and suddenly she saw the problem. He didn't use social media. Or at least he hadn't when he still lived with them. One of the perils of leading a double life – too easy to get caught if you're updating your location on your Insta page. History had shown him to be right about that. The only reason that she'd even got a sniff of his treachery was because Lila had put up a post about him on a retro band's fan page.

There was just one niggling inconsistency though. If he didn't use social media… 'How did you see the video?' she asked him.

'Someone sent it to Louise. She's beside herself.'

'I bet. So neither of you have looked at Lila's Instagram? Or her Twitter feed?'

He shook his head, and for once, Caro believed him. He'd never been in the least bit interested in anything like that. Said it was for losers. Caro doubted he was even aware that his other daughter was one of the most prolific internet users out there. At least, she had been until her spectacular downfall. Caro had a hunch that tonight's little performance had been the beginning of Lila's comeback in the virtual world.

She picked up her phone and put Lila's name into the search box. It took her straight to a feed that had been well and truly reignited. There was the video of Lila at the wedding tonight and it had… holy crap, over fifty thousand views. There were also thousands of comments, but Caro had no stomach for reading them.

Next there was a photograph of her pouting at the entrance to some nightclub in the city centre. Then another of her hugging a bloke that Caro recognised as a Scottish actor who'd landed a part in *EastEnders*. And finally, a last pic, taken twenty minutes ago, of her sitting on his knee in the VIP area in the same club. For someone who'd declared her undying love for Cammy just a few hours before, she'd sure got over him real quick. It seemed that it had done the trick though. She was getting the attention that she craved – even if it was for all the wrong reasons.

Caro turned her phone round so the screen was facing her dad – not that he could see it, given that he was standing a few metres away and clearly had no intention of coming any closer. 'She's sucking the face off a guy in Diamond – that's a nightclub in the city centre.' A simple way of describing its location came to her and she couldn't resist it. 'Actually it should be pretty easy for you to find. Just go to the restaurant where I first saw you with your other family that you'd hidden from us for three decades, then turn right, and it's just down that street.'

He nodded and she could see that he wasn't even going to thank her, congratulate her, say another fucking word that would be in any way meaningful or go some way to repairing the damage that he'd done.

Well, sod that.

'I met someone who used to know you today.' The words tumbled out before she could stop them. 'Actually, he knew Mum a lot better than you. It was back in Aberdeen in the eighties.'

His curiosity was enough to make him stop, interested to hear more. She was happy to oblige.

'His name is Seb Lloyd.'

Jack's face was still blank.

'Tall. Good-looking. He was the golf pro at a club that Mum and Aunt Pearl worked at.'

Still blank.

Caro felt her fury rise until there was no controlling it. Shouting and screaming wasn't her way, though – instead, she got very calm, and very quiet.

'He says he had a relationship with Mum.'

Finally she saw a flash of emotion on his face, then a snort. 'Never happened. Your mum was never with anyone else after she met me.'

Caro knew he was wrong, but she wasn't surprised that he was in complete denial. His ego was so great that she knew he wouldn't even be able to contemplate her mum looking at another man.

'He says it did and I believe him. He said you two had split up, you went off on holiday, then got back together again when you came back.'

Another flash of emotion, a different one this time as he searched his memory bank and settled on something that was lodged in the distant past. He shrugged. 'Maybe. But clearly it didn't work out because she came back to me. She always did.'

Caro eyed the empty champagne glass that was sitting on the table in front of her. Never had she wanted to throw an object at someone more than at this smug bastard.

She didn't.

Instead, she kept her façade of calm. 'Thing is, they were sleeping together right around the time that I was conceived. So there you go… you might not be the baby daddy after all.'

When she said it, she had no idea what to expect, but nothing she could have anticipated would have come even close to what she was seeing now. His face reddened, his lip curled into a malicious sneer, and his eyes darkened to the colour of his black leather bomber jacket.

'What the hell are you saying?'

'That you might have been stuck with some brat all those years that wasn't even yours.' For the purpose of stirring the pot, she was overlooking the fact that she'd just referred to herself as a brat. She knew the truth. She'd been a quiet, studious, well behaved kid, who knew her place and stuck to it. Not that he'd have known any of this because he barely gave her a second glance.

'You mean all those years I might have been supporting someone else's kid?'

Damn, she should have led with that and gone straight for the jugular. Of course it came down to money! It always did with him. It had long been one of her theories that he'd stuck with her mum all those years because he was hedging his bets and wanted somewhere to stay, cost free, in Aberdeen. Her mum had inherited their home from her parents, so they'd never had to pay a mortgage. In the days of the Aberdeen oil boom, when half of his time was spent up there, and house prices and rental rates were extortionate, that would have saved him a fortune.

'Yep, it would seem so. Isn't life a bitch sometimes.'

If his facial expressions were anything to go by, his brain was firing off like a malfunctioning computer now. He was clearly horrified. Furious.

'You know, *Jack*,' she said, emphasising the fact that she was using his name instead of 'Dad'. 'There's a bit of an irony there. All this time you thought you were the smart bastard, getting away with living a lie, when there's a very real possibility that all along you were the dumb joker that was being lied to.'

Sorry, Mum, she thought, sending up a silent apology. She just hoped that now, looking down and in full possession of the facts, her mum would cut her some slack and overlook her animosity to the man that Yvonne had loved her whole life.

'And I can't tell you how much I hope that was the case,' Caro finished, meaning every word.

For a moment, she thought he was going to argue, to fight back, but he said nothing. It didn't matter. Shallow and petty as it was, Caro knew she had finally permeated that indifferent shell, and hit him where it hurt. She hoped his insides were a fireball of rage and irritation.

Still saying nothing, he turned and opened the door behind him.

'Bye, Jack,' she yelled breezily, as he disappeared from view.

If they never met again, the last thing he would have heard was her laughing at him as he stomped away in fury.

After he'd gone, a kaleidoscope of conflicting feelings collided in her chest. Vindication. Happiness. Sadness. Anger. But most of all, satisfaction. She'd won a battle, both for her and for her mum.

That thought had just made this day so much sweeter. There was also a feeling of finality and closure. As far as she was concerned, and regardless of what the DNA test would prove, Jack Anderson was no longer her father. She didn't even share his name now. She was Caro Jones. That felt great.

The door opened again and for a moment she thought he might have come back to argue, rant, vent his indignation. But no. Cammy's gorgeous frame filled the doorway and strode towards her.

'Sorry! It took bloody ages to get cabs for everyone. It didn't help that Ida and Jean have decided that they're now the newest members of Little Mix and gave us a medley of their greatest hits. At least a dozen taxis swerved right by us.'

Caro wanted to tell him about Jack's appearance, but she was halted by his next statement.

'By the way, I saw your dad out there a little while ago.'

'Which one?'

Cammy smiled. 'The new one. I like him better.'

'Me too,' Caro agreed. The story of her altercation with Jack could wait until tomorrow.

'Anyway, he's wandering around and he looked a bit upset. Is he okay?'

Caro immediately jumped to her feet. 'I have no idea,' she told her husband honestly. 'But I think I'd better go and check.'

Thirty-Nine

Seb

Seb heard a rustling somewhere behind him, but he didn't turn around at first, too wrapped up in the solitude that he was feeling after a day of being surrounded by others. He hadn't experienced those connections, the everyday interactions of normal people, for a long time and it had taken him a moment to adjust. This had been the most bizarre, most unexpected, most surprising day of his life, the lows almost unbearable, but the highs taking him to a place he hadn't been since Juliet died. He'd been happy. Meeting a group of people who truly loved each other and who'd embraced him, pulled him into their world, had done something to his heart. Reignited it. Made it beat in a normal rhythm again. Of course, the very best thing about it all was the prospect of having a daughter, a family. He didn't even want to believe that it couldn't be true, because he wasn't ready to lose one of the most incredible gifts that he'd ever been given.

Another noise. He glanced over his shoulder to his left, expecting to see Caro or one of the wedding guests outlined in the moonlight, but it was someone he didn't recognise, at least not at first. Some bloke in a black bomber jacket was striding towards the side exit of the park, a route that would take him right past where Seb had just sat down. For a moment he thought it was Cammy, but he'd just seen him over at the main entrance a few minutes ago, herding a collective of revellers into taxis. He'd thought about stopping to help but, overcome by the need to stay focused and carry out his plans, he'd just waved and walked on into the depths of the garden, the path lit by the moon, a few tall iron street lamps and by the glimmer of thousands of fairy lights on the trees around him.

Now, as the figure came closer, he could see that it was a man of about his age, marching purposefully, his eyes on the gate ahead of him. Probably one of the staff from the Kibble Palace. Or perhaps just a bloke cutting through the gardens on his way home from the pub. The thought crossed his mind that if he was a mugger, Seb reckoned he could handle him. This bloke looked fit, but he was a few inches shorter than him and narrower in the shoulders.

As he got closer, Seb locked eyes on the stranger's face, searching for any sign that this could be an encounter that would take a nasty turn. It was only when he was just a few metres away that the light of a lamp post behind him brought into focus something that he recognised. He was older now, greyer, his face changed by the years, but Seb knew that he'd seen this man before many times. He very much doubted that the recognition would be reciprocated.

Thirty-five years ago, he'd watched Jack Anderson swan in and out of the club Seb worked in, his arrogance on display for anyone who cared to look. Yvonne hadn't seen that though. Seb had witnessed her face light up every time Jack appeared, and then dim again when he left the building. He'd known that his own feelings for Yvonne were a lost cause, but he'd had a glimmer of hope when she'd revealed that they'd split up. He'd known it was his only chance to make her see that she should be with him.

Sadly, he'd failed.

Yvonne had been his love for a short time, but then this man who was walking towards him now had claimed her back and she'd gone to him. Seb had hated him, but the irony was that Jack Anderson hadn't given him a second glance, hadn't even realised that he existed. Back then that had been fine. Now? Something in Seb flared, anger at the injustice that may have cost him a lifetime with the daughter he didn't know he had and he suddenly had an overwhelming need to let Jack Anderson know that he bloody well existed.

'Jack?'

A couple of metres away, the other man stopped, clearly surprised that someone would recognise him in such a random place.

'Yeah?'

Seb could see now that he was tanned and expensively dressed: a leather jacket, smart trousers, formal shoes.

'I'm Seb Lloyd. We met a long time ago at a golf club in Aberdeen. I knew Yvonne.'

He'd expected questions, perhaps a blank look, a shrug of the shoulders, but to Seb's surprise, Jack immediately went for confrontation.

'You're the one who's pitched up claiming you might be Caro's dad?'

Fuck. Seb immediately realised that Jack must have spoken to Caro already. He had a feeling this was about to get mighty interesting very quickly. He just hoped that his earlier confidence that he could take on this guy was well placed, or he could be facing a painful encounter in his immediate future.

'So is that a load of bollocks, some scam you've come up with, or do you really think you're her father?'

Seb thought about standing up, but decided against it. It was only going to inflame the situation. And besides, he'd rather have the element of physical surprise if this turned nasty. He stayed seated and tried to keep the emotion out of his voice as he went for calm sharing of the facts.

'It's not a scam. I only spent a short time with Yvonne, while you two had split up...' he thought he'd throw that in, add a bit of de-escalation to the mix, '... but the timings could work. We won't know for sure until we do a DNA test.'

He should apologise, explain that he didn't know Yvonne had even been pregnant when he'd left, say sorry for potentially rocking this guy's world, but from everything he'd learned today about this prick, he didn't feel the need. All he felt was protectiveness towards a woman who might not even share his genes. Perhaps this was what fatherhood was really about.

He waited for a reaction, bracing himself for conflict, anger, arguments. He was astounded when none of that came. Instead, Jack Anderson sneered as he carried on walking towards him.

'Yeah, well, good luck with that. And, mate, if you are her dad...'

Here it came. Jack was so close to him now he could see the moisture as he exhaled in the cold night air. Seb readied himself for some kind of contact, but… none came.

'… then I reckon you owe me a good few years of child support,' Jack spat.

With that he passed him and was gone, leaving Seb speechless with shock. That was it. No objections. No regrets. No clarification of details. This guy really did not care a toss about his daughter or the woman he'd been married to. Now, on top of everything he'd learned about her today, Seb truly had an understanding of what Caro had lived with. He also had an even stronger respect for her. To have been brought up by a man like this and still have turned out to be kind and decent and capable of real love and friendship was a testimony to what an incredible woman she was.

He would give everything he had for her to be his daughter.

Glancing skywards, he sent up a silent plea to the one person who, if the afterlife really did exist, might intervene on his behalf. 'I miss you, darling,' he told Juliet, silently. 'You were everything. You always will be.' He paused. 'I've no idea if you made this happen, but if you did, please know that I'll always be grateful.' It was true. Every piece of his soul was thankful that Caro had come into his life, not just because of what it meant for his future but also what it meant for his past. If Juliet had any influence on this, then perhaps it meant that she forgave him.

He could feel tears again and he wiped them away with the palm of his hand, but instead of his mind taking him to that familiar dark place of regret and sorrow, he felt a strange calm descend on him, an innate feeling that he was exactly where he was meant to be. It was time. Here and now was the place and the moment he'd been searching for.

He opened the zip of the brown leather bag that sat beside him on the bench and removed the small wooden box. He held it, closed his eyes, spoke to his love.

'Goodbye, Juliet. I hope you're waiting for me up there, but for now, I want you to rest in peace. I love you, my darling.'

With that, Seb stood up, opened the box and held it at arm's length, then spun around slowly, letting the contents scatter into the air of the city that his wife had loved.

When it was over, he felt a weight lift from his shoulders and the absolute relief that he'd fulfilled his promise. He'd brought his love home.

It was time to let go. Not of his memories, or his love for her, but of the guilt and regret that had been tearing at his soul. Juliet had loved him, of that he had no doubt. If the roles were reversed, he knew that he would want her to go on, to live her life for both of them. Now he felt with every beat of his healing heart that she would want him to do the same.

'Seb? Are you okay?'

Caro. He turned around and saw her standing there with Cammy by her side, and she was looking at him with concern. She cared. He'd only met her today and already she cared. He watched her eyes go to the empty box in his hand, and he saw that she understood what had just happened. She walked towards him, her hand outstretched. Wordlessly, he took it, and they stood like that for a few moments, Cammy watching in silence.

'You know, she would have loved you,' Seb told her.

'I think I would have loved her too,' Caro replied, a smile on her beautiful face.

'You would.' He knew that was true. 'And she'd be right here with me, hoping that you were mine.'

Caro didn't speak for a moment and he wondered again if this was all too much for her. The poor girl had been through a lifetime of emotion today.

'I've been thinking about that,' she said, and his stomach flipped. Had she come up with something that would dash his hopes? Had she decided to walk away, to leave the questions in the past and move on with her new life, without him in it?

'I don't want to do a DNA test.'

Nooooooo, a voice inside his mind screamed. A few minutes ago, he felt that he'd finally repaired his soul, and now, with those words, it shattered into a million pieces again. She didn't want him in her life. She wasn't even going to give him a chance to be her father.

He wanted to scream, to argue, to beg her to change her mind, but… he wouldn't. Because – bizarre as it sounded – he loved her already. And if loving her meant letting her make the decisions about their future, then that's what he would have to do.

'Okay,' he said, a strangled whisper.

Her brow creased with confusion, then she went on. 'Because I don't think it matters. Today, you've already been more of a father to me than Jack Anderson ever was. I don't need to know if we share the same genes. You loved my mum, for however short a time, and that's all that I need to know. So… if you'd like to be in my life from now on, if you want to be the dad that I never had, then I'd like that very much.'

His heart exploded, every doubt and fear melting away, replaced by an overwhelming, life changing rush of joy and gratitude.

As he stepped forward and hugged his daughter, tears streaming down both their faces, Seb Lloyd looked heavenwards again and sent another message to the person he truly felt was here with them. *Thank you, Juliet.*

Forty

Josie

'Oh, my God, my sides actually hurt,' Val announced. 'But I don't know if it's from laughing, or from the three pairs of magic knickers I've been wearing since five o'clock today. My internal organs are sitting up somewhere above my Wonderbra.'

Josie chuckled so loudly, a giggling Val had to shush her. 'Ssssshhhhh, you'll get us thrown out.'

'They'd have to catch me and wrestle me to the ground first,' Josie countered, feeling surprisingly sharp for a woman who was on the wrong side of champagne, cocktails and sleep deprivation. She hadn't glanced at her watch since the first chorus of what became a three hour sing-song of the hits of the last six decades. It had been better than any medicine and should, she'd decided, be prescribed on the NHS for everyone who'd received the news she'd heard this morning. What made it even better was that every single person she loved was right there with her.

Val and her husband Don had been the seventies lyrics experts, remembering almost every word of Tom Jones' and Elvis's greatest hits. Caro and Cammy had delayed the wedding night raunchy stuff to stay with them, Caro sitting on Cammy's knee and both of them singing at the tops of their voices. Jen and Chrissie, and their partners Luke and Tom, had kept the drinks coming. Seb had looked like he didn't know what had hit him, but, God love him, he'd joined in and seemed happy to be there. Stacey and some very handsome bloke she'd picked up along the way had slotted right in to the revelry. It was great to see the lass laughing like her old self. The poor soul had got her knickers in a twist over the last wee while, but Josie was sure she was going to be fine. She was made of tough stuff, that one. Just like her mum, Senga, who'd been through more heartache than most, and yet there she'd been, dancing her stilettos off, refusing to let anyone leave the party until the manager had finally shut down the residents' bar and politely asked them to call it a night.

And, of course, Avril and Michael had been at the centre of it all, two party animals just like their mamma.

Now, arm in arm with Val, they were doing the same walk of shame that they'd done countless times over the years that they'd been friends. Don had headed to bed an hour ago, but, as always, Val had stuck it out to the end, and now the two of them, joined at the elbow, were wandering along a hotel corridor, holding their shoes in their free hands, a bottle of champagne tucked under Josie's arm.

'In the name of God,' Josie exclaimed, as she caught sight of herself in a mirror. 'That's not how I looked at the start of the night. Look at the state of me!' She couldn't believe her reflection. Her smoky eyes were now a smear. Her lipstick was half off after all the goodnight kisses. Her hair resembled an explosion in a hay bale. 'I want to know what sick person kidnaps me, drugs me and puts me through a car wash on a night out. It's the only explanation,' she declared, making Val hoot with laughter again.

They reached Josie's room, and she swayed slightly as she put the key card in the lock.

'Are you coming in for a nightcap?'

Val winced as she pulled at her waistband. 'Only if I can take these knickers off.'

'Best offer I've had in a long time,' Josie told her, setting the two of them off on the giggles again.

For the second time today, Josie thought how lucky she was to have a friend like this. The laughs they'd shared over the last dozen or so years had been some of the best of her life. There had been heartache too, but it had been made so much more bearable because they'd been right there by each other's sides.

For Josie, friendships lasted a lifetime, and when she cared about someone – male or female – they became family and she stuck with them through thick and thin. Val was the very best of them and she needed her to know that.

In the room, she handed the bottle to Val, tossed her boots on the floor and flopped on the bed, just as another coughing fit consumed her.

'For feck's sake, Josie, will you get that seen to?' Val nagged her once again, while pouring the champagne into two mugs on the tea tray. 'You sound like you're on your last legs there.'

It took everything Josie had not to react to that. Now would be the time to tell her. They were alone, just the two of them, and Josie knew that Val would be right there for her, she'd share her grief and her sadness and she'd join her in her fight against this bastard disease until the end of time.

But...

She just couldn't do it. She didn't want to. There would be time for grief and heartbreak later, but right now it was more important to say what needed to be said, but in a way that wouldn't lead Val to the reality of the situation.

'You know,' Josie began, choosing her words carefully, deliberately injecting them with her trademark flippancy. 'That was a brilliant night. It really was. If I popped my clogs right now, I'd go a happy woman.'

Val chucked her over a packet of shortbread fingers as she snorted. 'Och, don't be daft. I know you're lying.'

Josie felt a clench of dismay. Had her friend tapped into her sadness today? Did she have a hint that Josie had a curling vine of dread that was wrapping its way around her, squeezing the life out of her?

Val immediately dispelled her fears with. 'You won't die happy until you've shagged Pierce Brosnan.'

'You've got a point,' she agreed, deadpan, her relief instant. 'Although, I do worry that he's getting on in years and at his age I'd be a bit too much for him.'

For the purposes of this intellectual discussion, they both omitted to acknowledge that Josie was several years older than the object of her desires.

'Val Brennan, I bloody love you, do you know that?' Josie blurted, her words steeped in hilarity. It was the only way to do it. Val understood her inside and out. If Josie showed even a glimmer of vulnerability or sincerity, Val would swoop in on it and she'd know.

'That's completely understandable. I'd love me too,' Val grinned, eyes sparkling with cheek and affection.

Josie felt the warmth of the moment dispel her fears. Val would be fine. She didn't have to say any more. Her best friend knew exactly how she felt about her and no more words were necessary to stress the point. Time to move on, and stick to what she'd said earlier to Seb. She was going to live each day, keep her illness to herself, and enjoy every moment until she couldn't. There would be plenty of time for her and Val to talk about the hard stuff in the future, but for now, she'd go with joy and laughter.

Val held her glass up to her. 'Congratulations, Josie, you pulled off the wedding of the year today. It was brilliant, it really was. If my Don trades me in for a supermodel, you can do my next one too.'

'No problem. I'll even give you a discount on my fee. So it'll be a large bottle of gin and five boxes of Tunnock's tea cakes.'

'Done!' Val agreed.

Josie smiled. 'It really was a fantastic night though, wasn't it? I mean, once we'd ironed out the glitches.'

'Just a few trifling issues,' Val teased. 'But, yep, well done, pal, it was one of the best.' She threw back the last drop of her champagne, dropped her shortbread wrapper in the bin beside her and pushed herself up to her feet, groaning as she did so. 'Right, I'm going to love you and leave you. I need to get back to my room and get these knickers off. My feet are turning blue.'

It was Josie's turn to snort with laughter. She clambered up, and went into Val's open arms. 'Goodnight, love. You're the best pal a woman could have, Val Brennan.'

'And you're a class act, Josie Cairney.'

Josie held her for just a few seconds longer than usual, taking in every feeling, every surge of love and affection for this woman.

Val gave her another squeeze. 'Och, we're getting soppy in our old age. Love you, Josie. See you for breakfast in the morning?'

'Love you too, pet, and yep, I'll be there.'

'Aye, well don't scoff all the sausages if you get there before me.' And with that, and another hoot of laughter, Val was off, waddling out of the room, the door closing silently behind her.

Josie picked up her champagne glass and took a sip, then sat for a moment. It had been such a trauma of a day, but now – and maybe it was the champagne – all she felt was a peaceful numbness.

She nipped to the loo, then came back into the room and refilled her glass, taking out her earrings and putting them down on the dressing table. Another sip. She pulled her bright pink trolley case on to the bed and opened it, then took out her toilet bag and her pyjamas. White silk. If a woman of her age couldn't splash out on her pyjamas, then there was something wrong with the world. Another sip. She undressed, pulled on the soft trousers and buttoned up the shirt. Another sip. She took a wipe from a packet in her toilet bag, and she cleansed her face, removing the last eighteen hours of make-up, feeling her skin tingling under her touch. Another sip. Then she carried her glass over, laid it on her bedside table and climbed into bed, the day rewinding and playing back like a movie in her mind. This time she fast-forwarded the sad parts and watched the good bits in slow motion, so that she could savour every moment all over again.

She glanced over at the bedside clock: 4.45 a.m. Almost morning. Not bad for an old broad of her age. Not bad at all.

Ignoring the creak of her bones, she reached over and flicked the switch that plunged her room into darkness.

She smiled. The world hadn't beaten her today. She'd won. And she'd done it surrounded by the people that she loved.

With that, Josie Cairney closed her eyes and went to sleep.

For the last time.

Forty-One

Stacey

If it wasn't for the beautiful Christmas tree in the corner, it would be difficult to believe that it was December. Everyone from the wedding party who'd stayed overnight at the hotel had gathered in a suite on the top floor, the windows open, sunlight streaming in like it was a summer's day in June.

Stacey watched Cammy hold Caro tightly as she burrowed her face in his shoulder. Seb stood over by the window, unobtrusive, respecting everyone's space. Just as her gaze fell on him, he quietly slipped out of the room.

Her mum and all the other 'aunties' were huddled on the sofa, cups of tea that wouldn't be drunk in their hands. Don and Jen were sitting on another sofa, one on either side of Val, like two towers of strength, there to support her. No doubt her grief would come later, but right now she was calm, head held high, exactly as Josie would expect her to be.

Poor Val. Stacey's heart ached for her. They'd first been summoned here an hour ago, and Michael and Avril had broken the news. Josie was gone.

It was impossible to believe. Josie was indestructible. Invincible. A force of nature. Crazy as it sounded, Stacey had expected her to be around for ever.

As soon as they'd let everyone know, Michael and Avril had gone back downstairs to sit with their mum until the arrangements had been made to take her to a place of rest. In the meantime, Val had told them the story of what had happened, undoubtedly the shock forcing her to hold it together as she spoke.

Val had got back to her room and realised that she didn't have her key card to get in. She hadn't wanted to wake up Don, so she'd gone back down to the bar and had a search for it. It wasn't there, so she'd decided she must have dropped it in Josie's room. After a couple of false starts, when she'd got off the lift at the wrong floor, she'd found the right room and knocked the door. No answer. Figuring her friend was asleep, she'd left and Don had been forced to answer his wife's knock at the door.

'It just didn't feel right though,' she'd said. 'Josie could be out for the count and still hear someone drop a pin in the next room.'

Back in her own room, Val couldn't sleep, couldn't shake the feeling that something was wrong, so she'd called Josie. No answer. It had been enough to escalate her fears to the point that she'd called down to reception and asked for someone with a key to meet her outside Josie's room. The night manager, the same man who had finally persuaded them to call a halt to the party just a short while before, had done as she asked, and that's when they'd found her.

'She was smiling,' Val had said, a wrenching sob finally escaping her. 'If there's a mercy, it's that it must have been over so quickly. There was only a half hour or so between me leaving her and going back.'

Since then, they'd all been together, mostly in silence, while they waited for Michael and Avril to return. Of course, they could all have gone home, but no one wanted to leave, all of them comforted by the very presence of the others. They were a clan. They stuck together. It was what Josie, with her husky voice, no-nonsense attitude and unswaying loyalty to the people she loved, would have demanded.

As soon as she learned what had happened, Stacey had texted the man who had slept on the sofa in her room last night. He'd joined their party and he'd entered into the spirit of it all, endearing him to everyone.

Even Josie had approved. 'You know what I said earlier about the right bloke…?' she'd told her with a cheeky grin and a wink.

Stacey realised now that – other than goodbyes when they'd all headed to their rooms at 4 a.m. – that was the last thing her aunt had said to her. The thought brought on the saddest of smiles. Aunt Josie. She was one of a kind.

Sorry I had to leave. I'll explain later, but it's nothing to do with you, I promise. Take care x

He'd immediately texted back.

Are you okay?

Damn. She was going to have to explain. She kept it simple.

My aunt has passed away and I'm with my family.

I'm so sorry. Can I help? Is there anything you need?

No. But thank you.

Okay, but I'm here. If you need anything, just call. X

That was exactly how he'd been last night too. Not pushy or demanding, just… a friend. A kind one.

The door opened and Michael and Avril came back in, holding hands, with Seb just behind them.

'Mum has been seen by the doctor and taken to the funeral home,' Michael said. 'We'll know more later. Thank you, everyone, for staying. For waiting here. It means so much to us.'

'Do you want a cup of tea, love?' That came from Senga, whose first reaction was always to try to help. Stacey knew now, more than ever, that she was so lucky to have a woman like that as her mum. They were all cut from the same cloth – Josie, Val, Ida, Ina, Agnes, Jean, Senga, Montana… The kind of women who had cores of steel and hearts of gold.

'Thanks, Senga. Although, I've got a feeling Mum would recommend gin for a time like this.'

They all knew that Avril was right – that's exactly what Josie Cairney would have said.

Senga handed them both cups of tea and then sat on the arm of the sofa, letting Avril take her place in the middle. Michael stayed standing, his handsome face pale and drawn. He glanced at Seb, some silent message passing between them that Stacey didn't understand, then he cleared his throat and began to speak.

'We've learned a bit more about Mum and what's been happening to her over the last few months.'

Senga saw Val look up at him in surprise. Whatever it was, this seemed to be news to everyone. Actually that wasn't true. Seb gave Michael an encouraging nod. It was clear that the newcomer to the group already knew what was about to be said. Stacey didn't have time to wonder why or how, too focused on listening to Michael.

'I'm sure you all know that Mum has had a terrible cough for months. Maybe years, actually. Well, after all of us nagging her…' There were many nods of agreement to that. He carried on. 'It turns out that she'd finally gone to the doctor and undergone some tests.'

Val's face adopted an expression of incomprehension. 'She did? She never said.'

'I know, Val. She never told any of us. I suppose we shouldn't be surprised by that. You know what she was like.'

It was all he needed to say for Val to nod sadly. 'Och, that woman,' she said with such despair and love that Stacey thought her heart would break.

'I know,' Michael said. 'She was a cracker, eh?'

That made everyone smile. It was strange how sometimes the darkest times called for humour – especially when it involved someone like Josie Cairney.

'Anyway,' he went on. 'She got the test results yesterday morning...'

'What?' Caro, this time, with more bewilderment. 'But how...?'

'She was late,' Val blurted, stricken. 'When she came to meet us yesterday morning, she was late. She gave me some reason for it – I don't even remember now – and I never gave it a second thought.'

Michael kept going. 'The tests showed that she had lung cancer. End stage. Incurable.'

Several gasps and sobs rang out around the room at that. Val simply put her head in her hands.

'I don't have all the details, but I do know that she'd decided against having any treatment, because she knew it would only buy her a couple more months. I also know that she didn't want to tell anyone, because she didn't want the illness to consume what time she had left. She'd decided to ignore it for as long as possible.'

'That woman was tougher than the rest of us put together,' Jean said, with undisguised admiration.

Avril took the baton from her brother. 'The thing is, now that we know all this, it makes so much sense. My mother would have hated to live a life that was hindered by anything. I just wish I'd realised why she was acting so weird last night.'

'Weird how?' Cammy asked.

Avril shrugged. 'She gave Michael and me a speech about how much she loved us, how proud she was of us.'

What happened next would stick in Stacey's mind forever.

'Us too,' Caro said.

'And me,' piped in Senga.

Val spoke next, her whole body sagging as something in her mind clicked into place. 'And me. I thought it was just the champagne that was making her sentimental.'

'Aye, me too,' Jean said.

'Same here,' Ida added, then Jen, then Chrissie, until just about every single person in the room realised that Josie had, in some way, said her version of goodbye to them last night.

The laughter started as a low hum of incredulity, then swept around the room until all of them caught the bug, tears streaming down faces, hands holding hands, heads shaking.

'Josie bloody Cairney,' Senga said, blowing her nose. 'Only she could make all of us laugh like this even when she's gone.'

Stacey leaned forward and wrapped her arms around her mum's shoulders, squeezing her tight, letting her know that she was there for her. She just wanted to hold on to her forever. It felt like life was way too fragile to let her go.

It took Michael a moment before he was able to speak again. 'I think she knew she was going to go sooner than the doctors said. Or at least, she wanted to be prepared. And I think that if you'd asked my mother how she wanted to leave this world, she'd have said peacefully, in her sleep, after a rip-roaring party with everyone she loved. We all know what she was like. She was the most brilliant woman I've ever known. She loved life, and all of us here, and she lived every day on her own terms. I think that she died that way too. And she wouldn't have had it any other way.'

Just at that, the door opened and a very respectful manager took one step into the room. 'I'm so sorry again for your loss,' he told them. 'Is there anything we can get for you? Anything at all?'

Glances shot between them all, subliminal messages being passed from one to another. It was Val who articulated their meaning.

'Some champagne, son,' she said. 'Can you send up a couple of bottles?' She turned from the shocked hotel employee to her husband Don. 'And, Don, love, if you could sort out my phone and get a bit of Tom Jones on it, that would be grand. Josie would expect nothing less.'

'Yaaassss!' That came from Avril, and set the tone for the others.

As the manager backed out of the room and Don fished Val's phone out of her bag, Stacey took her turn to speak.

'Last night, Aunt Josie said goodbye to me too. She said she loved me and she told me to live my best life. I keep hearing her say that now.'

The others nodded, the truth of that statement resonating with them all.

Live your best life.

That had come from a woman who had led by example.

Epilogue

Nine Months Later

The gardens were busy with members of the public, but the group of family and friends had congregated in a quiet area round the back of the Kibble Palace, by the pagoda.

Caro handed her daughter to Seb, who beamed with the kind of happiness that he could never have believed he would ever feel again. The last nine months... well, they'd been the most wonderful adventure. He'd gone back to Spain after Josie's funeral, but when Caro had called a couple of weeks later to tell him she was pregnant, he'd come to a decision. He'd handed in his notice, sold up everything he possessed and moved back to Scotland. By some stroke of magnificent timing, he'd managed to get a job at the club he'd worked at when he first met Juliet. He had a sneaking suspicion that she had something to do with that. Ever since Caro's wedding, he'd felt Juliet's presence around him, caring for him, protecting him. The drinking had stopped – he had no need for it now and he wanted to be sober to enjoy every moment of this new life.

There had been no more mention of DNA tests or doubts over paternity. As far as both he and Caro were concerned, he was her dad. And a grandad now too. He had a ready-made family and it came with a group of friends whose acceptance had helped him put together the pieces of a new life.

'You're good at that,' Senga teased him as she wandered to his side. He'd got to know her well since he'd moved back. It wasn't long since she'd lost her husband, so they understood each other, knew what it took to readjust to life without the person you thought you would grow old with. For now, they were friends, but lately he'd come to contemplate a future in which she could be something more. It would take time, but like everything else that had happened since he set foot in Glasgow just before Christmas, he truly felt that Juliet would approve.

Caro watched Seb gaze at his granddaughter with pure adoration and the sight of it made her heart swell. 'He's so good with her,' she whispered to Cammy, who was pouring drinks at the picnic table in front of them. 'How lucky are we to have him? Although, Auntie Pearl is still taking all the credit for tracking him down. She says she deserved a medal.' Caro caught Pearl's eye a few metres away and blew her a kiss. If Pearl wanted the credit, she was happy to give it – even if she still felt that there had been a whole load of divine intervention.

She was so glad that Pearl and Bob had travelled back from Spain to be here today.

They'd considered having a formal naming ceremony, then decided against it because it wasn't their style. This was their idea of the perfect day – sun, fresh air, everyone they loved, and drinks and food on rugs on the grass.

'I still can't believe that eight months ago, we didn't even know that she was coming,' Caro said. It had been the shock of her life, and that was saying something given everything that had happened to her over the last few years. She'd started to feel exhausted at the start of the New Year, but she'd put it down to transitioning from the stress she'd felt before the wedding, to the grief she'd felt afterwards. Christmas had been a tough time for them all, but they'd made an effort, knowing that Josie wouldn't have wanted them to mope. They were a couple of weeks into the new year, when Chrissie had noticed her pushing away her favourite dessert. 'Are you okay?' she'd asked.

Caro had nodded. 'Yeah, just not feeling like it. I've lost my appetite a bit. Think it's just with everything that's been going on.'

Chrissie had thought about that. 'And yet, you borrowed my size fourteen jeans last week because you said your size twelves were killing you.'

She had a point. Caro hadn't really made the connection, but now that she mentioned it…

They had both reached the same place and blurted out their thoughts at the same time.

'Could you be pregnant?'

'Could I be pregnant?'

She'd skipped back in her mind. Her periods had always been irregular and she hadn't had one for a while, but she'd put that down to pre-wedding nerves. Could those same pre-wedding nerves have been influenced by raging pregnancy hormones? So much made sense now.

Cammy had been absolutely delighted. It hadn't been planned and they hadn't been trying, but they hadn't been doing anything to avoid it either. They'd always thought that what was meant to be would be. Apparently, what was meant to be was an eight pound baby girl, six months later. They could hear Josie singing 'Que Sera Sera' the day she was born.

Stacey wandered over to the table and picked up a glass of Prosecco. 'Well, did you watch it?' she asked, wide-eyed and giggling. Both Caro and Cammy nodded shamefully, before Caro spoke. 'Yes! We couldn't help ourselves. God, it was tragic.'

'I know! But somehow...'

'Yep, we'll be watching it again tonight,' Caro said, in fits of laughter as she read Stacey's mind.

Stacey grinned, loving the relationship that she'd built up with this woman. They shared so much – interests, opinions, love for the same man and an obsession with the new reality series *Heartbreak Hotspot*. It was their guilty pleasure – a show that put a dozen people (six men and six women) who'd had their hearts broken, on an island in the sun and left them to it, the viewers lapping up the drama and voting one person off every week. The most notorious by far had been one Lila Anderson, who had got the gig after a video of her gatecrashing her sister's wedding had gone viral. Lila had become an overnight celebrity, the reality bad girl, falling out of nightclubs, dating a different guy every week, and having so many headline grabbing beauty procedures, she now had lips like a sink plunger and her boobs were a 34GG.

'Nope, I'm not doing it. I'm going to find something far more intellectual. Like footie,' Cammy announced, grinning, knowing he had to change the conversation. When these two got on to the subject of that show, they could gab for hours. 'How's the flat?' he asked Stacey.

'Yeah, we're loving it,' Stacey said, her eyes flicking over to Zac, who had managed to tie in a business trip so that he could be here today. It was his third visit since Christmas, but this one was special because it was their first time in the flat that Stacey was renting from Cammy and Caro. They'd moved into a bigger place on the floor below after the baby came. Stacey, meanwhile, had taken Josie's advice and was now splitting her time between LA and Scotland so that she could spend more time with Senga. It was made easier by the fact that she'd been inundated with offers of work in the UK after the video of her tossing Lila out of the wedding had become an internet sensation. People still used the hashtag #putthetrashout.

'I like him,' Cammy said, following her gaze.

'Yeah, me too,' she admitted, gleefully. This was a different kind of love to the one she'd felt for Cammy. It felt more... right. More real. And it definitely helped that he felt exactly the same way at the same time.

As she made her way back to him, she heard Cammy shout over to the woman in the bright pink suit with a hat the size of a satellite dish.

'Val, would you do the honours please?' They all watched as Val gently lifted the sleeping baby from Seb's arms.

'Ladies and gentlemen, could I have your attention please?' she said loudly, before being swiftly interrupted.

'Auntie Val, is that a real baby?'

'Yes, it is, son,' she answered the wide-eyed gaze of Josie's grandson, Harrison.

'We've got one of those too,' Harrison cried with wonder, pointing at his dad, Michael, and his mum, Mel, sitting cross-legged on a rug nearby. Mel was holding baby Daniel, born just a few months before Caro and Cammy added to the family. 'But Auntie Avril says that if he doesn't stop crying we can send him back.'

'Oh, you're such a grass, Harrison Cairney!' Avril had chided, swooping up her nephew and tickling him until he squealed. After years of being away, she'd been based in Glasgow for the last month, working on a new BBC drama. It was so bittersweet that she'd landed a contract here after her mother was gone. She and Michael had kept Josie's house, so that they'd always have a connection to their mum and that's where Avril had been staying. Every day, she ached with the loss of her, but sometimes she felt like Josie's spirit was so vivid there that she could hear her popping on the kettle and cracking open the biscuit tin.

Val took back control of the proceedings, refusing to give in to the tears that she knew were sitting right behind her eyes, ready to flow. She wouldn't let them. Josie would kill her if she crumbled now. She missed her best friend every single day, but she knew that Josie would want her to be strong, and take care of everyone who meant so much to them both. Starting with this little one in her arms right now.

'I'd like you all to meet my beautiful god-daughter,' Val began, beaming at all the people she loved. This was a special day. Josie would have loved it. 'This is Josephine. And if she's anything like the last Josie in our lives, then heaven help us all.'

Acknowledgements

Once again, my thanks to the fabulous Hannah Smith at Aria for her encouragement, patience and unfailing calm in the face of any crisis. Thanks too to the wonderful Vicky Joss for spreading the word with such skill and enthusiasm, and to Rose Fox and Jade Craddock who worked on the manuscript along the way.

Huge appreciation to all the bloggers and reviewers who have been so incredibly supportive of my work. And my love to all the amazing readers who continue to buy my books and who make my day, every day.

As always, gratitude to all my gal pals, who are never far away and who make my kitchen just like Josie's – a hive of tea, caramel wafers, drama, chat, support, scandal, occasional tears and a whole lot of laughter. I love you all.

And finally, to my guys, J, C & B – I never forget how lucky I am.

Love,

Shari xx

About the Author

SHARI LOW is the No. 1 best-selling author of over 20 novels, including *A Life Without You*, *The Story Of Our Life*, *With Or Without You*, *Another Day In Winter* and her latest release, *This Is Me*. And because she likes to over-share toe-curling moments and hapless disasters, she is also the shameless mother behind a collection of parenthood memories called *Because Mummy Said So*.

Once upon a time she met a guy, got engaged after a week, and twenty-something years later she lives near Glasgow with her husband, a labradoodle, and two teenagers who think she's fairly embarrassing, except when they need a lift.

Hello from Aria

We hope you enjoyed this book! If you did let us know, we'd love to hear from you.

We are Aria, a dynamic digital-first fiction imprint from award-winning independent publishers Head of Zeus. At heart, we're committed to publishing fantastic commercial fiction – from romance and sagas to crime, thrillers and historical fiction. Visit us online and discover a community of like-minded fiction fans!

We're also on the look out for tomorrow's superstar authors. So, if you're a budding writer looking for a publisher, we'd love to hear from you. You can submit your book online at ariafiction.com/we-want-read-your-book

You can find us at:
Email: aria@headofzeus.com
Website: www.ariafiction.com
Submissions: www.ariafiction.com/we-want-read-your-book

@ariafiction
@Aria_Fiction
@ariafiction

Printed in Great Britain
by Amazon